HARRIET HUME

HARRIET HUME

A London Fantasy

by

REBECCA WEST

Author of *The Judge*

New Introduction by
Victoria Glendinning

"...And like white witches, mischievously good..."
    –John Dryden

The Dial Press
New York

Published by
The Dial Press
1 Dag Hammarskjold Plaza
New York, New York 10017

Manufactured in the United States of America
First printing

Library of Congress Cataloging in Publication Data

West, Rebecca, pseud., 1892–
Harriet Hume: a London fantasy.

I. Title.
(Virago modern classics)
PR6045.E8H3   1982   823'.912   81-15299
ISBN 0-385-27410-6   AACR2

INTRODUCTION

Harriet Hume, published in 1928 when Rebecca West was in her mid-thirties, is subtitled "A London Fantasy"; it is a fable for adults, a vehicle chiefly for entertainment but also for the conveying of social and psychological observations. It is an exercise in the higher whimsy; although the story takes place after the First World War, this is not a "contemporary" novel in the usual sense. The language is mannered and archaic—which contributes in places to the comic effect—and the dialogue is not colloquial. Like a poem or a fairy story it seems outside time, and treats the supernatural as just one of those things. *Harriet Hume* belongs in the same imaginative territory as Walter de la Mare's poetic fantasies, as Max Beerbohm's burlesque of Oxford *Zuleika Dobson* and his *The Happy Hypocrite*. It is as baroque in manner and matter as the painting by Reynolds, "The Three Graces Decorating a Statue of Hymen",* from which Harriet, in the novel, makes a story within the story.

Apart from *The Judge*, which has a meticulous Edinburgh setting, *Harriet Hume* is the novel in which Rebecca West most clearly exploits her Irish blood and her Scottish childhood; for this particular kind of fantasy has some affinity with that of R. L. Stevenson

*Harriet says that the Graces in this picture are the Ladies Frances, Georgina and Arabella Dudley. The painting by Reynolds that bears the same title and corresponds to the composition described by Harriet is of the Montgomery sisters, Elizabeth, Anne and Barbara.

INTRODUCTION

and J. M. Barrie; and if James Stephens had ever attempted his own "London fantasy" in the style of his *The Crock of Gold*, it might have been very like parts of *Harriet Hume*. Not entirely, however; for Rebecca West's knowledge and grasp of politics, in both the wide and the narrow sense, were in the 1920s extremely sophisticated. The imagery, too, could be no one else's, as for example in her inspired culinary similes: the dim but upper-class Lady Ginevra is imagined "dancing at the Embassy, limp in the limp arms of one of her own kind, like two anchovies side by side in a bottle"; and the chaperones, at another party, "dozed in their corsets like jellies left overnight in their moulds".

Harriet Hume is also the most mysterious book that Dame Rebecca West has written. Since fantasy-art lends itself to the spectator's answering fantasy, it cannot be definitively "explained". It would be better to read the novel for yourself first, and look at the rest of the introduction afterwards, so as not to muddy the waters with what are only one reader's personal responses.

The story is mainly told through four encounters between the lovely Harriet Hume, a professional pianist, and Arnold Condorex, an ambitious politician. We first meet them after they have been making love, in Harriet's Kensington home. London itself is the element in which they move: Dame Rebecca West has said that she wrote this novel "to find out why she loved London". The Kensington of fifty years ago, leafy and tranquil, its streets and squares just a little run down, is evoked with love. Harriet, who lives in a converted section of an old house, the only access to which is through French windows that open on to the garden, says of Kensington: "It is like a cracked tombstone with a lilac bush bursting from it."

Harriet herself, and her room, are painted in tones of cream and gold. "Since her curtains were of amber taffeta, this made her room a cave of bronzy shadow, which the brightness from the windows on the garden shed washed softly as water." Her "rose-coloured nail" toys with a "nail-coloured rose", and "It was not a pity that her gown took the shade of China tea on the side of the curtained windows and the shade of pearls on the side where daylight had its way". Her gowns are always "parchment-coloured"; she is described as bland, docile, meek; if she had a fault, "it was that her oval face was almost insipid with compliancy". Later, in her grace and neatness, she is frequently likened to a cat. She is, it would seem, the essence of femininity.

Her lover on the other hand is dark, definite, vain, dynamic, ambitious, and very insecure; the "most miserable part of him" believes that "the whole world was furtively deriding one Arnold Condorex". As a consequence of the "private marvel" of their love, Harriet finds that she can, literally, read his mind; and in it she reads that he would cast her off to marry some rich woman who could advance his career. Their idyll is ruined. "But a man must rise in the world! Dear, God, did she not understand! A man must rise in the world!"

Six years later Condorex comes across Harriet again. The second tableau of London is in mid-winter; he walks into Hyde Park on his way back to his rooms in Albany (he has risen in the world) and sees the enchanting Harriet walking in front of him in the glittering, frosty park. Again she reads his thoughts: he is planning a profitable marriage to the Lady Ginevra, whom he does not love. Again the lovers' spontaneous delight in one another is spoiled. "Let the witch burn," thinks Condorex. "For she had come between him and every human being's right not to know quite what he is doing."

The next celebration of London, and their next meeting, comes when Condorex is married and a rising MP. His walk this time, on a summer evening of blistering heat, is from St James's Street, across Piccadilly and into Regent Street, and on to Portland Place where he now lives. He perceives the nobility of these streets; and Harriet, whom he meets near Portland Place and takes home with him, agrees that houses such as his are "just as beautiful as much good music and in the same way". They confirm their "real and infrangible union", which is not mystical but "homely and natural . . . as if our finger-nails were cut from the same piece". She can still read his thoughts: he is plotting to overthrow the senior members of his party, and she reads all his "guilt, and shame, and treachery". He begins to wish her dead.

There are cross-threads and complexities in this simple story line. The celebration of London's finest streets is a happy thread; but when Condorex feels threatened or oppressed these streets seem hostile to him. There can be few books in which London is so eloquently enjoyed, and few books where the pathetic fallacy is extended to include not only the weather and trees and flowers, but tarmacadam and skylines and Adam architecture. The pattern is further complicated

by the three myth-like stories of London that Harriet
tells: one about the ladies in the Reynolds painting,
one about a flock of headless sheep, one about the
stone sphinxes, animated in the small hours, "lumber-
ing on their soft paws" down Regent Street towards
Piccadilly Circus. Her poetic truths confound his
attempts to manipulate historic truth. For Condorex
has cheated his way to power.

Rebecca West is inventive enough to spell out the
precise way he does it, in a comic-ironic saga of
dodging and fudging and pompous obfuscation that
is ludicrous enough to be almost possible. They
discuss his political career in Portland Place. Harriet
asks, naively, whether politicians are not "all occupied
in finding a form of government which shall allow that
invisible thing, the will of the people, to express its
sense of the need for its own preservation . . . and
which shall not be deflected from this by the personal
interests of any group". He concurs, but thinks
privately: "It is strange that this fundamental stuff of
politics has never interested me. 'Tis the negotiation
that has ever charmed me, and the struggle for
eminence." Harriet can still read his thoughts.

After their fourth encounter—by now he is Lord
Mondh and holds high office—he knows his plotting
is about to be short-circuited, and that he is going to
be exposed, bankrupted and ruined. Yet, as he tells
himself, other politicians who still hold their heads
high are guilty of equally corrupt practices. "Rampound has done worse than this." Why is his own
minor roguery not tolerated? Rebecca West answers
this, through Condorex himself, in a passage that is
both witty and provocative and profoundly true for all
groups at all periods, most certainly—naming no

INTRODUCTION

names—including our own:

> . . . in each generation there is but one rogue and no more who is allowed to be great. One of the kind the common man is willing to pamper and adore for sometimes he himself tires of respectability, and then it is a comfort to him to see a rogue sitting in comfortable grossness with his ration of eight bottles of champagne and two wenches a day, all earned by cheating, and coming to no harm, nay, rising to power, wearing red robes at the Opening of Parliament. . . . For if a rogue can triumph so, the universe is not such a closed prison as they say, and one might find a road yet out of Surbiton. But, mark you, there must be only one of us, for if there are more, why, this ceases to be a heartening dream but another certificate that life is intolerable; since that it would be, if there were an army of scoundrels that had to be fed on earth's first fruits, before the virtuous might eat.

In their final interview at Portland Place, by night, Harriet and Condorex agree that they are "opposites". Harriet says that this is no great matter: "There is the North, and there is the South, and there is no war between them." But when Condorex's ruin comes upon him, the influence of his "opposite" becomes an obsession. He walks out from his house for the last time, along Oxford Street, past the Marble Arch, through Hyde Park to Kensington. His tragedy is all due to "the maliginity of my opposite"—Harriet. He sees enemies everywhere, he is disassociated, disorientated, "disorder personified", "all hate".

What is this opposition between Harriet and Condorex? It is perhaps the opposition between the personal life and the public life. For Harriet, public events were "a text that could at most be a footnote to her own life, an amusing appendix to the vastly more important things that happened when she played the piano, bit into an apple, was hot, was cold". For

INTRODUCTION

Condorex, his own position in relation to public events was the only index of importance. "A man must rise in the world!" '

Harriet was an artist and thought magically, he by calculation. She was anarchically unchaste, he upheld conventional morality as "part of his legend". She was flexible, unaggressive, floating; he was dynamic, ambitious, scheming. Passive, active; subjective, objective; the antitheses are reducible simply to her and him, sheer femaleness and sheer maleness. And neither, this story seems to say, is much good without the modifying effect of the other. Harriet puts this point of view to him in the end: "I may have been innocent, but I was also impotent. . . . Humanity would be unbearably lackadaisical if there was none but my kind alive." His "sturdy desire" to shape the "random elements of our existence into coherent patterns" was, she said, "the pith and marrow of mankind":

> You must admit that when you were not pursuing the chimera of greatness, you performed many very worthy achievements that enabled our species to establish itself on the globe more firmly. Did you not see to the building of bridges, the teaching of children, the suppression of riot and bloodshed? Is that so small a thing?

So she accorded the male principle its justification. But he questions it further, feeling guilty when he thinks of her life of contemplation: "Do not forget," he says, "that I found it impossible to work without surrendering to the principle of negotiation; and that it led me to murder, and logically so."

> For that principle of negotiation forbids one ever to let the simple essences of things react on each other and so produce a real and inevitable event; it prefers that one should perpetually tamper with the materials of life, picking this way with the finger-nail, flattening that with the thumb . . .

INTRODUCTION

And the logical conclusion of that process, as Condorex knows only too well, is indeed murder. "Ay, but the end of contemplating the eternal beauties, and doing nothing to yoke them with time," mewed Harriet, "is smugness, and stagnation, and sterility!" So the tide must go on ebbing and flowing between the two ways of being, to make each and either useful.

Condorex remembers Harriet's "pretty image about the North and the South, which could have kept me from identifying difference with enmity". It is very hard not to identify difference with enmity, not only between women and men, or within the body politic, but within one single person; for very few women are undiluted femininity, like Harriet. As a writer, Rebecca West has her North and her South, and in *Harriet Hume* she swings between the two; for it is a book that combines the purest and most anarchic fancy with the toughest of logical cause-and-effect. The two modes do not combine without conflict either in a relationship or in a personality, this side of the grave. But then Harriet and Condorex, in their eventual harmony, are on the far side of the grave, as are the two charming ghost-policemen.

Harriet Hume is an imaginative tour de force, a conceit that twines decoratively round some of the preoccupations that were to become central in Rebecca West's non-fiction writing in the years following: political treachery, treason, spying, retribution. *Harriet Hume* is a bridge-book; but on this side of the bridge the focus is on wit, style, grace and magic. And for Londoners, the streets and parks in which Condorex and Harriet walked and talked have a new significance, afterwards.

Victoria Glendinning, 1980

HARRIET HUME

I

THEIR feet, running down the wooden staircase from
her room, made a sound like the scurrying of mice
on midnight adventures; and when they paused on
the landing to kiss, it was still in whispers that they
told each other how much they were in love, as if
they feared to awaken sleepers.

But it was the afternoon that came in by the high
window on the landing, and it was amusing to
swagger back into the daylight, challenging it to
punish one for having been where one had been.
So he cried aloud: "See, Kensington goes on! It
has been waiting for us all the time! It has been
threatening us!" And certainly the aspen which
laid its lower branches across this window seemed to
be delivering some testy message by tapping on the
glass with its nearer twigs. "It is saying it will get
us yet! It is warning us—oh, look what is warning
us!" His right hand left her waist and pointed to
a gap in the foliage, where dancing leaves framed
a triangle cut from the line of houses that lay beyond
the garden wall. There could be seen of one house
the dumpy windows of the "best bedroom" floor,

which sunblinds made seem like three stout maids in green calashes waiting to put their mistress to bed. There could be seen of two houses the six tall windows of the "drawing-room" floor, opening on a balcony balustraded with the key-pattern in cast iron, to show that here England had met Greece, and that the introducing party had been the Victorian era. There could be seen of three houses the sturdy pillars of their porticos, varnished black to make a handsome harmony with the saddened primrose of the stucco front; their dining-room windows, broad and slightly protuberant, like the paunch of a moderate over-eater; and their stockade of area railings, boasting with their lance-heads that there were points, such as the purity of cooks and the sacredness of property, concerning which the neighbourhood could feel with primitive savagery. And for base of this triangle was the grey pavement in front of three-and-a-half houses, on which there now slowly stepped, from behind the screen of dancing leaves, a fat papa, no slimmer for being in a light summer suiting, a fat mamma, a deal less slim for being in flowered summer trailings, and a fat little boy and a fat little girl with bright cheeks and bright hair, who were pulling along by a jointly held lead a fat little white dog, which was sitting down on the ground and pretending to have a solid base. "It is telling us," cried Arnold Condorex, "that some day we will live in houses like that and be people like those. It is threatening us that some day we will spend Saturday afternoons not at all as

we do now, that instead we will go and take tea with
Grandmamma so that she can see our little——"

Suddenly Harriet Hume stood clear of him, her
mouth a little open, her eyes bright with wonder as
well as her delight in him. "Stop!" Her narrow
hand covered his lips so swiftly that though there
was no force behind the movement it startled him as
if it had been a blow.

Puzzled, he silently mumbled with his lips against
her palm, and raised his eyebrows. Was she going,
after all that had happened, to be delicate about
what hardly any women were delicate about nowadays?

"No, indeed," she laughed, before he had quite
finished the thought, and slipped aside her hand that
she might kiss him frankly; but slipped it back and
continued, "But I think—oh, Arnold! I am sure!—
I know the names you were going to say!"

His eyebrows went still higher and he gently butted
away her hand. "What names?" He disliked above
all things women who laid claim to occult gifts. It
was half way to saying they believed in reincarnation
and, when the wind blew from the south, themselves
remembered having been Egyptian princesses in their
time—ay! and having kept their own pyramid, too.

"No, indeed!" she said indignantly again. "I
make no foolish pretensions, nor ever did, my love!"
And she drew him back to the complete approval of
her by giving herself again into his arms, by letting
the pulse of her profound excitement shake through

her lips on to his. " But truly I know the names you were going to say just then, the names you were inventing for those fat children. Suddenly they seemed to be . . ." She laid her finger between her eyebrows. ". . . Here . . . like a patch of headache."

Mocking her, he kissed that finger. " What were they, then ? "

" Why," she cried, straight into his eyes, " they were Andrew and Phœbe ! "

His hands dropped down by his side.

" Am I not right ? " she pressed him exultantly.

" Right," he muttered. " It is a miracle ! " Awed, he scanned her glowing face. " My darling, that is very wonderful ! " But he did not like it. His eyes left her, looked out of the window at the gap in the foliage, though long ago papa, mamma, the little boy and girl, the white dog, had disappeared again behind the dancing leaves. " Pooh ! " he said lightly. " I must have told you of this. For I did not invent those names. They were those the curate had bestowed on his young in the village in the Cotswolds where we were taken for our holidays when we were babes, and they have stayed with me ever since as symbols for dull brats. I must have told you. . . ."

She shook her sleek head. " You have never told me ! Why, even as you say it, you are thinking, ' I have not talked of Lathom Cross for years ! ' No, my dear ! Of this I think there is no explanation !

It simply means that prodigious things are happening to us this afternoon! And why should they not! Why should they not!"

And with that she threw up her bare arms, clasped her hands above her head, and so ran down the stairs ahead of him. Following her, he marked how her shoulders were so prominent under her long tight bodice of thin silk that they might have been wings folded in on themselves and packed away for reasons of prudence : and thought that if she indeed desired to look an ordinary woman, walking on earth and of much the same specific gravity she had better not have cut her skirts so full, for their swaying buoyancy seemed to be supporting her. At least one could not credit that this was done by her tiny feet, which were so high in the instep and so finicking clear-cut at ankle and at toe, that one could fancy them not feet at all but spurs added as a last touch to a bird-woman built by a magician expert in fine jewellers' work and ornithology. Of all women he had ever known she was the most ethereal. Loving her was like swathing oneself with a long scarf of spirit. Yet, so far as loving went, how human! He had thought that when she had reached the foot of the stairs, which descended directly into the sitting-room, she would pause and wait for him, to have confirmed all that had been between them by more kisses. But instead she ran across the room to the grand piano, which with the two great arm-chairs and the divan was all it held, and threw open the lid, looking at him and pointing at the keyboard with an air of invitation. In a second, however, she remembered, and saying wistfully, " Oh, I had forgotten you did not play ! " closed the piano again ; and went to the divan and shook up the cushions for him ; and drew the curtains across the bay at the end of the room, for this old house that let her live in a corner of it was over lofty in all its proportions, and giraffe-high windows let in a slanting plethora of light trying to modern eyes that read too much. Since her curtains were of amber taffeta this made her room a cave of bronzy shadow, which the brightness from the windows on the garden side washed softly as water. Then she whisked her skirts towards the mantelpiece, where there were still two tall vases full of the flowers that had been given to her at her last concert, took out a rosebud, ran to him, snapped the long stalk and set it in his button-hole, and went back and found another for her bosom. And there at the hearth she came to rest, her rose-coloured nail toying with the nail-coloured rose, the involved wrist as finely turned as one would have been led to suppose from the carriage of her head (which supported a Grecian knot as hardly another head in a million), and the stance of her feet (of which one was turned out as far as could be, while the other rested behind it on the very point of the toe, as if she were a little girl at her dancing-class), while her other arm lay like a rod of spirally rounded ivory along the mantelpiece. It was not a pity that her gown took the shade of China tea on the side of the curtained windows and the shade of pearls on the side where daylight had its way.

"Oh, I am tired," yawned Condorex, rolling among the cushions.

"And I am hungry!" cried Harriet; and pointed to the open French window. "Well, see what came when we were giving our attention elsewhere!" On the topmost of the six broad, shallow steps that led down to the garden was the veiled golden brick of a half-pound of butter; a glossy white bottle of milk; a bag full of eggs. They were there because, fantastically enough, there was no entrance to Harriet's abode. So hastily had the old house been converted to feed the house-hunger that raged after the Great War, so far faster than any fast bowler had the contractor hurled in staircases and partitions of wood that had he left them alone had become match-boxes, that some problems of architecture had inevitably gone unsolved. Gentle and simple, therefore, be they great composer or "the vegetables," had to find the door in the wall of old Blennerhassett House through which only gardeners had gone until the General's widow died; had to master the trouble concerning the loose brass-knob; had to pass alongside the shapely groves and extended lawns that had still (for all that fences divided them into meaner spaces) the large formality of a country park to the flagged terrace from which rose these steps to Harriet's room; and before they could announce their coming must climb to the very top of the steps and run the risk of finding Harriet as she might be at the moment. This was indeed a risk. A baker's boy from Sussex Place had not been quite the same since he had rattled on the window to learn if he should leave brown or white, and Harriet, seated at the piano in her dressing-gown, had turned on him the face like a skull which she had worn ever since she had woken that morning sick with the sudden knowledge that the way she had always played the Fugato was wrong, and wrong, and wrong again. Better luck attended an old gentleman (K.C., V.O.) who had found Harriet in one of the great arm-chairs, her legs tucked up underneath her, in what would have been decency had she been wearing anything but a chemise transparent with a hundred washings, while she mended her one pair of silk stockings (for these were the terrible years when she was paying for the piano) that she had a minute before plucked from the clothes-horse in front of the kitchen fire; but he, alas, was quite the same after that experience as before.

"I may as well know first as last," said Harriet, "do you like your eggs boiled or scrambled?"

"Boiled," said he, "four minutes."

"We will dip our bread and butter in them," she said, settling the parcels in her arms as if they were a baby.

"It is wrong," he said.

Over her shoulder she asked him, "Can we strain at a gnat after swallowing a camel?" and the kitchen door closed tartly behind her.

14

He closed his eyes ; but it would be a mistake to
fall asleep if in five or ten minutes she would be bringing in tea, for he was so drowsy that he knew wakening
would be painful unless he slept for hours. Heaving
himself up, he stretched, yawned "Ah-ha-ha!"
contentedly, and hobbled over to shake back the
curtains so that full daylight should bully him back to
alertness. Then his fingers, which were not troubling
to make precise piano movements, slowly felt for
cigarettes in his case. They found what they wanted,
but he had no matches. But there were always enough
of them in the box on the mantelshelf. Harriet's
house was kept trimly enough. And the box, he
reflected as he closed it, was a credit to her taste ;
a very nice piece of Early Victorian foolishness,
lacquered papier-mâché sprayed with mother-of-pearl
flowers and golden leaves. He sighed, "Poor
Harriet!" For it had struck him that with the sole
exception of that superb monster, the piano, the little
things in her house were all so much better than the
big ; and nobody knew better than Arnold Condorex, for reasons which could be easily divined by
those who had visited his attic in the Temple, what
that meant. A carpet so flimsy that it reproduces on
its surface the least inequalities of the planks beneath,
and lean-arm-chairs and divan on which cushions
are no mere luxuries, when they are found in the same
room as exquisiteness that can be held in the palm
of the hand, trifles of art that cover no more than two
inches of table or six inches of wall, means that a

bright spirit has been born naked of material inheritance. " Poor Harriet ! " he sighed again.

But where had that birth, so beautiful, albeit destitute, been accomplished ? Though he knew Harriet so well and had taken more than a brief period of time to arrive at this knowledge, he knew nearly nothing about her, not even where, in the widest sense, the sense of class, she had been born. At times he had thought he had discovered that she was native of a class far above his own ; but not more often than he had thought she had betrayed an origin almost comically lower. It was odd that he had felt on both kinds of occasion a sudden exultant emotion, as if what he had found out had given him an advantage over her. But as he had never been quite sure what class he had belonged to himself it was natural enough that he should be confused about such matters. He bent over the book-case, which filled a recess between the fireplace and the French window, to see if it would give a hint of what kind of education she had had. But with the most perfect finality it contained no books : not one. Music it was that stuffed the shelves, save for the lowest shelf of all, which housed one week's issues of the *Morning Post*. At that he laughed aloud, half at the memory of the way she read them, half at his knowledge of why she read them. For Harriet suffered from a disorder of the sight which could not be corrected with spectacles since it fluctuated with her strength, so that a struggle with March winds or an hour's excess of practising would leave her sand-blind. Therefore, as it often happened that she was a little tired, she usually read her newspapers by spreading them on the floor, squatting tailor-wise at their edge in the pale pool of her skirts, and leaning her weight on her hand but very lightly, just so that her arm curved from shoulder to wrist in a scimitar shape, in order to move easily when she came to a column's end. Squatted thus, she peered down at the print with her eyes narrowed between immensely long eyelashes, and her sleek head veering back and forth, back and forth, to find the focus, though it looked as if she were nodding time to music that only she could hear. And she went to all this bother and disturbance of her neat room, solely to learn more of the friends her early fame had brought her. " Why, old Sir George is really a great man ! " she would cry. " He carried the Commons with him yesterday on the subject of China, on which (I must confess) I thought him such a bore only last Sunday among the lilacs ! " Most people are pleased enough when their lives can be counted as illustrative notes in the margin of what the world decides to commemorate in print and are overjoyed when they are incorporated in the main text ; but to Harriet, dear fool, that text could at most be a footnote to her own life, an amusing appendix to the vastly more important things that happened when she played the piano, bit into an apple, was hot, was cold. Arnold Condorex liked that about her reading, liked it as much as the sight of her waist rising straight from the watchspring she made, when she sat thus on the floor, by the neat coiling of her legs. 'Twas not for him to find repellent a disdainful and triumphant attitude to the world on the part of those who had been born with no silver spoon in their mouths.

Liking a pompous phrase from time to time, he muttered : ". . . as little human history as a nymph," and turned away, but stepped back immediately, for there had caught his eye, from behind the stoutness of the telephone directory and the turtle-shell cigarette-box that lay end to end on the bookshelf, three bars of Russian leather that might as well be the tops of photograph-frames. That indeed they were, and he made to pick them up but stopped himself, since one must not be caught prying, and instead brushed aside the directory with his right hand and the turtle-shell box with his left, and looked at the photographs where they rested against the wall behind. The midmost photograph was of a house, a stone house, a farmhouse, perhaps, or a lonely parsonage. No look of county about it. No drive. Patently no gardeners kept. No, he had long come to the conclusion she could not be of very high condition. But a good place, a clean place, as places are in the cold, clean North. That it was there could be seen from the background, which showed hills checkered with dikes to a height that only insane northern industry would climb ; and in the foreground the roses were plainly climate-curst. Surely the first night they met she had said something about Cumberland. A grim

18

place for Harriet to live; a grim place even for the woman whose photograph was on the left, though one could see that her handsomeness was stiffened with a buckram of moral purpose that her daughter lacked. Yet to be sure the elder was none the worse for that, since if Harriet had a fault it was that her oval face was almost insipid with compliancy. Yes, this woman was very handsome. What a life she must have lived all her days, shut up in that hole at the world's end with the man whose photograph was on the right, a bearded creature pretentiously austere, overblown with patriarchy, as avid for opportunities to raise a hand to heaven to bless or curse his children as a prima donna for arias. It would be very gratifying to go to a lonely village and stumble on such a superb woman. He heard through her imagined ears his knock on an imagined door; and could see with her imagined eyes his obscured handsomeness standing beyond the threshold in the night. " I beg pardon. I am lost. Can you tell me where I might find a room ? Oh, you are most kind." In an imagined kitchen he stood and quietly waited till she finished her task of putting the chain back on the door, and turned, and saw him; and bade him sit down, and when he was seated ingenuously moved the lamp along the table nearer him, till his handsomeness was wholly within its bright circle. One would not move until she sighed. Oh, to live for ever. There is so much to be done in the world.

Sliding the telephone book and the turtle-shell

box together again, he moved along to the mantelpiece and ſtared at himself in the mirror behind it,
smoothing back the raven hair that was apt (there was
a Levantine on his mother's side) to lie over his earſ
in something too like Disraeli's locks. Give him a
neckcloth and he might have been any of the ſtates-
men who were great when Corn Laws and Reform
Bills were all the go. He had the right aquilinity of
head which was preserved from suspicion of above-
earthness by the square shoulders, themselves preserved from the contrary suspicion of peasant grossness by the lean waiſt, the temperate hips. Also he
had the intense black gaze and the dark pluminess of
brows, beetling much for so young a man, that are
the very thing, as one has seen in a hundred prints,
for thinking about politics in a park under thunder-
clouds ; and he had to a T that ample, marbly Roman-
ness of profile which would make them think he had
written his speech in the library of his place, beneath
the cold eyes of the third earl, a buſt, and Cicero,
a remarkably fine tern. It was a type that would
have its day again. People were growing tired of
the serviceability that had been the only tempera-
mental wear for young politicians during the war.
They were ready now to be entertained by wit and
floridity ; and once they looked to one for entertainment what one would produce in the way of sense
had the dramatic power of the unexpeɛted ; and if one
could enaɛt at will the romantic geſture, so endearing
to the populace, of burning one's boats behind

one because of an inflaming principle, one would be safe for life. He pursed his lips, which were full, firm, and discreetly red, ending in two small vertical creases in handsome flesh, as do the cupid's bows of all the Elgin Marbles ; and faced the glass indifferently, not caring if it were there, as five years ahead he would face the Opposition Benches, not caring if they were there. " Oh, I am fortunate ! " he thought in a drawl ; and suddenly his mask cracked and showed his real face, that was as young as his real years. He reflected how fortunate he had been to gain Harriet, how nearly he had not met her, how kindly she had bent herself to his will, and how little he deserved her.

Tears stood in his eyes. He could no longer see anything in the glass. He told himself that though he had but little money to spend just then he could go out next morning and buy her a ring, and would not need to feel ashamed however modest it was, as her heart would understand how much he loved her and refer its modesty to the proper cause. Not in the least would he mind that she should know how little a way he had travelled on his path to fame and fortune ; he could even imagine owning to her how ridiculously few dress-shirts were in his wardrobe. Sweet Harriet, she would take any secret he gave her, fold it neatly as if it were a fine linen handkerchief, and pop it inside her bodice between the little mounts that were indubitably a woman's breasts yet did not prevent her form being very childish, and there it would lie, safe as a packet at the Mint ; and while

she wore it so her face would look at the world with
an expression of the most nearly universal benevolence
and the most gallant obstinacy, as if she were saying
that she would give it anything it wished save only
that. And at the thought of how pretty she would
look then, and of how little the ring would have to be
to fit her finger, he felt a serene contraction of the
throat, and two tears had to be dealt with by his
forefinger. "Dear Harriet! Dear Harriet!" he
muttered, and liked to see his handsomeness taking
the words out of his mouth in the mirror. Yes,
he was fortunate in that his handsomeness saved him
from being too painfully outstripped by her in beauty.
Yet still she was too good for him. He choked,
thinking of ways he might try to deserve her.

It was then that the whine of the hinge grew loud
enough for him to hear; and on turning his head he
saw that Harriet was standing still in the doorway with
a tray in her arms, and had, he guessed, from something
rigid in her attitude, been rooted there for more than
an instant. Immediately he felt, perhaps because
there was something witch-like in the stooping of her
slenderness over the weight of the tray, the coldest
apprehension regarding the feeling which had held
her so and lit a most perplexing brilliance in her face.
She was, of course, as blooming as every woman is
when a man has just proved that he loves her; that
is to say, a fairy masseuse had patted her flesh into
delicious infant contours on the cheekbones and had
shaped her lips into a smile suited to approval of

22

nothing less than divine conditions and left them bright as wet paint, as the bitten meat of cherries. But over and above that bloom she wore a radiance that had been but newly applied, and stood taut with a tensity derived from some galvanic force that still electrified the air about her, and had not been dissipated by time at all.

She was, he saw, about to speak. But on the explanation of what had happened to her he waited with no joy at all. For so soon as he had found himself surprised he had been taken in charge by that most miserable part of him which believed that the whole world was furtively deriding one Arnold Condorex and which ascribed to derision supreme power over the universe, against which love and justice might range themselves in vain ; and it whispered in his ear that what had transfigured the girl could be nothing less than this omnipotence of mocking laughter.

Blackly he moved to take her burden from her, and was about to say, with a stiff laugh, " Well, you have caught me looking in the glass," when she said happily : " Well, who would not, left alone in a room ! " and then cried out, as if she had been hurt, " Oh, I was not laughing at you ! Arnold, how could you think I was laughing at you ! " She ran beside him to the table, clinging to his sleeve with both hands, and as soon as he had set down the tray pinned herself to his bosom. " What have I done that you should think I would laugh at you and think meanly of you ? " she asked piteously ; and looking down into her wet eyes he knew that he was a fool.

"Why, nothing," he said, and gravely kissed her. "It is only that I am sometimes black and bitter and that . . ." What he had in his heart to say was that in his journey up from sordid God-knows-where he had had to overcome so many ambushed memories that it was not surprising if his fretted vigilance saw enemies everywhere. But it was hard for him to admit even to Harriet how long and hard that journey had been ; and Harriet relieved him of the need to, for she nodded her head and patted his hand as if he had already confided in her. "But tell me, dear, has anything happened to you ? When you stood at the door I had the queerest notion that you were so excited about something that you were going to burst out singing, or laughing, or crying——"

"Oh, yes, something has happened!" Harriet told him ; and drew away from him, solemn and open-mouthed with wonder, very much as she had done by the window on the balcony, not so long before. "You will not believe it ! But you will have to believe it ! " Then she looked a little disconsolate, as if she had divined that though he might believe it he would not like it. "Let us have tea first ! " she begged rather sadly ; but smiled brilliantly under her lashes, as if she thought that she would lead him to it, and it was not in human nature after that first amazement he should not like it.

Nor was it in human nature not to like the meal, to

24

which her little wrists moving about the tea equipage
gave the air of a doll's tea-party. Of the two cups
and saucers on her tray one was India red, and the
other that pale blue which Victorian ladies used freely
in their water-colour drawings of the Bay of Naples,
and she offered him his choice between them; and
bade him speak if he liked to drink his tea out of any
other colour, for there were four more of the harlequin
set in the china cupboard. Fondly she asked, " Will
you not have another, my dear?" though there are
no dairy Falstaffs who push excess to the point of the
third egg; and she had opened for him a new pot of
the quince jelly and the apple jelly flavoured with
orange, though only the other day he had heard her
lamenting that such conserves lose their flavour almost
as soon as they are exposed to the air. Tenderly he
reflected that her little head, which was almost egg-
like in its oval blandness, was as full as an egg is of
meat with the desire to please. But for that his
shrewdness rebuked him. There must be much else
besides. She had mastered the shining black leviathan
that just behind her proclaimed Bechstein its parent.
Like him she had crawled up the dark tunnel which
leads from obscurity to the light, and had performed
the feat more expeditiously. She must be in league
with formidable forces, he reflected with sudden
gloom, if her fragility could carry positions one
would judge impregnable save by the heaviest artillery.
If that were so, would it not be certain that she despised him, and that the illumination to which he had

been subject at the door was an explosion of mocking laughter? He pushed away his plate.

Excluding from his tones all hint of apprehension, he asked with an uneasy smile, "Now, Harriet, tell me what made you look so lovely at the door."

"Do not be apprehensive," she answered gaily. "It was something lovelier than anything that has ever happened to me before, and something lovelier than has ever happened to you, I will swear." Yet she was fearful; he knew that from the way her little hand was nuzzling into his palm. Did that not mean that she must be feeling guilty? "You must know," she continued, "that when I went into the kitchen I found that the big kettle had been left on the hob and had just come to the boil. This meant that I could make tea on the instant; my servant had left out the tray with all prepared; and it was but a matter of five minutes to boil the eggs. I reflected that I would not return to you as I had meant to do if I had had to fill the kettle with cold water, and there had been twenty minutes to wait; for I loathe nothing more than people whisking in and out of rooms. I believed too I could better occupy the few minutes opening new pots of quince and apple jelly, as I remembered that you liked one better than the other, and I knew that you are so amiable that you would pretend whichever I took in was that one, even if it were not; and here you must always have what you like best. Well, I was standing by my kitchen table, putting a knife to the string round the jam-pot, and thinking very tenderly of you as you rested here on my couch, when—when——"

Her fingers were floating towards her brow. He laughed aloud. It was that nonsense again. Well, he had been alarming himself unneccessarily.

"—I had that patch of headache here; and just as I was when we saw those children through those windows, I was in your mind. And because I was in your mind I knew what your body was doing. You were pulling back the curtains——"

He made a grimace that paid himself several compliments. For the smile which was its beginning showed that he was too canny to be deceived, that he realised she could see he had pulled the curtains as soon as she had entered the room, and thereby had been inspired to act her galvanisation and improvise this story; and the insincere attempt to suppress that smile which followed showed him a large-minded and tolerant man who would not be too hard on women for that in them which runs to telling fibs about the occult.

"Yes, truly," she persisted, with meek bravery, "I could feel that you were pulling back the curtains, and then that you felt a need for rhythm, that you wanted to enjoy a sense of ebb and flow without greatly exerting yourself. I had never before understood why people smoke. There were cigarettes in your case, but you had no matches. You thought of my pretty box on the mantelpiece that I bought at King's Lynn. You went to it, and lit a match, and thought how much better my small things are than my big ones——"

He pushed back his chair, he made to rise, his hand dragged his collar from his choking throat. The preposterous thing was true, and its truth was not bearable. He saw himself loafing about the room, prying and appraising, and it did not seem to him that one decent thought had passed through his mind. It was not humane to spy upon him so.

Harriet was at his feet, suddenly, like a bird that was on a bush and is on the path. Pressing her body against his knees, and slipping her hand into his, she compelled him to sit down again, and dumbfounded him by lifting a face calm as a primrose with happiness.

"You thought so beautifully about me!" she rejoiced. "You were sorry for me because I am so poor, and you reflected how alike we were in our utter lack of fortune. Ah, dear! I am so grateful to you for that thought. It is so rarely people think how needy I must be, on the little that is all musicians can earn until they are recognised as very great. They think I have no nice things because I am a sloven and do not care. They ask me on visits to their grand houses, where I have to give the servants what I ought to spend on a week's food. Oh, it was kind of you to have a mind to my poverty! And then you wondered who I am and whence I come. I have often wondered that about you, but since you did not offer to tell me I did not ask. But—yes, I will own that I have been a little hurt because you never asked me about

28

myself. I wanted you to be eager for all of what I was, as well as for all of what I am. So I was happy then, and happy when you remembered that at times you had thought me a princess, and at others a little trollop, for, of course, every woman would like to be both. There are some very enviable effects a trollop can make which are beyond the reach of a princess. Then you looked at my book-case, and marked how I read nothing except the newspapers, and remembered—oh, how flatteringly well!—how I must sit when I read them, because of my poor eyes. And you laughed at me a little, but did not like me any less, because I cannot be interested in anything that does not touch my life, and see nothing as real that does not hold a clue which leads back to me in my little house. It is, as you said, for news of Sir George that I read my paper.

"And then it was that you caught sight of those photographs behind the telephone directory and my turtle-shell tea-caddy. Oh, my love, when you saw them you showed such wisdom, such kind wisdom, though I fear you have bought it dearly! You looked at them furtively, you held the book and the box so that you might slip them back in place on the instant if I returned. Oh, that was right. When people seek complete knowledge of us it is ten to one they do it to find out the perfect place to shoot an arrow; so we acquire a habit of fearing those who make that search. With this new power I have to read your mind, I know that what you did proceeded from pure love for me, but had I come in unenlightened and you had not taken the precautions that you did, I might have winced. Do not be ashamed! You were acting as, knowing all, I would have you act. Then your eyes dwelt on my mother's face. You are right, she is more beautiful than I am. But your other thoughts were far too hopeful. There is nothing to be done. Poor darling, she believes each thunderclap to be a Divine warning. Myself "—she looked a little priggishly at her piano—" I would not care to allege that any sound had so simple a meaning. It is sad, for you are right about my father, who breaks the silence of our hills with a tiresomeness that has something their own air of enduring for ever. Then, thinking of her and him, you began to dream a day-dream of going to lonely places in the North and finding splendid women starved by climate and circumstance, like jewels dropped in peat, and redeeming them by coming dark and handsome into their homes by night. Dearest, I was so glad when you thought that, for it showed me how like you are to me! For never, I will now confess to you, have I travelled on the Underground without expecting the ticket-collector to throw aside that pert, snapping metal thing, and pop down on his knees, disclosing himself to be the Prince of Wales who (I admit very oddly) has chosen to find his bride by acting in that capacity, having had from childhood an ambition to marry that woman of the realm who has the smallest hand and the most darned gloves. We are both silly children, and how fortunate it is that we have found each other, so that we can play together without fear of being scorned by the other for our silliness !

"And we are not so silly either," she continued gravely, "for indeed we are marvellous, and should be able to command marvellous things ! Yes, all the things you imagined when you looked at yourself in the mirror should come true ! That fame, that power over the people, that house with the pillars and the pediments, and a park with the wooded knoll in it from which one can see five counties—there is no reason why you should not have them all ! Indeed you do deserve them, for thinking of another human being as you thought of me just after that ! Oh, Arnold, I stood in my kitchen and could not believe that I could have inspired such sentiments ! I felt proud and humble, and I cried a little, and I longed to give you a present that would not be just a present but would be appropriate to you, would be a present specially designed to please that quality in you which I find so pleasing ; and lo ! in that thought I found my mind meeting yours. You were thinking the very same thing about me ! At that I picked up my tray and told myself to stop day-dreaming ; but as I came along the passage I knew that I would find you standing by the mantelpiece, and that I would see in your face that you had been all overthrown and disturbed by the kindness of your feeling for me. I said aloud, ' Nonsense, he will be on the couch where I left him, and he will be drowsed and indifferent.' And then

my tray pushed open the door—and oh, Arnold!
Arnold!"

Her voice trilled up like a bird's, her face soared to
the level of his face for kisses. He delayed only for a
minute to gasp. "It is true. Every word is true!
And it is a miracle!" before he clipped her to him and
embraced her as if they were being swept off the solid
earth by a tide of prodigiousness. There was an
added marvel in feeling under his hand her heart-
beat which showed that though her spirit was so
marvellously transcending all ordinary human limita-
tions, she nevertheless kept as faithful a bond with
fact as the tick of a clock. Dizzied, he tried to recall
himself to order, the world to order. He jerked back
in his chair and loosened her arms. "Harriet!"
he protested, "this cannot be!"

"It is," she meekly claimed.

"But, my love, this is the real world! Over on that
table I see the horrid form which has been sent you by
the Income Tax Commissioners. The things are not
compatible. Such miracles of thought cannot occur!"

"But have I not told you what you were thinking?"
she answered calmly. "And can there be any other
test?"

"Yes, you are right!" he cried. "That is the only
test, and you have satisfied it; and, in the satisfying
of it, have given me such good news about my soul.
For I have believed it only a lair of monsters, and you
have shown it to be a scene where a sylph may wander,
and not take fright." Again he drew her to him;

and they remained very close, until he drew apart, took her hands in his, and gazed very reverently on her face.

"You are right," she said pertly, "it is odd that I look so like a doll when I have qualities above the ruck of dolls."

He bit his lip. "Do not laugh at me!" he begged, and asked very solemnly, "Harriet, how do you do this thing?"

"Are you so greatly interested in how it is done?" she asked carelessly, playing with his cravat. "To me what is done seems more interesting than the doing of it. But I suppose," she said, swinging herself down from his knee, "that it belongs to this order of happening." She tripped to her piano, uncovered the keyboard, and retreated again until she stood with her back against the wall. For a minute or two she breathed so deeply that it seemed likely to go hard with the seams of her little bodice, while intention made her face remote from him; and then, in a voice far lower than her usual, she began to recite:

> I have a garden of my own,
> But so with roses overgrown
> And lilies, that you would it guess
> To be a little wilderness;
> And all the springtime of the year . . .

The moment provided a triple occupation for Arnold Condorex; for he was delirious at having the extremes of love and strangeness revealed to him in an afternoon with such heavenly lightness and benignity;

and he was reflecting how remarkable it was that her skin, the billows of her skirt, and the glossy varnished wall behind her, were within but a tone or two of each other in colour, yet presented a spectacle in which the eye could dwell with a sense of the most abundant variousness; and he was embarrassed as he always was when he heard anyone repeating poetry, since his lack of memory for words prevented him from ever recognising it, and his pride made him itch to say he did. But he was snatched from all these occupations by his half-horrified perception that from the unattended keyboard of the piano, whose mistress stood ten feet away, was coming music. Not melody, to be sure, but a progression that corresponded with the line of her voice, echoing clearly enough each note she dwelt on for any space or with any richness. The sound was less brisk than that which a finger evokes by striking a key. Rather was it as if some inhabiting spirit of the instrument had resolved no longer to tolerate the age-old conditions by which human virtuosity steals all the credit of its tune-fulness, and was essaying to make its music by itself, and found its new art difficult. But that it made a sound could not be gainsaid. He made an uneasy exclamation.

"No, indeed," laughed Harriet, leaning against the wall and flinging wide her arms in laughter, "this is no speciality of the house. Any piano will answer any voice that speaks to it deeply enough. There are cords in my throat, and cords in my piano. Set the air shaking with strong enough pulses, and both cords will shake alike. I . . . I imagine that something of the same order explains our private marvel." Though her eyelids drooped, she would not let them have their way, but tilted her head back, so that under them she could still regard him steadily. Since a blush would spread, she covered her cheeks with her hands and spoke bravely between them : " We have been shaken by the same pulse, and it was not a weak one."

He was at her side. Taking her in his arms, he whispered, " Did I not tell you all the time that was miraculous ? "

Gently she evaded him, putting up a hand between their lips, but only that she might ask him, a little piteously : " But you, my dear, can you not read my thoughts at all ? "

Smiling at the idea that such things could be hoped of him, he shook his head.

Her eyes were mournful. " I have so strange a feeling that you could . . . if you would . . . but let that pass ! " She sighed, and let him utterly enfold her.

" Oh, we must always——! " he groaned.

" Ah, let us not ever——! " she breathed.

Their trembling forbade them to finish their sentences ; which was of no great moment, since that aspect of their situation was so far from unique. They clung together, attempting to regain their calm, until Harriet, rolling her eye over her lover's shoulder towards her window and her garden, saw something she did not expect and gave a shrill scream.

"Look!" she cried, and pointed at what to him was nothing.

"My dear?" he asked.

"The shadow of the purple lilac is lying straight across the terrace!"

"These odd-job gardeners," he jested, "have their lapses. They do not tie up shadows as they should."

"But, my dear, that means it is evening!"

"Evening! It cannot be evening! It is perhaps late afternoon, it may be about half-past five." He drew out the handsome watch the Duke had given him when he left the Ministry for the War Office and could not take his indefatigable secretary with him. "Why, it positively is twenty minutes past seven! But that is impossible! Why, how the time has flown!" They exchanged a glance of raillery. "I hope, my dear," he said, putting his watch back in his pocket, "that you are not now going to play tricks with time. A man must have something to tell him where he is."

"I do not see why," she answered, but did not keep up the argument, for she had a little lost her spirits. "My love, if you have to go to Lord Downderry again this evening you must go on your way. I will never keep you from your duty. What's that? You are remembering that he said to-night you need not come till ten? Oh, that is excellent."

"And do you not call it excellent also, that other

thing which is in my mind?" he asked. "Which is, that since your garden is pretty enough to be a worthy setting for your prettiness, I would like to walk with you there till I must go."

"I will not disturb the classic relationship of the sexes to that degree," replied Harriet. "Whatever gifts I may have, I will leave you to say aloud the flattering things you think of me, and will pretend to be surprised when I hear them. So I am amazed to hear that you wish to walk with me in my garden, and confused by the reason you give for it; and I would be obliged if you would hand me my shawl."

She wound it about her till she had as little arm as a seal, and led the way down the steps into her garden, which was bloomy with deep shadows. At the first flower-bed she stooped to dismiss a weed from service, brushed the mould from her fingers with some distaste, and grumbled because the duties of a gardener could not be performed with a feather-duster. Then they took to the lawn and strolled up and down, keeping admirable step though he was so much taller, and being very pleased over little things. They paused at the wrought-iron gate which the Bridge Club that occupied the main wing of Blennerhassett House had set up, for the sake of ornament, in the middle of the fence dividing their share of the old garden from Harriet's; and they enjoyed the long shadow, like a lyre with many strings, which it cast on the lawn behind it. By the crest some of its convolutions formed Arnold was able to tell from what demolished great house in the neighbourhood it came, and at that Harriet was able to tell him how clever he was. Then he gave her his arm very kindly, and they took another turn.

" We are as contented as old married people," he said, after a silence.

" Much more so, I suppose," she answered.

" You are saucy, Miss, you are saucy," he rebuked her. " Are you not afraid to be as saucy in the very face of the refining influence of Nature ? Are you not abashed by the elevating society of the birds, the flowers, the trees ? And, by the way, those three trees at the end of your garden are exceedingly beautiful. I have often thought so, but I have never seen them look so splendid as to-night."

Her eyes flashed on them. " You know them, of course ? They are the Ladies Frances, Georgina, and Arabella Dudley. Sir Joshua Reynolds painted them. The result of his labours is in the National Gallery under the title, ' The Three Graces Decorating a Statue of Hymen.' "

He scrutinised them. The one on the left was low, and extended its branches up to the taller trees on the right as a kneeling woman might offer a gift to a woman standing beside her ; and that taller tree seemed with its own branches to pass on what was given to the tallest tree, which was evidently of the order of those who take and do not give, for all its branches save that which took the gift stayed close to its trunk as folded arms to a body. There was also a suggestion of humanity in the way they stood on the turf with

38

more than arboreal elegance, as if their roots had in
their time been attentive to a dancing master; and
their leaves at this evening hour looked more like
flowers than leaves, being crudely aureate where the
sunset struck them and a deep blue where it did not,
and not like real flowers either, but such fantasy-
engendered blooms as nymphs might use.

"You are right," he pronounced. "If it is not a
secret of the household, may I ask how they came
here?"

"It is a long story," replied Harriet, "and in part
almost improbable. They are here in consequence
of a lamentable train of events that began on the
evening of a day which——"

"Ah, you little liar," he cried in delight, "are
you well away on one of your fairy tales?"

"—of a day," continued Harriet, "which by an
interesting coincidence was the third birthday of the
Lady Frances, the second of the Lady Georgina, and
the first of the Lady Arabella. Their nurse had left
them sleeping like three cherubs to go down to the
servants' hall for supper, and was sitting at ease over
her meat when the slut she had left in charge came
rushing into the room screeching and blubbering
that though she had nodded over the fire for but an
instant they had all been gone when she awakened.
It would be useless and horrible to describe the events
of that night. The mother of the infants went off
in swoons like a minute-gun for the rest of the night;
their father took a fowling-piece and bade the chap-

lain do what he could in his department of life while
he himself beat the park with a party of keepers. All
were reunited in what I would like for convenience
to describe as a hopeless dawn, did I not fear that owing
to a certain pictorial masterpiece of last century that
phrase will confuse your mind with suggestions of a
fishing-fleet. The mother embarked on one last
and technically supreme swoon, and the father,
whose feet were exceedingly wet, testily called on the
chaplain to go on his knees again for one final preca-
tory effort, when a cry from the garden brought them
running to the windows. And there, on the lawn,
lay the lost infants. They were sleeping peacefully
and bore no sign of injury. The only singularity
about their aspect was that their melon-like little
contours were linked by a thick cable of flowers.
But that, in the relief of finding them alive, seemed
unimportant enough.

"But alas! it was far from unimportant. For from
that hour onwards those three daughters of the
nobility were never happy unless they bore with them
some such garland as the one that had been found about
their infant limbs that uncanny morning. When they
were children this did not matter. It was considered
an affecting proof of sensibility; and though nurses
complained of the trouble it gave, there was in those
days a superb excess of nurses. It became, however,
increasingly inconvenient as they grew to womanhood.
To begin with, it was not the thing; and their wretched
mother went to the extremes of trouble and expense

to travel all over the British Isles to places where they were holding garden fêtes, where her daughters could appear before the eyes of eligible young men in circumstances that would make their eccentricity seem but a tasteful concession to the spirit of the occasion. Her task of concealment was made nearly impossible, however, by the inflexibility with which these young women held to their whim. They insisted on taking their garlands in to dinner with them ; and what it did to the napes and neckerchiefs of the gentlemen (often heirs to large fortunes) who sat between them was to their father and mother a source of inexpressible grief and irritation. Moreover the affair was, to those who were in a position to be perfectly acquainted with it, of a very sinister complexion. For though the Ladies Frances, Georgiana, and Arabella frequently changed their ropes of flowers for others, being able to make new ones with such rapidity that it seemed as if unseen fingers must be aiding them, it was never because the old ones faded. Those preserved an undiminished freshness that was not natural ; and, worse still, thrown down in any garden, instantly took root and became a dominant factor in the landscape. You have, when visiting the great houses of London, seen some flower-beds that by the brightness and variegation of their blooms struck marvel into your heart ? You may be sure that in their time they had evoked an emotion far surpassing your own in the horror-stricken bosoms of the three girls' unfortunate parents. Yet it was not in human nature for them to put an end to the evil by such drastic measures as may come into your mind; for though their daughters were among the greatest beauties in England so long as they laid hold of their garland, without it they were not above the common run of comeliness.

" Shall I stop, my love ? " asked Harriet. " I am sure you are too wise for fairy-tales."

He shook her arm as if he were a child and she his nurse, that had teased him by stopping when Cinderella entered the coach.

" At length, however, the powers that thus compromised the landed gentry of England by so unwholesome an association with magic defeated themselves. Three young noblemen of immense estates met the three girls at a garden fête in Wales where under the directions of an eccentric landowner enamoured of the romantic movement they were able to trapse about among brand-new Gothic ruins from dawn to dusk. Since the fête lasted for three days, their parents were able to bit and bridle these infatuations till they became good safe carriage-horses of honourable attachments. The betrothals were instantly announced, the marriages followed smoking-hot. At first the young women, who had been brought up in a proper state of innocence, received the news of their good fortune with indifference; but when they were instructed that there are certain occasions in a woman's life when she cannot be accompanied by her two sisters bearing a rope of flowers, they looked at each other with the most sickly apprehension, which, indeed, was justified. For the full beauty of not one of them survived her honeymoon. Even on the wedding-morn it seemed to have waned. They were still handsome; but they were not, as they had often seemed when they trod the sward of parks in their floral panoply, immortal goddesses. Society was good-humoured towards them; but it was bruited abroad that they were disordered in their intellects by a lady who had been present at a mantua-maker's, when they were choosing ball-gowns, and heard them agree in complaining very mournfully that such and such a trimming was *not so durable as flowers*.

" Their lives droned on. Since they had no special advantages as wives, their marriages followed the ordinary course, and it was not long before their husbands visited them only out of good manners to furnish them with a civil annual childbirth. The Lady Frances was alone, therefore, when round about her fortieth year, certain details of her image in the looking-glass suddenly struck her; and it was a soft-footed maid-servant entering her room ('twas in the town house in Portland Place) who found her weeping and uttering the extraordinary lament ' For so simple a matter as a garland to let us grow like this ! ' In a year's time, Lady Georgiana came along to see her sister; and the soft-footed maid-servant found them sitting side by side before the mirror, their arms round each other's waist, both weeping and uttering complaints of the same incomprehensible nature. In another year's time, the Lady Georgiana came and brought her younger sister, whom she seemed to be tending as one who is familiar to a misfortune comforts another who is new to it. The soft-footed servant was none the wiser for this visit, since almost as soon as the three sisters confronted each other they burst into vigorous tears and more of these wild and nonsensical dirges, and Lady Frances ran across the room and opened the door; and without remarking on the circumstance that it knocked over the maidservant, who was in a sitting-position, thrust money into her hands and bade her send a boy to bring a barrow-load of flowers from Covent Garden on the instant.

" When the flowers were brought the three sisters were sitting in the midst of their children, whom they had sent for as suddenly as they had commanded the flowers. They were simultaneously weeping over them and uttering the most disparaging comments on them, which were not unjust, as indeed there was not a remarkable boy or girl among them, but which were expressed in oddly obscure terms. ' Ah, had they but let us keep our garlands, our births would have been better!' On the sight of the flowers, however, they grew solemn, though indeed these were nothing but a hodge-podge of what is a-blowing and a-growing in the month of June. They dismissed their children, and bade the maid-servant light all the tapers, as they had fine work to do. They were not heard to speak again, save by their husbands, who, happening to visit the house together that evening in course of making arrangements for a friend's duel, thought it ill-mannered not to pass greetings with their wives, since they were under the same roof for once, and went up to Lady Frances' room. As the three men knocked at the door they heard a crepitation of dismay, and nothing more. Jealousy, which can so strangely be aroused by the uncherished object, flamed up in all of them. They turned the handle without waiting for permission. The three women, white and rigid, stood facing them behind a table, from which a cable of peonies and poppies coiled to the floor. This was some feminine foolery, and their terrors no more than the respect that good wives pay their husbands. One of them prodded the flowery snake with his buckled shoe. ' What is this, my dear ? ' ' It is for the children.' Ah, shame ! These are the last words recorded of the Ladies Frances, Georgiana, and Arabella Dudley, and they were not candid. See, their branches are stirred with confusion.

" Their husbands were the last to hear them speak. They were not the last to see them. That was left to the butler and the footmen, who, shortly before the dinner-gong should have sounded, looked up the staircase and saw their mistress and her sisters coming down, in greater beauty than they had been for many years, and carrying a cable of flowers unknown in this country, so thick that it must have taken days to weave. The lackeys say that not only did it seem their obvious duty to open the front door for the ladies; but that a power compelled them to it so that they could not have done other for a million pounds; and that in any case they could not have pursued them, for hardly had they seen the three figures changed to white translucency by the moonlight which was silvering the Grecian vistas of the street, when the front door shut of itself with a formidable clang and would not open again for half an hour. By that time, we know, all was over. The ladies had crossed the Park, had proceeded down the Brompton Road ('tis believed they had some thoughts of Knole or Penshurst) and on the outskirts of Chelsea were waylaid by a band of Mohocks, who, seeing their shining forms at a distance, set off at a run to make closer acquaintance. 'Tis from a written confession of one of them, that died within the week at St. Bartholomew's Hospital, his blood frozen by what he saw, that we know the truth: how the three ladies ran from the road to this very spot, which is my garden, which was then a patch of waste land between two cottages; how the Lady Arabella was forced to her knees by the violence of her terror, and the Lady Georgiana was abased nearly as low, but the Lady Frances—look, she is the tall one on the right—seemed upheld to perfect erectness by an invisible power. But of the nature of this power horrible revelation was made to the Mohocks, who

46

shrunk back aghast (since they were pious lads except for their disposition towards robbery and rape) at her next action. For she cast out her arms in an attitude of prayer, but not to heaven! Nay, her hands and her eyes petitioned the ground on which she stood, and plainly were petitioning some force that had existence other than in her fancy. For while the Mohocks huddled together, attempting to recollect the Lord's Prayer, there took place a transformation of the surrounding vegetation which must have been miraculous. The coltsfoot that had bloomed and died three months before, rose again; and their resurrected gold shone beside the shadowy mooniness of the daisies, which were the season's proper wear, and the black flimsiness of poppies that had come before the corn. All the blossoms of the year were there in the darkness, and a patch of nettles at the Mohocks' feet climbed in an instant till the white flowers looked them in the eye, ungenial as spearheads. The three ladies joined hands in the attitudes you see; they had been greatly praised for the poses in Sir Joshua Reynolds' picture. The earth about them trembled, to a degree it swallowed them. When it gulped and stopped the remaining parts of them suffered an abrupt extension towards the stars, then knew the calm integrity of being trees. And there they stand.

"To rejoice with them would be easy, but it would not be right. For the thing was a cruel blow to the pride of their families. To this day, the Dudleys are as close as oysters about it. Ask Lord Dudley about it, and he will pretend no knowledge of it. Persist, and he will send for a policeman———" she dissolved into a gentle giggling.

"Well, it is a tale with a happy ending!" said Arnold ; and they halted and looked up at the trees. "I would like to be a tree in your garden ; and never make a fool of myself or get into mischief again."

"You will not be a tree in my garden," said Harriet, "but you will never make a fool of yourself or get into mischief. And now I have told you a fairy tale, and you must go home. Truly, it is time."

"I will not be able to go home at all," he told her, "unless you let me first walk with you three times up and three times down your long fine lawn. Do you know, Harriet, I have never been so sorry to leave anybody in my life, since I was a little boy and used to go to spend the afternoon with my old uncle who had been a soldier and fought with Roberts at Kandahar, and I would kick and scream and blubber when my mother came after tea to end our talks of bloodshed and rifles and Ashantis. You are as dear to me as if I had known you all my life, which I have not, and as exciting as if I had seen you for the first time this afternoon, which I have not either."

Harriet squeezed his arm ; and without saying a word to each other, but in very comfortable communion, they paced the lawn as he had desired. Evening, when she had begun her story, had rested upon the scene as bloom on the grape, but it had now assumed a more dominating part. The sky had been bleached of its daylight blue, and though it had not yet been invaded by the dark tone of night its translucent pallor was pricked here and there by a star to show that this would not be long delayed. In the garden each colour was yielding up its essence to the darkness. The upward-looking faces of the flowers were merely pale, and so too were the downward-looking faces of the leaves on the trees. The soil in the beds and the tree-trunks were merely night-coloured; and the lawn they trod showed that if grass had a ghost it would be the same greyish hue as, it is commonly accepted, are the ghosts of men. From each of Harriet's windows leaned forth darkness, which held wide the gaping doors at the top of her blanched stone steps; and in the main wing of the house, though now a line of golden lights winked all the length of its ground floor, the same inhabitant looked forth from the windows of the upper storey in the shadow of the colossal pediment.

Suddenly Arnold Condorex burst out laughing. " Do you know," he said, " that when you were telling that story I found myself believing it were true ? "

" Do you know for certain it is not ? " smiled Harriet. " I am glad it entertained you. Indeed, our time together has been very satisfactory, even to the very end. For are you not enjoying now a very pleasant sadness ? I do not know anything more delightful than to be sad at this time of day." She uttered an ejaculation of pleasure as from the line of golden lights there came the sound of music. " Exquisite ! A waltz ! And an indifferent one ! My heart will presently melt."

" Music ? Do the inhabitants of Kensington then play bridge in time to music ? " enquired Arnold.

" Oh, there is much done there other than bridge," explained Harriet, showing signs of local patriotism, " and it is by no means attended by the inhabitants of Kensington alone. I hear the Blennerhassett is surpassed only by the Embassy as a magnet for fashion."

" What ! " exclaimed Arnold, coming to a standstill " Is that the Blennerhassett ? "

" Does it surprise you so much," she rallied him, " that a club which has its home in Blennerhassett House should be called the Blennerhassett ? "

" It should not, certainly," he admitted with a laugh, " but I have heard so often of the Blennerhassett, though I have never seen it, since I am as yet," he said with some moodiness, his eyes resting on the golden lights, " the companion of the nobility only in their labours, not in their pleasures. And when one thinks of a focus of such pleasures, one does not think of it as adjoining one of one's own quiet haunts."

She looked at him sharply. " Does one not ? " she said wistfully ; and continued, as if to console him, " But to-night, however, the most elegant will not be there. What, have I confused you so that you have forgotten the day of the week ? This is Saturday.

The truly popular are now at varying distances from London : to take their situation at its most favourable ; in the panelled bedrooms of great houses. Here there are only those who, happy enough in being born within the palisades of society, have not that further happiness of having been in any way blessed at birth. The females of this breed were begotten by fathers who do but smirk the chubbier when they find on the breakfast-table a letter from their bank managers, so certainly it is to report increase ; and their mothers are knots in a far-flung net of creditable cousinships. But they are not beautiful enough, or they are more than plump enough, or their dancing is too gross a contradiction of the motion of the spheres, or their bridge is but a stumbling-block in the path of their neighbours. So at the moment they bear down on us, not radiant, but not disconsolate, for they have companions, albeit those are the males of their own sort . . ."

Speech dried on her lips. Her natural guardian angel, her own grace, forsook her suddenly. She staggered, tripped on a minute inequality, and would have fallen to the ground, had he not caught her in his arms. From the dead weight her almost weightless body had assumed, from the blue shadows that lay on her closed eyelids and round her lips, which remained parted as in horror, he perceived that some monstrous blow had felled her. But what the blow was, or who had struck it, he did not guess until she looked up into his face, and shuddered, and cast

away his arms. Then he remembered, and understood.

She stood for a moment apart from him, rubbing her
hands as if to wash away his touch and keeping her
face away from him; then made an obvious effort to
still her bosom, and turned back to him, offering to
slip her arm in his with a kindliness that half his lost
and miserable spirit hailed as the damned might hail
a draught of water, while half of it tried to think of it
meanly, as smugness, vanity, and joy at having put
him in the wrong.

"You must make one more promenade with me,"
she said, giving him a pallid smile, "for you promised
yourself six journeys about the lawn, and you have
made but five. Come!" and gently she forced her
arm in his.

Poor Harriet's house looked dreary as they walked.
That was no wonder; for in the brief striking-match
time it takes to think a thought there had been broomed
out of its doors and windows a great deal of prettiness
and happiness that till then had appeared to be part
of its fittings. Till then it had seemed certain that
there would never be need for Harriet to sit in darkness, since there were inscribed on the air of her apart-
ment scenes which, shadows of memory though they
must be, were so bright in their subject that they
were as good as a couple of chandeliers. There
had been that first time she had looked up from
her piano and seen him standing outside the French
windows at the top of the stone steps, holding a

bouquet of roses he had purchased at the shop round
the corner (he had wished to buy it from some more
magnificent florist's but did not know the etiquette of
transportation) and looking sullen, because he dared
not stare into the room and he was mortally afraid
lest she should be closeted with some person of more
consequence than himself. She had flipped at three
joyous notes in the treble before she ran to open
to him. There had been the moment when she had
come downstairs after half an hour spent in making
ten moons of her nails, and discovered him sitting
at his ease by her hearth, toying with the long gloves
which she had left on her piano. She had chided
him for coming in with neither knock nor ring, and
for laying his rough paws on the fine leather; but
he had drawled that he would observe no ceremony
with one who lived like a gipsy, half in her garden,
and that she was a sloven to leave her gloves about,
and a deceiver to call them gloves, since it was notorious that in Kensington there was a race of gazelles
with a snake-like habit of casting their skins at certain
seasons of year, and one such had in this room cast
the covering of its fleet fore-ankles. "Ay!" he had
said, and held up the strips of leather against the light.
She had glowed to perceive that he was taking
pleasure in little things about her even as she took
pleasure in little things about him, such as the contrast at that very moment between the affected
insolence of his lip and the shining brotherliness of
his eye. That had been a good moment, and there

had been better this very afternoon; but she could not recall those without the certainty of tears.

So she surely had been justified, poor Harriet, in thinking that at any time when her fire would not draw, when the fairy of the switch would not obey, she would have warmth, she would have light, simply by filling the air with these shapes that had once so glowingly occupied it. Alas! It would never be so now. What woman can bear to recall the most flattering moment of a love affair in which, time has revealed, she did but play the part of a maid who is kissed only because the mistress is not yet ready for the suitor? And there had been that in Arnold Condorex's thought which offended against the order of nature, as it is comprehended by the hearts of females, almost as soon as they are aware that there is a different class of beings who wear blue bows upon their cot-covers instead of pink. From that beginning they know well that it is natural and just as the supersession of the spring by summer, that the less beautiful should be abandoned for the more beautiful. It is no good deploring it, nor, indeed, is it worth deploring. For spring dies, summer dies, autumn dies, winter dies, the year is gone, another is come; for youth passes, ripeness passes, age passes, a generation's gone, another is come. All is ended in a general levelling. So secretly, whatever they may say aloud, they think a deserted wife who weeps a loss springing from the eclipse of her charms to be a fool who kicks against the pricks. But when they come across the reverse of the process and see a man leaving a beautiful woman for one less beautiful, not because his sight is deranged by love but because he thereby gains an end, then they feel such disgust as is excited in our males by the horrid habits of the Bulgars. Not thus is nature's way. The skin, than which nothing is more loyal to nature, rises in gooseflesh.

She had felt therefore a general horror, as well as a personal anguish, when, his cold eyes turned towards the lights and music of the club, he wondered how soon he might chance on some undesired woman as she was describing, who could be quickly got and would be a stairway to better things. The plain daughter of a Privy Councillor had been his thought, which had expanded into a consideration of what ways he might use, did he meet such a dowd at Lady Derrydown's tea on Thursday (for one never knows), to enjoy Harriet till the last safe moment and then disembarrass himself of her. No, she would never now be able to warm and light her rooms by recalling how they had been tender to each other.

They had completed the first part of their promenade and had now turned their backs on the dark house, but it was no more pleasant walking this way than the other. She had to cast her eyes down on the ground so that she did not have to look at the three trees which she had named the Ladies Frances, Georgiana, and Arabella Dudley, for now she could not bear to think that she had told him a fairy tale. It is the special hardship of women that it is their destiny to make gifts, and that the quality of their giving is decided by the quality shown by those who do the taking. No matter how full their hearts may be of tenderness and generosity as they hold out their gifts, if the takers snatch it without gratitude, then the givers count as neither tender nor generous, but merely easy. Indeed Harriet had not meant to be easy, but she was not fool enough to refuse to see that this evening had proved her so ; and she felt that the proof lay more in her having put herself about to entertain him with a piece of fancy than in her having made certain other disclosures which might have seemed more important.

She bit her lip ; and beside her Arnold Condorex's mind growled that she was not being fair to him. No man on earth would ever surpass him in appreciation of her peculiar quality ; would more ecstatically know her bland as a runnel of cream from the lip of a jug, and at the same time so wild and ethereal that she could not be the product of the tame human womb, but must have been begotten by a god in a wind-tost grove, and then again so primly perfect that she could not be the product of the crude human womb, but must have been worked by the finicking human hand, like fine needlework or old silver. No man on earth to whom she made benevolent concessions would in his soul more immediately have doffed his hat and gone down on his knees, sensible that he was in a church. But a man must rise in the world! Dear God, did she not understand? A man must rise in the world! Despair swept through him as he realised

56

that certainly she would not understand; and it became absolute as he realised that neither did he truly understand it himself. He would have been far better pleased had it been his intention to stay faithfully with his Harriet till some force that could be honoured parted them, rather than to betray her for a Privy Councillor's plain daughter, whom for some reason he now saw as a large and raw-boned English sheep-dog.

Yet the latter intention was unalterably a part of himself. He could no more remove it than he could uproot his own breath. Why should he be so welded with a programme which, in thinking on it, he felt he did not in the least relish? Could he veritably care so much about the duty to rise in the world if he was capable of such hearty longing to act counter to it? But with a groan he realised that he cared for nothing else. It dominated him, he was its instrument. There might have been a vast superior spirit which had invested him and was so much greater than himself that its loins sprung from his shoulders, and it used his whole body as legs to carry it about on its business of rising in the world. Yet even if that were so, must he lose Harriet? Could he not keep her with a lie? But, great gods, now she had this power, he could not lie to her. Nay, at this very moment, she must know that he was debating whether or not he might successfully lie to her!

Looking from side to side in his distress, he noticed that they were at that instant passing the door in the wall, and he most heartily wished he might wring her hand in perfunctory farewell and dash for it, leaving for ever this garden that had become accursed. But he had left his hat and stick on the sofa; and it was a presentation stick. The trouble of getting it must be accomplished first.

"I will fetch them for you," said Harriet, and started towards the door.

He said, "Let me!" But over her shoulder she gave him a smile that was not unkind, and yet was proud enough to forbid him to persist. No, indeed, he could not thrust himself again into the rooms he had desecrated. He watched the pale figure pass through the settling twilight, and perceived that she was carrying herself with the straightness of those who feel themselves utterly bowed down; and he covered his face with his hands.

When he could bear to bring them down again she was standing in front of him, his hat and stick dark against the pallor of her gown. She laughed tenderly, as if she had found him playing a game familiar to them both, and murmured, "My love, you must go now." To judge from her bearing all might have been well between them.

"My love, I must go now," he echoed hoarsely. They looked long at one another. It struck him that they were exchanging glances of more agonised sincerity, more desperately truthful reference to their mutual regard, than they would have shared had they been parting as true lovers. Could not something be done with all this honesty, with all this acute sense of each other's being? "Oh, Harriet!" he cried. "Can we not——? May we not——?"

She grew very still. Her head drooped, so that through the more than dusk he could not see her face at all. A bird sped across the sky above them, croaking some monstrous tale of avian disaster, but she did not look up at it. A freshet of wind stirred her skirts, but she did not smooth them. It might have been that she had died on her feet and was being upheld in air by friendly sprits till one came who had loved her most, and had the right to lay her on her bier. And indeed, as Arnold Condorex well knew, she was telling him that, so far as being his loving mistress was concerned, she was dead.

"Ah, well!" he sighed. "So must it be!" He put out his hand and took hers, and raised it towards his lips, and said solemnly, seeking her eyes through the darkness: "May God bless you and keep you wherever you may go, for being so kind to me this day."

She answered him in his own words: "May God bless you and keep you, wherever you may go, for being so kind to me this day," and raised her mouth to his.

They were as a Greek vase, he the sturdy vessel, she the scroll of ornament wound round him. But that vase was shattered an instant after its making, when he broke away from her inquisitorially, to know if, when the music changed in the damnable club

beyond the wrought-iron gates, he had wondered
whether he danced well enough to acquit himself to
the pleasure of the Privy Councillor's plain daughter
or should take lessons. Had he not wondered that?
It seemed as if he had not, for her face was smooth as
junket in its bowl. He had not thought it then, but,
by God, he was about to think it now! He cried
out, "I must leave this place!" and turned blindly
towards the door in the wall. It did not in the least
assuage him that she sped beside him, guiding his
blindness, finding the latch for him. For he felt his
intention to rise in the world like lead in his bosom,
and he knew she must know it was there, and must
know that if he stayed another instant he would be
snarling at her in his soul, blaming her meanly and
unjustly for this clairvoyant power, though well aware
that she had come by it through pure accident, and had
lost as much by it as him. Was there no end to the
nastiness in his brain-pan?

Now he was out on the pavement. From the darkness behind him she cried gaily, "Fare you well, and
mind you are not late for his lordship," and slammed
the door. He leaned against the wall, drew out his
handkerchief, and passed it over his brow, which was
wet with sweat; and stood awhile and groaned.
What an end of a gallant adventure! Was it possible
that he could be really a good secretary? And had her
voice not broken on the last few words?

His brow was not indeed truly dry until a later
hour that night, when the unusually affable greetings

of Lord Derrydown made him conscious that he was confronted with one of those occasions when, by being useful to the great, we can advance nearer to that blessed time when they are useless to us and can be scorned. He became himself again. Assuming the meek and serviceable aspect of a retriever, he listened while Lord Derrydown informed him that that evening a crisis had arisen in high places which he, and he alone, could bring to a happy conclusion. It was, of course, known to all that a tour of our Eastern possessions was about to be performed by a certain personage of high rank, whose mind enjoyed the pellucidity of an ideal Italian sky. Not enough matter was ever present in it to mar that dazzling vacuity by a single cloud; and while this state of affairs made persons who sat next him at banquets invariably describe him as delightfully simple and unaffected, it created a less favourable effect when it was revealed in the course of oratory. It was, in fact, a case where a competent secretary was not only desirable but indispensable; and one such had long since been engaged. But at the last moment—it was horrible to think how near the time of embarkation— the worst had been discovered concerning his habits.

His habits, repeated Lord Derrydown, and he drooped his blue and wrinkled eyelids to show shame and horror. Arnold Condorex did the like with his, thinking without mercy, " The old fool looks like one of those sheep's skulls that one finds lying on the downs." His lowered gaze fell on the dispatch-box

that was relique of this master's tenure of the Chan-
cellorship of the Duchy of Lancaster, and he knew a
spasm of desire as urgent as any he had ever felt for
a woman. "God, had I but family behind me!"
came from his breast as if a harp-string had twanged
there; and was followed by a richer and more swelling
note. "But listen! That has begun which promises
you shall do very well in spite of your low birth!"
Barely could he control himself sufficiently to go
through the proper motions of raising his eyebrows
in surprise, and of rolling his pupils from side to side
in modesty, as Lord Derrydown went on to explain
that when the Prime Minister and the Secretary of
State had consulted him as to how they might best fill
the sudden vacancy, he had named, and had been
conscious of extreme self-sacrifice when he did so,
his own secretary as a person of sterling ability and no
habits, no habits at all. His heart cried out in rapture,
"The old fool has offered me to the Prime Minister
as a bribe to cozen him to do the Archbishop of Can-
terbury's will and wreck the Bill for permitting a
man to marry his grand-dame by an amendment that
it will apply only if she be of crooked stature and
swarthy and there be no likelihood of pleasure in it.
I am right, then, about my own quality!" Scarcely
could he knit his brows, protrude his lower lip,
bury his chin on his chest, and make the other adjustments of his countenance necessary for his impersona-
tion of a devoted servant downcast because his master
(to whom, God knows, he would deny nothing if he

could but choose) had asked a service almost impossible for him to perform ; so high was his soul soaring, and so loud was it singing, " I am rising in the world ! I am rising in the world ! "

Then a misgiving came on him. It was as if one, sitting in a fine room he had lately furnished and preening himself because all was well and all was paid for, should see between two of the floor boards a dark pool trickling. Where had he been infected with this monstrous doubt that rising in the world was not the supreme good ? Why, that very night, along with some other very disagreeable happenings, in the garden of Harriet Hume whom now he need not see again. " In two days ! Sail in two days ! " he exclaimed, echoing the old fool's words. But prudence alone made him speak as if he were appalled ; for if a man must buy his outfit for the East and do much other official business in two days, then fitly he may say good-bye to a lady, with whom in any case he has exchanged no serious vows, by telephone.

Yet that was not how he said good-bye to her, though, God knows, that was how he tried to do it. Panic prevented him. For several times the next morning he gave her number to the dark capricious instrument, but it became no channel for the sirop of her voice and continued to make its own animal noises. On the fifth occasion he said to himself, " This is strange, for at this hour she is usually at her piano," and then the sweat stood on his forehead as it had done the evening before, when he went from her gate. During the night his will, having no fancy for what had happened on the previous day in Harriet's garden, had been busy unpicking the stitches which sewed together his recollections, and had left them in loose pieces round his brain; but now they seemed bent on putting themselves together in the same abhorred shape. For was it not that Harriet was able to tell through her new clairvoyant powers that it was he who caused her telephone to make its angry pheasant-whirr; and for that reason was now sitting still upon her stool, her hands suspended above the keys of the piano, her mouth trembling as she wished that he who had ruined her peace yesternight would leave her quiet to-day? He groaned; and immediately knew himself a fool. For calm fell on the growling in the ebonite, and little Harriet said " Halloa " as cheerful as a sparrow. Oh, he had dreamt all this about clairvoyance. She gave a great many " Ohs " and " Ahs " to his great news, and seemed to understand most amiably that he had no time to pay a farewell visit to her, and tittered very prettily when he spoke of the previous afternoon. " All's well that ends well ! " said he, putting down the instrument and sitting back in his chair.

But had it ended well? He started forward because a dread had pinched him that all was very ill, that he had veritably witnessed a suspension of the proper order of nature, and that he had trodden a flower to the ground very brutally because of it. For had she not answered the telephone only because her sight into his thoughts had told her he was suspecting why she did not answer it ? He snatched up the instrument and again gave it her number ; and the instant after he and she knew that most abstract form of confrontation which happens when two people stand with receivers to ear and transmitters to mouth but do not speak. "If my dream be true and no phrensy," he thought wildly, and with cunning, "she will say 'Yes, you may come to tea to-day' before I have asked it of her," but there was silence broken only by such a faint noise as a mouse might make, not knowing what to do, until it struck him that she knew he was putting her to this test and was at her wits' end to guess what was wisest, When he rapped out his request aloud he had a frightful sense that he was making it a second time, and that she acceded with the patness of one who has thought a question over.

Yet surely his dream was phrensy. When he came down to Blennerhassett House that afternoon with a stack of roses from a truly magnificent florist (he had begun to spend his money with the recklessness of one about to make a great fortune or to die) he found Harriet very pretty, and a trifle silly, and as comfortable a companion as one could wish. Prattling not too intelligently about India and elephants and Nabobs' jewels, she fiddled about her garden cutting lavender-flowers till the basket she had slung on her forearm was full, and then fluttered indoors to put them on her windowsills to dry ; and then she sat behind her silver equipage and gave him very good home-made

65

scones and country butter, and giggled a great deal. Looking on the suavity of her face and the meek pliancy of her form and manners, which were such that if one found her in one's way one might surely pick her up and loop her round a hook on the door without encountering physical or mental resistance, he said to himself, "It muft be that the other night my intellects were disordered. Certainly there is as little sinifter in my Harriet here as there is in drinking sugared tea out of a pretty cup. She could not read my thoughts. I doubt if she could read her primer." But something tender in him, that same part which had before the mirror designed to buy her a little ring for her little hand, rebuked him. "Whatever happened laft night, whether it was magic or the dropping of an ill-considered word, you betrayed to her that no woman is as much to you as the prospect of rising in the world, and you betrayed it in an ugly hour, and in a roughish shape. Decidedly you have brought no good fortune to the girl. For only yesterday she was as kind to you as may be, and to-day you tell her you muft immediately sail for the Indies. You cannot say that you have treated her handsomely." At that he could not help but fall a-moping.

Juft then Harriet, smiling like a doll, raised her hand to her head and withdrew the sole pin that held in place her Grecian knot; and the sleek serpents of her hair slipped down over her shoulders and covered her bosom, their curled heads lying in her lap. In but one neat, fluent movement she again

compressed its fineness and impaled it ; but not before
he had called himself a fool for thinking that the loss
of a lover could mean much to any creature so rich
in all the moſt seduċtive attributes of her sex. With
an easy conscience, therefore, he rose to his feet and
bade her good-bye ; and remained in a ſtate of cheer-
fulness until, when he was re-entering his flat in the
Temple, his hand left the latch-key ſticking in the
lock while his chin sank on his breaſt and he ſtood
ſtaring very ſtupidly at the door. It had occurred
to him that if she had read his compunċtion for leaving
her so soon and so abruptly she could not have devised
a prettier and kinder way of relieving his mind.
Yet of that aċtion, though it drearily assumed in his
mind an air of complete probability, he thought not
as one usually thinks of pretty and kind things.
When, once across his threshold, he vehemently
slammed the door, the vehemence was because he
imagined himself slamming it on the prodigiousness
of Harriet Hume.

II

Not till six years afterwards did Arnold Condorex
see Harriet Hume again. It was nearly otherwise,
for within two years from their parting his footsteps
were led to the door in the wall of Blennerhassett
House, and it was sheer singularity, of a kind that he
blushed to remember, that forbade him entering it.
'Twas at the time when the Powers were revising
certain matters to do with Asian frontiers under the
eye of Geneva; not the least of which matters was
that eternal source of discussions, that litter of cocka-
trices, the Mangostan Treaty. It had annoyed Mr.
Gladstone in 1878; and it annoyed the Secretary of
State for India in our day not less, perhaps even more,
because at least Mr. Gladstone appears (from his
speeches) to have known what or where Mondh was.
Mysterious Mondh! How came it that it was the
very pivot and keystone of that monstrous Treaty
which casts a longer shadow across Asia than Mount
Everest, yet was not marked on any map nor present
in the narrative of any traveller? Such was the question that the India Office was gloomily addressing to
its own bosom. It might have seemed more profitable
to address it to the bosom of a Mango, but that was

purely a theoretical possibility. For the sake of the British Raj no white man must ever admit to a Mango that he does not know everything. Once the secret were to leak out, the insolence of the Mangoes at present studying law and mathematics in this country would become unbridled, and there would not be a rupee or a virgin left between Middle Temple Hall and Cambridge; and from Mangostan disloyal expeditions would set out for Moscow, which certainly would not be able to do anything with them, but ought not to be encouraged even by that much. For these reasons it caused inexpressible joy in the India Office when it was credibly reported that a certain general on the retired list of the India Army had been heard, during his last visit to the Oriental Club in 1912, to say that he had once spent a month in Mondh; and that he was still living and resident in South Kensington. Immediately the Secretary of State for India had summoned Arnold Condorex (who was by now an expert in Far Eastern affairs and had been transferred to the India Office with such a magnificent transcendence of normal processes as took Elijah up to Heaven) and bade him to hasten to pluck the secret from the old man's mouth.

It was on his return from his errand that he found himself at Harriet's door. By then it was the burning afternoon of a dog-day; the shadows on the pavement were blue as water. Yet he had thought he would walk a part of the way home, just the length of a few squares and crescents. For the general's house had

been a sealed cube of age. The butler who had opened
the door had looked past Condorex with as much suspicion as his enrheumed eyes could hold, at a knife-
grinding machine that happened to be standing in the
road; for he himself had witnessed the quarrel between
the knife grinder and the Friend of Man that Canning
writes of, and he felt too frail to deal with anything like
that nowadays. The general's daughter blushed and
turned away her face as she passed him on the stairs,
so long was it since any human being outside these
walls, save only Debrett and Burke, had known
of her existence; and he knew she had this very day
formed a dreadful resolution that if nothing happened
in the next thirty years she would dress herself all in
white and fling herself from the Italianate tower which
gave a romantic finish to the villa. The general
himself lay frog-cold in a room as hot as a Turkish
bath, and was not truly alive, but caught in the hinge
of the door between life and death, and groaned as it
swung to and fro and let others in and out, but never
him. After being in such a house it seemed good to
move one's limbs and sweat, and also Arnold wished
to walk that he might think, and even talk aloud, if he
wanted to do so. For he had a matter to settle with
his conscience.

From the end of the first half-house it had been
plain that the old gentleman's memory had betrayed
him, and that his experience was not of Mondh but of
Pondh; poor, unwanted Pondh, whose conspicuous-
ness on the map amounted to a kind of looseness,

since it was not once mentioned in the Treaty. Would he advance himself if he returned with this information? Would he, indeed, be advancing the cause of the British Empire, of civilisation, of peace, were he so almost rudely honest? The situation could surely be dealt with more helpfully by an exercise of the qualities which make a good secretary. His own convenience and the higher ends of man would be subserved by a certain slight adjustment of the facts, with no harm to anybody save the raising up of difficulties in the path of some secretary in a position like his own fifty or sixty years hence; and he regarded the destiny of a secretary too highly to shrink from provoking the incidents which are most characteristic of it. Raising his eyes to the sky, which was a deep and unsullied blue, he said in a clear voice, " Let Pondh be Mondh." No feeling of regret rebuked him; and he continued on his way at a pace remarkable on such a warm day, wondering without resentment and even with discipular piety who had been Mr. Gladstone's secretary in 1878, until he was struck by something familiar in the aspect of the wall by which he was walking. A pretty green creeper ran half the length of it, and at intervals drooped pale waving tendrils a fore-arm's length down into the street, so that it looked as if a harem had drugged their eunuchs in a body and had stolen to the confines of their prison to have their fingers kissed by a queue of lovers. He came to a standstill, and addressed them very amiably, for he was now in excellent humour:

"I have known you, my dears, when you were not half as well-grown as you are now, and far more discreet. In those days your little hands reached no further than the top of the wall, where they used to flutter very appealingly. I have seen the same performance in boarding-schools where the pupils stay late into their teens. I said as much, I remember, to someone. . . ."

And someone, he remembered also, had giggled. Someone had been Harriet Hume. This, then, was Blennerhassett House, which he had not known because he had approached it from the opposite direction to that he had come from when it had seen him nearly every day, two summers before. And here, a step or two further on, was Harriet's door, which he had often had to pause before in order to compose an aspect that he knew to be disordered by the excessive beating of his heart. It was newly painted, a tasteful green. The minx must be in funds. With a reminiscent smile he decided that he must try his luck and see if she were at home. For all of Arnold Condorex's advancement had been earned by his talent for negotiation, and with none could he negotiate more successfully than with himself. He had dealt with his own soul most ably on this matter, begging himself to forget that and to remember this, to let that go because it had a sharp edge and would draw blood whenever it was picked up, but to keep that because it dovetailed with this or that to make a profitable whole. So now he thought of Harriet Hume only as a creature lovely as a swan and mild as milk, trim in disorder, prim in amorousness, a personage in the world because of her talents, and a little goose to those who knew her well ; with whom he had been fortunate. It had served him to remember that, because it had made him confident with women. And there had been, he had it written on his present mind, an awkwardness on the day of his good fortune, since by some slip of the tongue he had betrayed that he thought more of his advancement than of her or any other woman in the world. It served him to remember that, because it had made him careful with women. And he had not really lost much by his awkwardness, for it had been but two days later that he had had to sail for India. It had served him to remember that, because it had made him believe in his stars. Because of these selected memories, and because the last two years had given him much evidence that he could win nearly everyone to be his friend, he laid his fingers without reluctance on the handle of the door. Surely Harriet had been the gayest person he had ever known. He burst out laughing and said to himself, " Egad, I will tell her I have made Pondh Mondh," thinking of the transaction much more merrily than he had thought but a few minutes earlier. But immediately his fingers fell to his side, because he perfectly knew what he was going to see when he opened the door.

The garden was not changed. It had still, in spite of its partition, that air of being a corner in a wide and rolling park ; and it was still, as a town garden should be, less an exhibition of flowers than a green sanctuary. And it was not empty, any more than it had been when he frequented it. In the shade of the Ladies Frances, Georgiana, and Arabella Dudley was a deck-chair of yellow and white striped canvas, on which he was sure, though its back was turned to him, there reposed a young man enjoying the liberty of shirt-sleeves ; for there dangled beside it an almost bare arm obviously belonging to a male. The down on it, he thought sombrely, were one to approach near enough to see it, would be fair. A book and some weekly journals lay on the grass by the chair. He made himself at home, this young man, whoever he might be. Indeed the afternoon seemed to be passing here so pleasantly that the mouth could not help but water. For nearer the centre of the lawn was a light iron table pierced by a giant dust-and-orange umbrella, the same as may be seen on the terrace of any French hotel, and by this stood Harriet, looking infinitely ductile with contentment.

She had not lost an atom of her innocent loveliness. She was very much the same in her appurtenances also. For she was wearing, as she had always done, a parchment-coloured gown that showed her shape to the waist and then became a thousand pleats of fine muslin ; and it still seemed incredible that there should be a grown woman's feet in those tiny sandals ; and at her bosom she had pinned, as he had seen her do a dozen times when she was in a good mood, her favourite rose, an open-eyed and golden flower with a grainy brownness at its centre, exhalent of honey. The only novelty about her aspect was her peasantish broad straw hat which she had pushed back until its elastic was strained low across her throat, and it hung like a great O behind her shoulders; yet that was not so novel either, for it had seemed to him that he had always been aware that she would look just such a melting dove of deliciousness if one hung a peasantish hat like a great O behind her shoulders. Of the same dubious truth it was that he had never seen her do exactly what she was doing at the moment; which was to look down into a tumbler and swirl it round and round, because there was sugar to be melted and she, the lazy slut, would not run back to her house for the spoon she had forgotten. Yet, if he had never seen her do that, how did he know so well that, though she would not run back to the house in her own interest, her little ankles would twinkle up the steps to her French window in no time had it been he who held a glass of her lemonade in his hand and had need of a spoon?

In fact, she was unaltered, and she was exquisite. But can the semi-sacred charm of familiarity, can true delight, attach to that which has been apprehended by a process other than natural? He retreated a pace from the door, regarding it with loathing. Surely it is established as firmly as any article of our faith that the only occasion on which a door is not a door is when it is ajar. It has no license to be a lens through which the unseen can be seen, it has no permit to tamper with time and exhibit that which has not yet been encountered. Addressing it in firm tones, he said, "I will not trouble to go in, on such a fine day she will not be in town," and passed on, bending his brows again over the business of making Pondh into Mondh; a transaction which he never admitted to a soul, neither with laughter, as he had meant to admit it to his Harriet, or in solemnity.

So he passed on, and did not see his Harriet until a December afternoon, criss-crossed with the residue of its yesterday's light snowfall, more than four years later. Heavens! how well he felt that day! He tingled with good health and energy and prosperity. That was why after he had had luncheon with old Lord Ketchup in Hyde Park Gate he left by foot and crossed the Kensington Road that he might walk part of his way back to Albany through the Park. Lord, he felt well! All turned to satisfaction in him. This very walk afforded proof of how neatly his days were dovetailed in these times, and what good cabinet-making these adjustments had achieved. He would take a stroll through the Park, which would keep his figure slim; he would look in on his club, the Senile Abercorn, to which by marvellous good fortune he had been elected three years before in spite of his inconsiderable age, and take his ease where no one at his birth could have predicted he would take it, and be civil to such notable people as he chanced to see; and then he would go at leisure to his rooms in Albany

and oversee the preparations his valet had made with
the pigskin (none had sprucer luggage than he had
now, who came to London with a tin-trunk) for this
all-important Christmas visit to Ireland; and later
he would find himself, with everything he needed for
both body and soul, surely the best-found passenger
in the night mail for Holyhead.

A regime always as provident as this, he reflected
as he trudged along, had made him whom they had
early ceased to call a man of promise only because his
promise had come so soon to fulfilment. Prudence
and hard work, these two had set him well on the way
to rise in the world to a height that all would have to
note; and what was so blessed was that he had had to
pay for it with no sacrifice at all. He had sacrificed
none of his principles; and once or twice had taken
a firm and fearless line, careless of public opinion,
that had proved very popular. Nor had he been
obliged to sacrifice his robust health to his assiduity.
His marvellous sense of bodily well-being was proof
of that. The elasticity of his own tread intoxicated
him, and he was enchanted to observe that in the short
space of Kensington Road he had need to promenade
before he entered the Park he outstripped two or three
young men who seemed to be still in their twenties.
Though the air was stinging, his circulation was so
well able to resist it that he could enjoy the beauties
of nature as wholeheartedly as if he were walking on
a June afternoon; and indeed they deserved enjoyment. " It can all be done in one single line," Winter

was saying of the trees, " if one is careful to keep the point of the pen on the paper, and charges it discreetly with the indian ink. And line, of course, is the thing. But it cannot be done all this way unless you choose a good˙solid dull sky as a background. You will be driven to the weak, water-colour methods of my poor sister Spring if you confuse your background with dots and dashes of sunshine ; and if you flood it with a gross plenitude of blue as Summer does there is nothing for it but to go in for her shapeless and strong-coloured flummery of leaves. And if you let all get sodden with gold, as Autumn does, then there is nothing for it but to paint like Turner and be damned. But if you care for line, why here it is." And there it was, on each side of the road through Hyde Park, in black traceries on dun that made the human attempts at acuity in the form of the spiked railings below seem bluntness itself; and yet further off, out of the foreground of the eye, where they marked the course of the Ladies' Mile and Rotten Row, they melted into a lacey darkness soft as soot.

Because the grass beneath them was brindled with light snow, this darkness seemed intense to the point of vehemence. Now that the earth itself had taken on the colour of old age the tree-trunks themselves, which at other times are the least spectacular forms of growth, created such a feeling of resolute increase as is given ordinarily by some prodigious show of leaf or flower or fruit. They might have been black flames

78

thrusting upwards through the effete soil, from some subterranean power-house which was far too much in earnest to paint them with the ruddy hues that belong to fires of a more superficial kindling. The scene, full as it was of a sense of the life of earth in spite of being crowded with signs of the suspension of all opulence, suggested a plutonic energy that could work exultantly in spite of receiving none of these encouragements which man considers necessary to sweeten his toil. That impression was heightened as there thundered along the riding-track beside him a party of horsemen whose faces were contracted with pain at the bitterness of the air, and yet were magnificent with pride at their government of their mounts and pleasure in the speed to which they had compelled them. It increased his already enormous satisfaction with the afternoon that not for more than a minute did he feel that cringing resentment which those who walk commonly feel at the sight of those who ride, since he could remind himself that now he was among the riders, and had himself often caused others to cringe. He rode remarkably well for one who had acquired the art of horsemanship far more lately than in childhood. He need have no anxiety about following the hounds in Ireland. The thought of his progress in this and other matters made him feel himself like a great horse, magnificently sound in wind and limb, thudding down its hooves on soil that Providence had seen was neither waterlogged nor broken by frost, in a gallop that nothing would stop.

He had intended to go along the Row to Hyde Park Corner, and would have done so had he not seen, whisking into the gate in the railings which admits to the more mannered elegancies of Kensington Gardens, a neat figure, which made him burst out laughing and exclaim, "By Gad! that is Harriet Hume!" He burst out laughing because she was so very pretty, and he did not want her. He did not want anything that he had not got. He had it all. "I must have a word with little Harriet," he told himself, and crossed the road, for he had nothing else to do, since clubs will wait. Moreover, even seen through the blurring palisade of railings, she was a creature of such special and skimming grace that it was the height of luxury not to desire her because he was about to have as good. "She walks fast, she is like a deer!" he said, as he passed within the gates and found that she was already a small figure at the end of the broad elm walk that leads down to the Serpentine. Gaining on her, he continued to congratulate her and himself by perceiving her quality. "She dresses well," he said, "she understands her type!" For she wore a little black hat that was three-cornered yet was not so fanciful that it offended, and he wondered no longer why she kept her elbows pinned to her side, after she had raised a muff to her face and buried first one cheek and then the other in its softness. How trimly she was speeding before him, and with what good temper! She was cold, and she desired to be warm, but there was no sullenness about her

objection to her state and her desire to change it.
Simply she hastened through the air with a movement
more dancing than usual and her cheek laid to a muff
as amiably as if it were a lover. Oh, she was a good
wench, this little Harriet!

Just then a breach in the trees showed him a vista
extending to the very brim of the Serpentine, where
certain people standing at the water's edge, because
of the flatness of the shore at this particular point,
had the appearance of waiting on a quay for a boat;
and a certain disposition of the trees and bushes on
the opposite bank, grouped beneath a perspective of
spires and towers that seemed inside the Park though
they were in fact far beyond its boundaries, deceived
topography and conjured up an illusion of a fantastic
island to which the expected boat would ferry them.
"Is this where we embark for Cythera?" his mind
asked him with odd inconsequence and emphasis;
and he had an even odder notion that if that were not
to be so it was only because he and Harriet had
already made their embarkations, and that other selves
of theirs than could be seen were even now drifting
down a dark stream, their faces pale in a colder and a
later hour than this that chilled them now.

But his mind shook itself like a dog, and he leaped
back to his gratifying game of approving that of which
he had no need. "I will not speak to her for a while,"
he said exultantly, "I will walk just behind her,"
for that gave him a pleasing sense of contrast to the
days when, had he seen her walking in front of him,

he would have had to run forward even under horses' heads and cars' bonnets, and slip his arm through hers, that at the first possible moment he might have her lovely face tilted to him and hear her Oh's and Ah's. But he could not long remain in that mood of exultation, for there were a thousand incidents in her promenade which competed to distract him. The first thing that happened was that an ill-favoured Irish wolf-hound, putting his fore-paws on a pool of ice, found them sliding away from him and howled in consternation until Harriet tripped forward and jerked him to trustworthy ground by the collar. She bowed her head to whisper to his pale and pompous eyes in his own language that not for one instant had he lost his dignity; and he snuffled in her hand to compliment her on her perfect accent. Then she bounded on, turning her little head right and left to enjoy the icy flavour of the day. The path was running beside the lake now, and all was hard-chiselled. The weakest little woman among the ducks, the most down-trodden wife of them all, who hardly dared call her quack her own, could not indulge her natural disposition to swim without making a V adamantine as an irrevocable decision on the nearly frozen lake. There was no wind-crisped water here, only ribbed glass.

This world clear-cut as her own ankles, cool as her own hands, was naturally pleasant to her. For quite a time she dallied by a clump of reeds which a matrimonial scuttering of ducks had deluged with spray which had frozen on the very instant, and had now the aspect of a French prism candlestick. " She is like a child," he thought tenderly, " things that glitter are dear to her." But she was tempted from her reeds by another beauty peculiar to this season, at which her nostrils dilated with not less delight. So few people were abroad this bitter day that there were no parties breaking the landscape by following convenient and arbitrary paths, and there were no performances of chase and counter chase by the industrious ballet of London dogs. Hence the eye could without disturbance apprehend under the boracic sprinkling of light snow the gentle contours that God had given to the place, and the noble avenues which Capability Brown had seen in his fancy when he planted his saplings. The great Metropolis was annulled. The park-keeper's delicious lodge, with its proportions squat as a Royal bonnet, its pediments and arches reminiscent not of the temple but the grotto, might have been pinned to the bosom of a gentleman's estate in the Midlands ; and one would not have been surprised, had one approached it more nearly, to find the frosted turf indented with the hooves of the Pytchley. " Why, she is like a very little child," he thought, laughing. " I will lay a wager from the manner she looks toward it that the lodge has instantly become a type of rural simplicity to her, and she is wishing that the King would hear her play and give it to her as a present, and she could live there like a nymph on milk and nuts and berries ! The sweet fool! Well, I wish I were the King and could give her what she wants. Ah, what ineffable grace!"

For she had come suddenly to a standstill, had risen a little on her toes, and had drooped her head, as if she were fixedly regarding something on the path before her. She wavered slightly, like a steady flame. So prima ballerinas stand before the *pas seule*, if they are excellent.

"Shall I speak to her now?" he asked himself. "Before heaven I cannot long postpone myself that pleasure!"

But she had glided forward and was off again, at such a swallow's pace that he had much ado not to lose distance on her. "It is strange that she can dance along so fast on such high heels," he panted. "Ah, but I love her for wearing them so high. I remember she was always well aware that to be elegant a woman must walk on very high heels or on none. But she was mistress of all such wisdom. I have never known a woman with more exquisite understanding of the female person. Ah, *dieu merci*, she remits the pace."

For she had laid her head on one side, and was slowly rubbing her cheek against the fur of her collar, with very much the motion of a puss that has been stroked under the ear; and her feet were moving no faster than her head. Thereafter she dawdled. A snail could have passed more expeditiously by the slope where the obese birds that dress in shades of coffee-and-milk have their club. "If I catch her while

she is still there," he hoped, "she may tell me a fairy-
tale about those quacking fellows. She is full of fancy.
I remember one night when she loved me and took
great pains to please me she told me a most diverting
tale about three women who were turned into trees.
Ah, she is cold, she shivers! Lud, is she ill? She
puts one hand to her brow as if she rubbed away a
headache, and with the other she seems about to cast
away her muff in a desperate though graceful movement. Nay, she cannot be ill, she is all too well, for
she is springing ahead at a rate I never can equal...."

In a minute or so he knew he had spoken the truth
and had to come puffing to a halt. "It is no use!
I cannot afford to be seen pursuing a female in Hyde
Park, and I must admit that even if I could, I should not
catch her. Well, it is a great pity, for now I see the
little trollop, I find I love her far more dearly
than I supposed I did. Why, the good wench stops
and looks around! I shall have her yet!" For in
truth she had again come to a standstill, and had turned
on her track as if to follow with her eyes a wolf-
hound of more than common princely bearing; and
at this very moment the face that hated to deny anybody anything for very long had broken out into
the kindliest smiles at the sight of him, and a little
hand in a little grey glove was left in mid-air, to wait
until called for.

"I must own," he puffed, as he came within grasp
of it, "that I did not guess it was you when I began to
dog your steps. I only asked myself, who was the

last woman in London to carry a muff, and if I might not pay my respects to her for her wise vanity."

"I do not carry a muff because I am vain," answered Harriet, "but to preserve my hands. They are, as you know, my sole treasures."

"Your sole treasures?" he asked in mock rebuke; and indeed he had been reflecting that he had vastly underrated the perfection of the details of her person. "What, when you have those feet, that nose, those eyes——"

"I do not play Bach with my feet," she retorted mildly, "nor Mozart with my nose. But let us talk of you, for truly you are looking so well that it is subject-matter for quite a long conversation. You are looking remarkably well! And how glad," she said, with naïve surprise, "I am to see you! I did not think I should be half so glad. Come, let us walk in the Italian Garden for a little. It is over there behind those railings that are made taut green ropes by their overgrowth of ivy. I go there out of kindness now and then. And now tell me all. Are you very happy?"

"Nay, I cannot tell you anything," he said, "until you have first told me how you can be kind to a garden by walking in it."

"Why, look around you!" she bade him, with an air of quiet common sense. Obediently he glanced round them, smiling foolishly, and in contentment, at the pavement of stone flags where they were about to walk, and the lily-pad tanks that were sunk in it, all having its rectilinear design reinforced by the straight line of snow that was ruled on the shadowed side of everything. "Is it not indeed an Italian garden? And Italian gardens that are laid out in England are invariably soured by disappointment, for they have the same romantic expectations which are found in the hearts of all women who, though born under our skies, have yet exotic appearances. Have you not often heard a black-avised woman say, 'You know my grandmother was an Italian,' and seen her eyes turn hungrily to the door to make sure if the stranger newly come through was not tall and fair as the fortune-teller said? It is so with Italian gardens. They hope to one man that they shall be the stage for a life as like opera as makes no matter. This very garden dreams without end of being the scene of a duel between husband and lover in doublet and hose while a fair and dishonest wife clings to an urn and climbs up and up the scale. Well, see who are here. Nurses and children, dogs and their owners; and a dog is the very antithesis of opera. A cat would get the idea in ten minutes, but a dog would never cease to ask, 'Why?' and that is a difficult question to answer when it concerns opera. Look to whom they have raised a statue! To Dr. Jenner! Though I am bound to say he looks not out of harmony with the place to-day, for he has plainly gone mad in the night. See how he sits and muses on a lapful of snow. For these reasons I make a point of coming here every now and then and walking up and down as if I had lost my lover, and I do not think I am mistaken when I say it looks happier by the time I go. But, dear Arnold, do not let us talk nonsense any more. Tell me all that has happened to you."

" I wish we might talk nonsense for ever," he said wistfully, and looked about him. They were standing now by the curved balustrade where the two nymphs with cannon-ball breasts sit knee to knee and pour from ample-bellied urns invisible waters which, falling to earth, become the Serpentine. He had a great desire to ask who these nymphs might be, and hear the little liar tell to what great Whig families they had belonged when they were flesh, and why they had taken to a life of stone. It seemed to him that he needed a fairy-tale as a starving man needs food. But how to fit all in with the Holyhead train starting when it did? He could but sigh. Some alteration had come on his spirits, for now it no longer seemed to him in the least a matter for congratulation that he had what he had and had not Harriet. But he reflected that did he lose what he had and come to Harriet she would grudge no effort to subdue his grief, and he was glad that he had chanced that afternoon to walk in Kensington Gardens, for it had meant something like the finding of a loving little sister that had been hidden from him far too long. His gladness grew to an ache in his heart and tears in his eyes, as she slipped her hand under his arm and squeezed it very kindly. "But I do not want to speak of myself," he said, "for I want to hear news of you. Do you still live in Kensington?"

"Oh, yes," she answered earnestly. "I would not ever move from Kensington. I adore its decay and its gardens. It is like a cracked tombstone with a lilac bush bursting from it. But you, I suppose, have moved again and again, and always up and up."

"Indeed," he told her frankly, "I live in Albany in comfort so much greater than any beginnings gave me any right to expect that I thank my God every morning I awake and see my curtains being shaken apart. I have been very fortunate ; yet I do not believe I shall think myself half so fortunate as I have been thinking if you cannot say the same to me."

"Oh, I do well," she said indifferently, "I am a servant in a good house. So many people come to see my masters, Bach, Mozart, Beethoven, and the rest, that someone will always be needed to answer the door."

"I have seen your photograph on posters outside the Queen's Hall," he said.

"I have seen your photograph everywhere," she said, "and heard many speak of you, and always well. Old Sir George thinks highly of you."

"Sir George !" He laughed, like a growing boy who finds the schoolmaster that last year towered over him is this year down by his shoulder. More than a few notables seemed like that to him these days.

"Do not laugh at Sir George," she warned him quickly. "He has lived to be very old, and no one has ever talked of taking away the honours he was given when he was young. But I have not gone

only by what other people have said, I have made my
own investigations. Do you know that I read every
word of your great speech on the Fortress of Mondh?"

"You did?" They exchanged a foolish smile.
At a distance of even five paces one would have sworn
they were still in love. "Sitting on the floor? With
one hand on the carpet, and the arm curved like a
scythe?"

"Ah, you mock at me," she lamented. "I have
told you, 'tis no affectation when I sit like that, 'tis
because of my poor eyes. And I had a concert the
day before, and was as blind as a bat, yet I read every
word!"

"And what did you think of it?" asked Arnold,
with an eagerness which was absurd, since he knew
that Harriet was very silly.

She sighed reverentially. "It reminded me," she
said, "of the interior of St. Paul's Cathedral."

"You mean," he enquired, "a certain spacious-
ness?" She nodded. "Ah, yes," he agreed. His
eye travelled across the grey glass of the Serpentine
to the limits of the prospect, to the dark web of the
elms by Rotten Row. Reverie appeared to claim him.
"'Twas by that speech," he remarked, in that saun-
tering tone by which men disguise themselves when
they talk of what seems to them the height of por-
tents, "that I first attracted the attention of Lord
Sourdeline."

"I am not surprised," cooed Harriet.

His lids drooped still lower over his pupils, which

were bright with pleasure at what they had seen on the horizon. Yet more casually, yet more slowly with his lips curved as if the syllables tasted like caviare, he said, " I am going over to Ireland to spend Christmas with Lord Sourdeline." But suddenly his face fell, he looked down on Harriet with the greatest possible concern, and cried, drawing her close to him, " And you, my dear, have you arranged yourself a good Christmas? You are not going to be alone? "

They had stopped by the edge of the lily-pad tank that is in the centre of the garden, and is shaped like a rose. She looked up with eyes as solemn as a prayer-book, yet he knew she was laughing at him. " Ah, what is Christmas, for one who lives alone like me? " she asked. " I shall arise at my usual early hour, and I shall let out the cat. Ah, gentlemen like you do not know the importance of the part played by the cat in lives like mine! Then I will take my little besom and sweep the snow from my steps, for I am neat; and after I have had my simple breakfast I will sit down and practise my trade for fear that by neglecting my fingers this day I will go hungry some later day. And towards noon," she droned, " I will take a china plate from my dresser, and I will carry it alone to the pastrycook at the end of the street, and will bring it domed with a dish-cover, tarnished and with a loose knob on the top, very miserable-looking and streaked with a meagre slice cut from a bird communally roasted for the very poor.

'Twill not take me long to eat it. Not long enough. Then, for my second course, I will take from a paper-bag one of the tragic mince-pies of the very poor, that is a deal of wan pastry to two currants, a lean sultana, and a smear of sweetness. There were two in the bag once, but I ate the other on the previous night. That was my Christmas Eve——"

"Will you stop or shall I throw you to the lily-pads?" he asked. But indeed she could say no more for laughter. And he was laughing too, and looking on her very tenderly, for he could not conceive a prettier way by which she could have informed him that he could go on his pleasure with a light heart, since her pleasure was already bespoken for her, and yet given him no grossly actual detail on which his jealousy might get to work and make bad blood between them. "And they will be very happy," he sighed to himself. "After dinner they will sit together in one of her great chairs before the fire, and they will drink champagne from the same glass, and she will not want to drink it, but will plague him to watch the shining bubbles. Ah, deary me, deary me!"

She shook her head at him, but smiled; and she withdrew one hand from her muff, held it on a level with her lip, arched her wrist, and looked obliquely at some trifle of time-keeping that could be seen so between her wrist and her glove. The movement was of the order of silken contortion that a cat uses when it washes itself, and he could not bear it when it was followed, as, of course, it would be, by a cry that she must instantly be gone.

"Stay a little," he said, "for you must not go until you have told me what you are." She smiled with her accustomed good-humour, and he shook his finger at her. "Nay, you cannot smile this away! I am in earnest. I desire to know what you are, for I am sure you cannot be what you seem. You seem a little slut, but no one loves little sluts as I love you. I think you have some value above your seeming. I suspect you of being the embodiment of some principle, of having behind your head or under your feet an invisible scroll bearing the name of some quality such as the young women in the mural decorations of some public buildings are prudent enough to display visibly? Are you love? Are you truth? You are not justice, though you might be mercy. Are you poetry? Or are you philosophy?"

She made him take the hand she was offering in farewell. "Write me down," she told him, "as all that Arnold Condorex rejected."

One whose occupation it is to rise in the world has need to cultivate an art of dealing with rebuffs which is not less complex than the art of fencing. It has its tierces, its glizades, and its parries, though these consist not of action but of its negative, being affectations of such various degrees of insensibility as will make the assailant feel that he has scored no point and aroused no resentment; and all these he had mastered. He believed that he was turning on her a

front as calm as a marble bust of a mayor in a town hall.
Yet on the instant it was not his hand that was holding
hers but hers that held his, and she cried in a voice
that remorse had made more like a woman's and less
like a nymph's than he had heard from her lips before.
" How I have hurt you! And how noble you are,
to be so hurt by your fear that you have hurt another!"

It was all outside the field of reason, and nothing
that he had ever intended to occupy his time with
further. But he found himself choking, and the snow-
powdered landscape lost form and ran before his eyes
like a sadly-coloured fragment of stained glass, as he
said, " Why, Harriet, I have always been a little hurt
for this very reason that I feared I had hurt you!
Are you sure you do not think that I have offered you
some slight? For I have never felt easy in my mind
about the end of that very pretty day we spent together
in your little house, when you were so kind and so
beautiful. It seems to me that when we walked together in the garden after tea I said or did something
that made you think I held you lightly; and that I
was not very clever about dispelling your rightful
indignation. And then—and then——"

He stole a look at her, and would have been glad
enough if she had interrupted him; but that she did
not do, though she patted his hand very amiably.
So he laid the flat of his hand to his brow and stam-
mered on, " —and then strange things happened before I sailed for India, which did not mend the matter.
I had most odd fancies, for which there could be no

foundation in the world. I believe I must have been mentally distraught, for they were the flightiest imaginations conceivable. Indeed, I had a right to be not quite myself at that time, for I had worked too long with Lord Derrydown. 'Twas like living by favour of a whimsical sheep. But, dear Harriet, can we not come to an understanding over this? For, indeed, I love you dearly, and there is no woman I honour above you, and whatever I said to the contrary was but a slip of the tongue that had no meaning. Will you not believe me, my dear?"

Harriet raised her muff to her chin, wagged her head at him over the top of it very gravely, and said, "I do believe you with all my head and heart."

He answered her with murmurs expressive of satisfaction at her satisfaction. But an instant after she had dropped her muff so that it swung from the cord about her neck, and was holding her hands as if to make him take a present from her, and crying: "Why will you still feel hangdog? Listen, I will tell you all. I will not deny that when you left me the state of my mind was deplorable. I retired to my bedroom and put on soft slippers, as women do when they form the intention of weeping for some considerable length of time, and then found that my situation was more serious than I had supposed, since there was no toffee in the house. For I would as lief not weep at all as weep without toffee. Your sex is greatly to be pitied for its inexperience of that beautiful sense of rhythm and counter-rhythm (not at all unlike the

pleasure derivable from a fugue) which is ours when
we punctuate our movements of spasm by popping
into our mouths those hard yet buttery cubes, and
thus restore to our system the natural unguents drawn
from them by tears. I could find not a thing in the
larder suitable for episodic eating save a jar of sweet
pickles ; and when I had helped myself to two or three
of those I was conscious less of a broken heart than
of a weak stomach. I will own I felt very pitiable for
an hour or two."

"Indeed I am greatly to blame ! " groaned Arnold
Condorex, grinding his teeth, bowing his head, fairly
rolling his eyes in penitence.

"Will you not be sensible and listen ? " she begged
him gaily. "Nay, do not think that I am being brave !
You cannot conceive how soon I abandoned the
business of weeping, and invoked that prudent side
of me which I have had to cultivate, since I am but
a poor girl with my way to make in the world. I was,
you see, almost discreditably not without resources.
Graceful I am, but nothing uncommon in my grace.
I "—she sucked her thumb till she could find words—
"I am a little less common than a china shepherdess,
but I am not rare. You may see me on a hundred
thousand mantelpieces, with my Leghorn hat and
my tarlatan gown and my wide sash that show off
my slenderness, and should it happen that the tall
gentleman in very tight trousers at the other end of
the mantelpiece fail to survive the touch of the new
housemaid I am left alone for no longer time—than—

96

lies—between—my—owner's—visits—to—the—market—town——" her breath failed her for shame, and
her thumb went back to her mouth.

"What are you trying to tell me, you little jade?"
he asked, smiling rather wryly.

"I am trying to tell you, my dove," she said, bracing
herself to it, "that although I had been transported
out of my soul by your endearing attributes, I had
never destroyed my address-book. Its pages," she
remarked in an offhand manner, "were not blank."

He knitted his brows as if he did not understand,
and since he was no fool that can only have been
because he did not wish to do so.

"You had hardly been gone more than two hours
before I had spoken by telephone with a young man
and given him permission to call on the following
day and instruct me concerning the Polish Corridor,
since some amiability of mine had inadvertently made
him believe me profoundly interested in that subject,
on which he was an expert. 'Twas the beginning
of a delightful friendship. I wish you had known him.
You would have liked him so much," she said, in
the disingenuous tones in which women urge socia-
bility on those who are in the natural course of things
unlikely to delight in each other's company.

He looked at her quizzically.

She stepped backwards, blushing. Then bit her
lip and said, "How well you know my quality!
No, 'twas not as easy as that. I do not wonder you
do not believe me. Yet what I say is true, I did not

grieve for very long. I will tell you how it really happened that I found peace and you have no need to reproach yourself. I did not become tranquil nearly so rapidly as I have pretended. It might well have been that I had thrown myself into the arms of this young man with that violence which is for the soul the same form of suicide that leaping from a high balcony on to rocks is for the body; but instead I was very cool with him; you would not believe how cool I was. For after I had put down the telephone it occurred to me that I would not find it easy to sleep, and I remembered that that morning when I was combing my hair the manner in which I played the Hammerklavier Sonata had seemed most shameful, and I resolved to practise it. So I blew out the candles that I might rest my eyes, which were a trifle sore, and I sat down at my piano and played it over and over again, while the rising moon painted a black and silver pattern on my floor. After an hour or two I stopped, and there was nothing in my world save exaltation, for even as the black and silver pattern had stamped itself more brightly on the boards as the moon mounted the skies, so the pattern of the adagio had grown clearer and clearer in my mind as my comprehension had soared upward to its zenith, and now my finger-tips had no more to do than copy it. I have never felt more comfortable in my spirit. I had no thought of you until my Grimalkin mewed at my window, and to admit him I had need to face the garden where we had so lately walked together, and

fallen out. But I was not confused. Gazing calmly
on it, I said, ' Do you not see that advancement is to
him what music is to you? You would let no man
come between you and the heavenly strains of Bach
and Beethoven and Mozart. 'Tis factious, therefore,
to feel aggrieved because he will not let a woman come
between him and what he holds as not less sacred.'
I therefore felt no longer at a disadvantage, and it
appeared incredible that I had intended to dedicate the
night to tears. I went up to bed and slept a matter of
nine hours. But before I did that, I remember, I
stood for quite a time at the window, with my tired
Grimalkin in my arms, while I watched the garden
relax from the sharp brilliance of moonlight to the
quaker shades of dawn, and thought of you as kindly
as you could possibly have wished. Well, so it was ! "

He was saying heartily, " Why, I am very glad, dear
Harriet, that you took the matter so sensibly," when
her face, which had been looking up at him as fair and
open-eyed as the golden rose he had sometimes seen
her wear in her bodice, clouded with disappointment.
" You do not believe me," she wistfully exclaimed.
Then suddenly a lightning flash ran through her frame
and after jerking high her chin blazed from her eyes.
" Ah, I see what it is ! You do not want to believe
me ! Some part of you, unworthy of the rest, takes
pride in having incommoded me, and will not permit
the better part that loathes to think so accept my
assurance. Oh, what perversity, to cling with love
to the idea that you have inflicted pain ! I will not have

it so!" But her gaze, not less suddenly, grew soft.
"Why, I perceive that all this time you have been
torturing yourself regarding this small business!
Again and again you have awakened in these most
superfluous hours between two and four in the morning, and said to yourself, 'I dealt ungraciously with
Harriet Hume,' and suffered a heartache. Oh, my
poor sweetheart, my pet lamb, my honey-bird!
And I perceive too, that when that heartache wore
off as all heartaches do, you turned over and prepared
to enjoy complete repose, but were prevented from
that pleasure by fears that I must needs hate you for
having used me so, and that I might raise my
armies against you. 'Dear God, there is Sir George,'
you have groaned; and thrashed about until dawn.
Oh, my poor stricken deer, why do you look ashamed?
That is a thought most natural to such as us who had
to fight our way towards eminence through enemies.
But I will put a finish to all this, I will not let you for
another moment canker your mind with pride in
phantom cruelties. Listen, while I make the proof!"

Uneasily he smiled, "I do not believe I shall be able
to listen to it, for you are looking very pretty!"

She knew his praise of her was not without its
viciousness, but her face remained as brilliant under
its animation as a daisy under a dewdrop, she was so
sure that all would go well when she had had her say.
"You must know first," she told him, "that you have
greatly disguised from yourself the nature of the
catastrophe that befel us in my garden; for which you

need blame neither yourself nor your deeds, since it occurred for no other reason than that I had suddenly been granted the power to read your thoughts."

Arnold Condorex burst into laughter, so extravagant that it cost him his balance. He would have staggered away from her, had she not clipped his cuff between her palm and her fingers. "Yes, I recall you had that curious fantasy!" he told her, choking with indulgent mirth.

"'Twas no fantasy," she insisted mildly. "I had that power, and have not lost it. This very day has seen me exercise it unimpaired. Did you not see me, as I walked before you through these gardens, stop suddenly and tremble, like a fish caught up from its pond on a line? It was the hook of your own thoughts that had fastened in my back, so actually that I would not have been surprised had it torn the shoulders of my gown. I knew it was you that followed me, and I knew the thoughts that were running in your head. Come, tell me," she coaxed, lifting to him a face as bright as a new penny with knowledge of her impending triumph, "did you not look at that pretty little cottage which stands among the lawns and guess that, being silly, I longed to live there in the sylvan way, making repasts of such nuts and berries as are to be found in Kensington Gardens? And did you not very handsomely wish you were the King, and could give me all I wish?"

Roughly he freed himself and stepped away from her crying, "I did not!" and then, seeing the game was up, said sullenly, " I did ! " and, putting his hand to his head, querulously exclaimed : " But I cannot see what that proves ! "

" Sweet," she chirruped at his elbow, " hark at the important proof it makes ! I am not so temperate in nature as I seem. There are those who have seen me skimming like the wind from some incident that had galled my pride, my hair streaming like a comet (allowing for the difference in colour) from my distracted head, my eyes rolling in frenzy, and my rigid fingers clapped over my ears. I must confess— without regret," interpolated the little prig, " for I believe it has improved my renderings of Beethoven— that I am not immune from agony. Had I loved you as passionately. and had you injured me as cruelly as you suppose, there was and is one figure in your thoughts who would instantly have transformed me to the tear-flecked Mænad I can sometimes be. Ah, my love, are you not fortunate in your affairs of the heart ! "

There was a pause before he replied, " I do not understand you."

Rapt in a vision, she was for the moment not attentive to him. " The intensity of your thought," she trilled, " makes her visible to me as if we were walking skirt by skirt here on the pavement. I have made all manner of close observations on her. She has as small a hand and foot as mine, as finely arched an eyebrow and as shining an eye, and like me she has no reason to fear had she to take her turn in a gallery of antique statues. Only she is golden as the sovereign our fathers used, and thus beyond dispute outshines me; and she has that majesty I have always known I lack. But am I frenzied at the thought of her! No! Exquisite she is, and she is yours, and I rejoice!"

But Arnold Condorex, or so it seemed, was turning into stone. He repeated, "I do not understand you. You do not speak of anyone I know."

"Why must you dissemble your happiness to me," she cried tenderly, "when I mean so well? I will not tell a soul but my cat if you do not want it known. I only speak of it to assure you how very happy I am that you are going to be happy! For I saw all, dear Arnold. I saw the vision of the future which comes and goes at the back of your mind, sustaining you against all present tedium; of the six pearl-grey and soot-black pillars of St. George's, Hanover Square, and how one day soon they shall be washed by a boiling surf of the mob that loves to see the gentry married; of the interior of that match-making building, that shall be incandescent with white flowers and crammed to the doors with persons of consequence; of yourself, standing so properly at the head of the aisle, no more and no less composed than is suitable for the moment; of her at whose coming all the doves swoop down, remembering that though they have for some time been associated with the Anglican Church they were at first the birds of Venus——"

No lark, shot down from the invisible niche in the

skies where it had poised to sing its heart out, was more suddenly silenced than was Harriet then. With her mouth a little open, she stood staring before her at the Serpentine, which now looked very much the colour of a dead fish.

Till then these two had been very snug out there, in the Italian Garden, more snug than it would seem possible for two walking abroad in this world of sword-sharp airs, splinters of ice, and lawns grizzled like old men with rime. Because of a certain warmth their meeting had engendered in their hearts, it was as if a line of invisible bonfires were blazing on the stone flags and were making an alley of good temperature for them. But now those fires were dead. Nothing disguised from them that it was nearly Christmas of a winter that had been murderous to the poor, and that they were standing in the uncabined atmosphere with only a little haberdashery between it and their pelts. This was because another fire had died. Its hearth had been in Arnold Condorex's breast, and in its time it might have been called loyalty, or gratitude, or nobility, but had now no need for a name, since it was ashes, and would presently be dispersed by the winds and be as if it had not been at all. For if he meant to marry Lord Sourdeline's only daughter before he went to Ireland, why, then, he was a traitor; a double traitor, since she was betrothed to the only son of old Lord Derrydown.

Striking her bosom with her minute clenched hand, poor Harriet moaned, "I know all, yet I know it a second too late ! 'Tis the artist's special quality and defect ! " Faltering, she turned towards the entrance of the enclosure.

Coldly he said, " Let me attend you to the gate."

Walking beside her with dejected head, he supposed she knew it all ; how he had heard from another like himself, who had a firm intention to rise in the world, and had told him with a trading gleam in his eye, that the far-famed golden Ginevra, whose beauty had been the astonishment of English earth since her seventeenth birthday, had fallen moonishly in love with him after having heard him deliver his speech on his first visit to the Fortress of Mondh, and had these three months kept his portrait under her pillow, where her betrothed's had never been. She knew, too, he supposed, that the informer had made a winking claim of credibility for his story by saying how it had been garnered for him by his sister, who was employed in some mean capacity about Lord Sourdeline's household. Oh, God ! How resolutely the enterprise took on itself the form of a Hogarthian picture full of the colours of soiled linen, depicting a party of servants armed with weapons of the kitchen, spits and pokers and tongs still daubed with grease, creeping up a backstairs to the fine door of the library ; where their master's noble head would nod over a Latin book until they ran in to gag and rob him ! And how infinitely low the informer had looked when he had gone on to say, his eye gleaming as if he had achieved some triumph of vendition in Petticoat Lane, that the

Lady Ginevra was by no means as gifted in her intellects as in her person, being very gullible indeed, and that her father could deny her nothing! Hogarth again!

As they went by the last of the tanks, Harriet faltered and was obliged to rest upon his arm. To cover her agitation she behaved as if she had paused to watch a governess who, good creature, was attempting to train the fat boy and girl who were her charges in kindness to the brute creation by throwing bread to the water-fowl afloat there in the shadowed ebony water. "How I admire," said Harriet with a weak smile, "those who bring food to the birds! It shows that when they begin a walk they know where it will end, which I never do."

But the governess had turned her gaze on them, and had on seeing the marks of deep emotion on the faces made a long leap through the ether to some universe thickly upholstered with seductions. She became petrified, her scattering arm stiff as a pump-handle, while she considered whether it were better for her charges to continue in the practice of Franciscan benevolence or to be removed at once from the neighbourhood of persons she believed guilty of uncontrolled passions. The manly vigour of Arnold, the singular loveliness of Harriet, suggested to her that if a seduction had indeed taken place it had probably been of a very thorough nature. She cast from her the last dry white flakes with such a convulsive movement that they feathered the convex waistcoat of an old gentleman who was passing by, and with cries of "Come, Andrew! Come Phoebe!" hurried her charges from the enclosure.

"God, this woman is making me conspicuous!" exclaimed Arnold with the natural fearfulness of the male, and by a not too gentle indication of his desire to move swiftly saw to it that she too got on her way out into the gardens.

She faltered, he supposed, because she felt the force of his loathing. For certainly he loathed her, since she had spoiled something to which he had given the most prudent management. He had met the eye of the informer in a most prudent and gentlemanly way, cold, wearily, yet not inimically, and had poo-poohed the whole affair. "I have no mind," he had said firmly and sensibly, "to present myself as a suitor to a family that would not accept me as an equal." And against the news that Sister Sukey would soon be here on holiday and might have more to say over a dish of tea he had built up a marble wall with words only technically of regret, saying that he was likely for some time to be too greatly overburdened with duties to be free for social entertainments. If he had later given the informer a letter to the Director of the Department for the Engenderment of Larger Oysters and had himself pressed his suitability for one of those sought after measuring posts, it was but to mitigate the absolute nature of that rebuff.

Ay, there was nothing wrong about his proceedings, present or future, were they but looked at from the

right end, which is the further side of the performance.
A tree is the most natural and wholesome of growths ;
but if one walking in a park should come suddenly
on an elm that swept the ground with its inverted
foliage and raised against the skies roots hung with
clods of earth, he would run. Say he had gone to Castle
Sourdeline and in the celebrated domed entrance hall
with the fluted columns of verd-antique, had first
had sight of the far-famed golden Ginevra where
she stood between Canova's Hebe and the Pozzuoli
Venus (not now considered genuine, but very fine),
and had looked into her eyes with a gaze prolonged
beyond the ordinary by astonishment at her perfection, yet sanctified with reverence ; say he had later
ridden with her in the delicious vales of County Wick-
low, but never out of sight of their party, and had
danced with her, but had looked steadily on the white
and gold pilasters and their rich capitals, and never on
the fair and pleading face she raised to him ; say he
had been quick to act on the first moment he could
no longer conceal from himself how the land lay,
and had gone to the lady's father and betrothed and
made a manly confession of his feelings, and left
immediately, and entered into no clandestine corre-
spondence ; say he had never seen her again till these
persons were alarmed lest their darling should fall into
a decline, and themselves summoned him—why,
what would be that sequence of events save the
romance of a high-minded young man who had not
parted with a pennyworth of his honour to pay for

his happiness. If it seemed otherwise, it was Harriet's infernal witchcraft that had transformed it, and had, now he came to think of it, engineered this whole situation. For he would long ago have married a plain woman with family behind her, and so forfeited his freedom to approach Ginevra, had it not been (though he had not till this moment admitted it) that he could never bend eyes on such without remembering that dusk in the garden of Blennerhassett House, when she had burgled his mind and seen he meant to do that very thing. Damnable witch, she had enchanted him into feeling a sense of loss and shame for what is no crime, but the world's constant practice, only abused in priggish books, like the laying-out of wealth to usury! God, why do we not burn witches now?

Meeting his eyes just then, for she had turned at the egress to offer him her civil adieux, she grew pale, shuddered, and jerked up her chin. It was as if a flame licked her bosom and threatened the pretty face of which she was so vain. She looked away from him to the Gardens, to the near glade where several hardy children of the russet-apple kind scattered abroad among the trees while one of their number pressed its face against a trunk; at the near lawn where five fat terrier brothers rolled tipsily in the sherry of the winter sunlight. When her gaze came back to him she seemed to be turned to stone by her wonder that those simple things could be on the same earth as his thought. Therefore he kept it very clean in his mind while he raised his hat and left her silently. He would show no mercy to her whom he now hated so much that he could not speak. Let her burn. Let the witch burn. For she had come between him and every human being's right not to know quite what he is doing.

III

YET it was he, not she, who constrained their next
interview; and yet it was not he, for the day had
altered him out of his usual self. That day was arid.
No rain had fallen in England for five weeks. In
the country the deepest dell had lost acquaintance
with humidity. In grottos and fountains plants
that had grown to think possessed of moisture as a
property languished in desiccated forms as different
from their usual aspect as age from youth. The appearance of the town, though masonry does not wither
on its stem, was not less desolate; for at the end of
every vista hovered a sinister presence which seemed
to be shaped by malignity out of dust, and that dust
ruddier and more inimical to man than is found in
London. It was as if the genius of the Sahara, hearing
that drought had of late extended its empire to this
island which had seemed to have water as its constant lover, were come here to gloat. Over the Green
Park it stood and mocked at those who had come from
their mean homes to seek alleviation there, and finding
the air they had trusted to be 'cool, hot as a fever
patient's breath, the grass they had trusted to be
lush, repellent as some old ragged carpet, fell into

postures not less fatigued and tortured than they assumed on their own hated pallets. Where Bond Street and Grafton Street are joined it waited for those pedestrians who laboured up from Piccadilly and told them : " Did you think yourselves fortunate that you are not as others are and do not have to work in the heat of the day, but can parade at your leisure this alley lined with vanities ? Well, then, enjoy your fortune ! What, will you not ? You reel, you put your hand to your head, you call a vehicle ! Weaklings, I fear, weaklings to a man ! " Did one open one's mouth to gasp for air, this genius was with one in a trice and forced its hot harsh immanence within one's throat, as lion-tamers place their heads within the jaws of their broken beasts. Did the wind one had prayed for blow at last, it was not before the presence had bitted it and bridled it and used it as its steed.

Even Arnold Condorex, whose body knew as little of subjugation by the elements as a bull's, relaxed his posture and closed his eyes as his vast Chimborazi-Mecklenburgh took him through the Mall, that was now almost as merely earth as a dried river bed. " Had I remained obscure," he mused, " I would most probably be swimming now in some green swirling of waters on the Cornish coast. I used to be an uncommonly strong swimmer, I remember." He sighed, and felt his body somewhat dead and gross in his thick ceremonial clothes. Brushing away the moisture the presence had laid upon his brow, he longed for the lean body that was no longer his, for the waters he might not visit. "But I could never have suffered obscurity," he argued, "I shall not rest until all men have admitted that I am their peer; ay, and beg me to make admission of equality." Upright, straight lines appeared at each end of his lips, as one may see in Japanese representations of great warriors, and he became rigid in contemplation of an unseen glory.

His car had stopped. He raised his head with a jerk and was startled to find that they were in St. James's Street, outside Boodles' Club, which is the most elegant casket ever designed for the spirit of convivial gentlemen. Its excellencies struck home to him as such things do when seen for the first time or unexpectedly, and for a second he sat lost in them. How discerning is that suggestion of the pagan temple which it makes with its pediment and its fluted tympanum which make apt allusion to the imperfect Christianisation of the English gentleman and his ineradicable loyalty to Venus, Mars and Bacchus! How fondly and pleasantly its use of mellow brick and plump bow-windows maintains that this pagan element is ever by such as enter Boodles' corrected by sound domestic and social considerations! And how the perfect proportions of the whole warn on the one hand against baseness, and on the other hand against enthusiasm! "Surely it is not a shameful thing," said his soul, "that I want to forge links between myself and that well-ordered society?" He felt a pang of surprise at perceiving a not ignoble reason for his ambition. But now he had need to find something to say to his chauffeur, who was holding open the door.

"And who," he quizzically enquired, "told you to drive me here?"

His servants adored him so that the poorest jest of his made them sparkle like women in love when their lovers condescend. "You did, sir," grinned the man.

Condorex raised his eyebrows, and shrugged his shoulders, and sat still. He supposed it was so; that when he had left the House of Commons he had been utterly ravished by abstraction. Well, who would not, who was to-morrow going to make such a stand for principle as had hardly been made since the days of Burke? Besides, he had feared that if any one spoke to him they would remark his agitation, and would remember to-morrow that he had been agitated full three hours before he had had reason, according to the manifesto he was to give forth to-morrow. But Boodles' would be a worse place than the House for him to-day. A horde of them would be within, belonging to the old wing that must now be done with, or the sons of such. Beyond a doubt there would be the good young Lord Ladyday, son of old Derry-down, who would greet him with that jolly horse laugh he had learned at Melton Mowbray, that exchange and mart of equine and human characteristics, where hunters find their way across country like great generals, and gentlemen take care to discuss over the mahogany no topic that slights by its complexity the

intellectual standards of the stall and horse-box.
What a fellow! " Because he approved my high-
principled conduct with Ginevra before our marriage,"
thought Condorex, " need he come snuffing about me
now like a pony that sees one whom it remembers
to have given it sugar, to find I have some new dainty
of good behaviour concealed about me? " With a
start he became aware he was looking up to the bow-
window of Boodles' with a face contorted by hatred.
" What," he exclaimed, " are you losing your capacity
for self-government! For certainly you have never
had greater need of it! " He would have given a
great deal to drive straight home and sealed himself
in his library, and sat and smoked and looked before
him, till the hour came. But if he had done so maybe
that old man with the radish-coloured pate sitting in
the bow-window who looked as if he slept (but old
men are often very profound liars) was not sleeping
and would say that he had seen Condorex drive up
to the club that afternoon, and by God he was mopping
and mowing and humming and hawing, and in the
end drove off again; and to-morrow it would be remembered and the manifesto disputed. Therefore
he must go in and enquire for a letter and come out
with one in his hand, very cool and collected, before
he drove home. Certainly there would be a letter
within, for that active body, the Rutlandshire branch
of the Union of Anglican Housewives Opposed to All
Amorous Delights, invariably addressed him there.
It was perhaps their one chance of writing to Boodles'.

But when he stepped on to the pavement he became conscious of the Saharan presence, standing nearly as high as the meridian over Piccadilly. He stared up into its set and brassy frown. The quality that made men follow him was his proud disposition to accept vast challenges ; as he had accepted the truly vast challenge of his lack of fame and fortune. In firm accents he said to the chauffeur : " You need not wait. I will walk home."

The placards held by the pale newsboys at the corner of St. James's Street and Piccadilly were limp as if paper itself had need to sweat this weather. " Ay ! " he said to himself as he crossed the road by them, keeping his head down before the fierceness of this presence as he had never previously lowered it save to wind and sleet, " these lads are the servants of time and move according to its tick-tock, but they do not know that in one quarter time has changed its pace and will lag intolerably until this evening. In Bond Street there was hardly a soul abroad, but he did not find it desolate. " I do not feel the sun so very strong," he mused, " I believe that I was born with more vigour than other men, and will retain it longer. I am sure I do not feel myself any weaker now that I have lost my youth." Positively the vehemence of the day was to his taste, he enjoyed the harsh contrast between the shadowed side of the road, which was dark blue like a thundercloud, and that where the sun fell, which had all the colour burned out of it and was pallid as caoutchouc. He turned aside at Burlington

Street and sought Regent Street along the tailors' alleys, and saw scarcely a body save a little black-coated man or two whisking in and out of doorways with pattern-books under their arms, with an air of being martyrs to decency and loyal to the duty of clothing the nakedness of the English gentry though the sky blistered ; until he came on a dreadful scarecrow walking in rags so soiled it might have had a night's lodging in a mill where they ground greenish flour. So indifferently did it walk through the furnace-breath that one perceived its capacity for suffering to be already fully exercised by the misery which was its constant state, and to be incapable of registering increase. But by a glittering impudence it affected when it saw itself observed, winking its fevered eyes and curvetting its scrawny neck, it showed how well it knew the nature of that state, and therefore that it must sometime have known another. "Disgrace must be a strange enchantment," said Arnold Condorex, shuddering ; and he crossed the road.

Regent Street was now deserted, save for a runnel of matrons that had trickled down from some terminus to which they had come on excursion tickets, which the railway companies continued to offer out of habitual enterprise and they continued to accept out of habitual thrift, although the destination was now nearly hell. These women looked like ghosts, for the strong light bleached what colour age and this habitual thrift had allowed their skins, their lips, their hair, and shone back from the shiny surfaces of their worn garments. "And indeed," he thought sadly and kindly, "there is something ghostly about their condition, too. For to be born into an obscure family and not to attain any eminence in one's lifetime must be to know something as different from full existence as the life of ghosts." Across the way was one of those blanknesses behind stocky-plank palisades which it is as disconcerting to come upon in a familiar street as it would be to pick up a familiar book and come on the stubs of twenty torn-out pages. "Why the building, whatever it was, must have been pulled down some time from the progress of the work. Have I grown unobservant?" he asked himself in perturbation. "But no! I travel always in the Chimborazi-Mecklenburgh with papers on my knee, or a secretary whom I must instruct, or distinguished company whom I must respect by conversation." Athwart the emptiness a crane drew its vast diagram, and lifted up a jerking container almost into the face of the Saharan presence, that here, perhaps because of the amount of dust rising from the work, seemed to be clad in yellow like the robe of a Tibetan monk. He watched the tilted shape climb up and up as he sauntered along the empty road, and said to himself, "It is strange I have never been afraid of heights."

It had been his odd whim to go to his home in Portland Place by the Queen's Hall side of upper Regent Street, though 'twas the other side that led him more directly. But this he abandoned when he had crossed Oxford Street and found in his path a hushed

crowd of the dusty matrons who, because of his
important bearing, fell back as he advanced. In a
cleared space before a shop-window a tall policeman,
his blue eyes glaucous with pity, his red face fish-like
because he struggled with tears, stood above one of
the matrons who lay stretched on the pavement, her
head on a rolled coat. The thick soles of her shoes
were turned extravagantly outwards, but sometimes
twitched as if to say, " Shall we walk again, or shall
we not ? " and her breath debated, " Shall I flee ?
Shall I stay ? " so that her pale tongue flickered like
an asp's between her parted lips. The cylinder between
her feet and head, where the issue was being decided,
was so shapeless that the argument seemed likely
to be sluggishly conducted. Two slits on the awning
overhead wrote wavering lines of sunlight on the
pavement beside her ; they recalled candles by a bier.
Condorex said to the policeman in a quiet and confident
voice, " Has the ambulance been summoned ? " The
policeman saluted and said, " Yes, Mr. Condorex." They
exchanged a sober, responsible, and quite meaningless
nod, and he turned aside. He wished the harsh afternoon
light had not painted London the colour of a grave.

Once in Great Portland Street he took out his handkerchief and wiped his brow. " But it would not
have been terrible had it not been mean," he told
himself. " 'Tis meanness that makes life fearful, ay,
and death too. If I had just seen a great man struck
down by the assassin's knife I would have felt grief
and horror, but not this desire to go down on all

fours and vomit like a dog. Death would be different with an Abbey hushed, and the pomp of a public event. There is nothing upon which Fame cannot put a better face." Presently he wondered why he was walking in such an ungenteel highway when there were turnings that would bring him into the splendid breadth of his own Portland Place; and shuddered at the one he took. It was a narrow street of high houses that ran across Portland Place to some further thoroughfare, and through the crystal lens of the heat it could be seen that not a living thing moved in all its long length. Nothing was there but the hot stones of the houses and the pavement, which looked so nearly white in the strong glare that it was as if their outer surface had been burned away. It was hard to believe that the actual flames as well as light had not been used to cleanse it to this state of barrenness, and the suspicion was increased by the blue mist which floated through the glassy brightness. It recalled to him a highway he had seen in Pompeii, and he was displeased by the comparison. " This is a world that is utterly untempered to those who live in it ! " he complained. " This day is far too hot ! People are dying of it." And he himself had begun to perspire far too freely for comfort. " Things can go wrong," he mourned, " women can die in the street, catastrophe respects no one and is ingenious——"

At that point he stopped, for the very good reason that there had entered the street from a by-lane, and was now walking a few yards ahead of him, a woman with a remarkably neat shape. She did not look to be a lady, for she was clad in a gown of parchment-coloured muslin that was something too free and simple for a person of condition to wear on the street. One might guess her the wife of a jolly waterman, to whom she had at noon delivered his dinner in a striped handkerchief, going to the edge of the wharf and sending her voice through the tiny trumpet of her hands across the bright haze-wreathed waters to the alley among great ships where he sculled. Or it might more probably be, since she was strayed too far from the Thames to let that be likely, that her husband stood all day on a paint-splashed ladder in a pompous room, wielding a white brush to make dingy garlands good as new, and was comforted because she sat below and plied her needle and sometimes sang; and was the more comforted because he did not know that the gaiety of her song proceeded from certain rakish dreams (such as often visit poor men's pretty wives) of what might have happened had she queened it in such a great house. Yet maybe that for all the informality of her dress she was not of the people at all, but was one of those ladies who will converse with the plumber in their nightgowns and on being rebuked open innocent eyes, and beg it to be noticed what a good family man he looked. In any case she was deliciously made, and at that moment was moulded in the prettiest pose imaginable; for she was holding something to her bosom with her right arm, which gave her right shoulder a lovely, languishing contour,

and her left hand was raised to her face, an accident
which revealed that she was one of the two women
in a thousand who have a dainty elbow. He felt that
he had been working too hard of late, that he would
get old before his time, did he lose touch with life as
he had done of late. But what was she at? Her left
hand had dropped and had thrown something small in
the gutter, and how she seemed to be searching in
whatever it was she carried at her bosom. Now,
undeniably, she was popping something into her
mouth. Gad! the saucy wench was about to enter
Portland Place eating cherries out of a bag. And Gad!
she was Harriet Hume.

In a trance he followed her, remembering now
that she had been very present in his mind only the
night before. About two o'clock in the morning he
had dreamed that three very comely women, the colour
of weathered sculpture, had sat in his room at a table
that was not there, weaving a cable from a heap of
pale flowers. It had seemed to him that he was awake
when he saw them, that he had raised himself on his
elbow to watch them better, and had remained so
for some minutes. But on his real awakening he had
recalled that these were but figures out of a fairy-tale
which had been told him by a woman in a garden;
and that the woman was Harriet Hume. At the sudden
recollection of her a bitterness like crushed almonds
had filled his mouth, his mind. Yet, when he had gone
to sleep, he had struggled back to wakefulness only
to tell himself that to-morrow he must contrive to pass

by the Queen's Hall and try to find her picture on the
hoardings there, as he had used to do when he went
more by foot than now ; and he had felt as one who
promises himself a delight, a comfort.

Now he felt no bitterness at the sight of her, nor
could quite recall why he should have done so. They
had fallen out on each of their last two meetings, he
knew, but he was now a better negotiator than ever,
and had long since cozened himself out of an exact
remembrance of the issue at fault. The matter fell
therefore under the care of that habit of his by which
he took for granted that if he had offended anyone
he had done it out of policy and had gained an advantage by it, and that it would be both prudent and an
exercise in technique were he to be reconciled to them.
Moreover. he knew a very lively desire to slip close
to her and whisper a compliment in her ear ; and he
had suffered a great depression of his spirit when he
had seen her walk before him in such beauty and
thought himself debarred from her because he dared
not risk his high repute by speaking to strange
wenches. And Lord ! she was at her tricks again !
For she had come to a standstill, and after regarding
the area-railings by which she walked with a good deal
of seriousness, had hung on one of the spearheads a
fine red doublet of cherries, which dangled from it like
an ear-ring.

He quickened his step and caught her up, the more
easily that as soon as she had done this thing she had
apparently been rooted to the ground, and stood

like a tableau vivant with her eyes nailed to the spear-head her foolishness had decorated. There was still no one in the street, in front of them, or behind them. The houses seemed asleep. He laid his hand on her waist and asked: "Will you not tell me, Harriet, why you did that?"

She was trembling violently. "Because," she forced through her chattering teeth, keeping her eyes fixed on the pendant cherries, "to-day I read an article in *The Times*—and had a deal of trouble spelling out the hard words—which told how a Parsee gentleman, turning his subtlety to work on plants, has discovered they, too, are not exempt from this ailment named consciousness. And if plants, why not sticks, and stones, and metal? And if so, what a life of drudgery they lead, how confined by us to the grooves of the uses we find for them! So I thought I would admit one area-rail to the high human pleasure of feeling finer than its neighbours. . . ." her voice died.

"Are you then the same dear fool as ever?" he enquired tenderly. And then, as the distress of her bearing came home to him, he exclaimed with compunction, "But how I have startled you! Did you not hear me coming?"

She did but raise her eyebrows, and smile faintly.

"My dear," he continued in great concern, "we are both very foolish to be walking abroad in this great heat. Will you not come to my house, which is just across the way, and rest yourself?" He added to himself. "I must guard over myself, lest I am indiscreet, for my fidelity to Ginevra is part of my legend, and these things never stay hidden. But I believe I will find pleasure in admiring the delicious thing I once possessed. Indeed I was very fortunate! I had forgotten the perfection of her bosom."

Till then she had kept her face turned from him, and because of that and of the deep brim of her poke-bonnet, he had seen little of it save the lobe of her ear and the tip of her nose. But now she offered herself fully to his eyes. Decidedly she was not looking her best, for heat and weariness had printed shadows under her eyes and round her mouth, which lay on her fine skin like watermarks on paper; and certainly she had not painted, and perhaps not even powdered, since the morning. She lowered her lids and let him gaze. "Ah, the poor doxy!" he thought pitifully. "Is it not shameful that so lovely a creature should not have a maid to help her rise at leisure, and a carriage to take her on her ways, and money enough to give her all she wants without toiling for it! I will take her home, and set her in a big chair, and I will give her tea. 'Tis a miracle, the effect of tea on females. But how like an angel she is looking now!" For she had opened her eyes and was regarding him with the most loving smile.

"Come, take my arm," he said; and thought, "I know not what my butler and my footmen will say when they open the door and see her standing in this muslin gown. I hope they will not think she is a light-o'-love I have gathered on the pavements.

But it would be a pretty thing if a man cannot take home an old friend for fear of his manservants." She slipped her arm in his, and squeezed it very affectionately. He bade her lean on him, and chided her for venturing forth on such a day of bludgeoning heat, while he was wondering: "Why did we quarrel? Why, surely 'twas on account of some singular gift she seemed to have, which was nothing less than true second sight, so far as could be seen. Ay, she told me I would marry Ginevra before we had ever met, I remember. But why should we have quarrelled over that?" He shook his head blandly. "I cannot call the circumstances to mind." But suddenly eagerness pierced him so that he gripped her arm. "Would she read my future to-day, I wonder? I cannot recollect how she did it. With tea-leaves? In a crystal? I think not. We were standing in Kensington Gardens chatting when she told me about Ginevra——"

But Harriet had come to a standstill again, and her eyes were set on a taxi-cab that was coming towards them. "I think 'twould be better if I went straight home," she mewed.

"Why, Harriet, have you taken a dislike to me that you have changed your mind?" he exclaimed, and within he mourned: "She is not coming, she will not read my future, and God knows one would fain learn one's future when one is throwing all overboard for the sake of principle! Things go wrong. They go wrong most pitifully. That woman was dying where she lay in Oxford Circus." He shuddered. Harriet was standing in front of him, sending a very grave look up into his face. "My dear, we are very nearly at my door, you had better come in," he told her, and groaned inwardly. "Leaving the future on one side, what shall I do if she does not come in with me! The time will never go by until it is six!"

At that a hammer struck in his brow; and he knew it would strike so every minute of the next two hours that he was alone and undistracted.

"Oh, I will stay with you, my dear!" she cried impulsively, and clung on his arm again.

"That is a good girl," he said, comfortably paddling along, "and she shall not have far to go either, for my house is number one hundred and twenty. Now, my love, you are surely not going to be tiresome again!" For once more she had come to a standstill.

"Nay, but——"

"What is it, my pest, my plague?"

"Why, 'tis my bag of cherries!" she confessed. "I cannot take them into your house. 'Twould offend the propriety of your menservants."

"Never think of it," he said stoutly. "We will take them in, we are no slaves."

"Nay, my sweet," she fluttered. "I cannot expose you to such inconvenience. See; I can bend down and feign to tie my shoe, and leave the bag between the railings of the house where we are standing, and no one will see us."

"You shall not do anything of the sort," he said

solidly. "I have a mind to eat cherries with my tea, and I desire they shall be these same cherries that I have seen in this bag; which, my dear, you have carried so imprudently that there is a faint purple stain beneath your left bosom, that might well lead a passer-by to conclude that you had stabbed yourself for love. Tell me, did you not buy these fruits at a barrow?"

"I did," admitted Harriet. "But I chose a coster-monger who looked a clean man, and had a clear blue eye."

"I thought as much," he announced with some satisfaction, "they are fruits of low origin. (That is a very cheap paper-bag.) Nevertheless, they look to be as excellent cherries as I have ever seen, just as this dusty trull on my arm, who has not flour-bagged her nose since dawn, and who eats fruit out of a bag as she walks down a most genteel throughfare, ay, and casts the stones in the gutter, is the most beautiful and the most kind female I have seen for years. But pray do not giggle any more just now, even though I have praised you, and you are naturally transported with delight, for we are at my house."

"Is this your house?" breathed Harriet, looking upwards. "This one? With the fanlight that makes lace look heavy, though it is of iron? And the two rams' heads by the door-posts, that look so gentle and so sly? To think that this is your house, which I have admired times out of number as I hurried by!"

"Ay, it is considered beautiful," he said eagerly; and added, with more than a little timidity, "but

I suppose you do not think it so beautiful as your music."

"Why do you say that?" she cried. "It is just as beautiful as much good music and in much the same way!"

They stood looking up at the door in silence for a minute or two. "'Tis the true work of the Brothers Adam," he explained at length; "within you will see that nothing in the house is left untouched by the prevailing harmony." He thought to himself: "I could not have lived here had I not risen in the world," and at that was pricked by the same stab of surprise as when, outside Boodles', he had recognised that there was more than ignobility in his ambition. Suddenly he felt very tired, and wanted to go into his house and rest alone in Harriet's company; and loathed to think that to get his wish he must first confront his butler and his footman who bore to one another (or so it seemed for the moment to his irritated mind) a resemblance in blankness contemptible in anything but boiled eggs. But he remembered that in his wallet he carried a latch-key that till then he had hardly ever used, and thus it was that, when he and Harriet softly closed the door behind them, there was nothing in the hall save its own beauty, and the motes dancing down the noble staircase.

"Oh, it goes far beyond all expectation!" she exclaimed. "The wrought-iron of those banisters grows like ivy! And not like common ivy either! Like that which twines the thyrsus of Apollo."

"And note the door-head of the dining-room," he urged in an undertone. "'Tis much admired. Its fellow is at Lansdowne House, though somewhat larger." As he spoke he pulled off his hat and gloves, and threw them on a chair. "And look, my love——"

"Ah!" She was clinging to his arm with both her hands, staring with round eyes along the passage, up the staircase. Yet all that was doing was that his hat had rolled off the chair and made a clatter.

"Why, you sweet fool!" he whispered to her. It gave him a strange pleasure to stand there whispering to her although there was no real need for lowered voices. "Sometimes I think I derive no great good-fortune from standing where I do in the universe. But that position brings some advantages. (My dear, how pretty you are! How very pretty!) And one of them is that were ten serving men to spring upon us here in this hall, and I were carrying away that vase, and you had your frail arms about that mirror, it would still be they who had to go, and we who stayed. Is that not an advantage, my peerless one?"

In his manly desire to comfort her he was holding her in his arms a little too much, all things considered, after the fashion of a lover grasping his mistress; and she, with that disposition to insipid compliancy which was, perhaps, her greatest fault, was reclining there very much after the fashion of a mistress grasped by her lover.

"I know I am foolish," she sighed.

"Foolish is not the word," he said judicially. "You

are a goose. Have you never asked Providence why it has pleased Him to afflict you in this manner ? "

She giggled. Her cheek was but an inch from his shirt-front. Since he poutered his breast like a pigeon, it was his fault they met, and it was she who broke away and (though she cast yet another glance up the staircase as if she saw an armed man descending it with sword prepared for flesh) cried out gaily : " And now for the rooms ! They cannot be as fine as this ! "

" They are far finer," he answered, and led her along the passage to his little library. With his hand on the door-knob he paused, made comical eyebrows at her, and groaned, " Now am I utterly at your mercy ! How I shall despond if you do not like it ? "

When the door was opened she clapped her hands and trilled, " How could you dream I would not like it ? "

" Because I love it," he said sombrely, " and I am foolish about it as men are about the things they love."

She ran about the room. Watching her, he exclaimed, as one who laments a loss, " How well you accord with it ! " But being as rapt from personal things as if she attended to a musical affair, she did not listen and went chattering on, " Oh, this is the true suavity, the blandness which one pays for when one sits down to play the good music that was made before the Romantics came ! There is such true observation of existence here ! See, in that arch above the bookshelves in the alcove there, how he has remembered the arch of the sky above the plains ! See how he

decorates the curve of the arch with a golden border
so that we think of the sun on its journey through the
day ; and how he then cuts the half-circle into twelve
golden slices by a very orderly design, as if to say we
must break the day into hours and gild each with
beauty ! And how the pilasters on each side of the
shelves claim that if we constrict our lives by the sound
and temperate exercise of the faculties, as the ancients
showed us, we shall not be crushed by the sky, but
shall support it so that it is the less likely to fall !
'Tis humbug, of course, for what he cared for was
not the tonic moral quality of this method of regarding
life but simply its comely effect, but how good it is !
What vast imaginative references it makes ! For does
not that rounded end of the room seem like an altar
to some austere god of Greece, and make all that is
done here like a votive offering to him ? "

He assured her, though she had forgotten he was
there, " Ay, I have found it a great inspiration."

She looked strangely at him. " In your political
work ? "

" What other ? "

It seemed, though that was against reason, as if she
were saddened by his answer. She looked away from
him, and turned her eyes again, though with less
concentration, on the beauties of the room. " And
these plaster decorations on the panels ! They are
like the banisters, they seem to grow like vegetation.
But these are more fine than ivy, they are like the most
delicate creepers——"

Fondly he asked, "Does the creeper still swing low over your garden-wall?"

"Every Spring it does," she nodded, "until three very personable young men come to cut it back. Often I have wondered who they were, and why the regular gardener did not do it. But now I know they were the Adam Brothers slipping through time for something they could use. There is much of this in-and-out work between the centuries——" but she was trembling so that she could not finish.

He scrutinised her, and saw that in the last few minutes her face had grown monstrously troubled, and had been drained of all her usual felicities of complexion; and he cried out in the liveliest self-reproach, "Curse it, I had forgotten that you are only a silly slut who has walked too far in the heat, and that I had brought you here to rest! Come, lie you down on my couch. Though I fear I am not giving you all the refreshment I hoped, for it seems to me that excessive light is the only property of this detestable day which is excluded from this house. I can all but see the tides of heat rocking against the walls. Come, my love, let me put a well-fed cushion beneath your head. Are you better now?" But her upward smile, though she nodded, was still some way from perfect serenity. "Ah, I have it!" he exclaimed. "You feel the need of tea. Is it not so? I had forgotten the dependence of your sex on tea!"

"Ah, yes!" breathed Harriet meekly, "you are always right! I am feeling the need of tea!"

"You see how well I understand you after all these years!" he told her proudly, tugging at the bell. "Now you will learn, my dear, how far it is from being true that in a house where ten servants are kept bells are answered ten times as quickly as in a house where there is but one of the breed; and while you are learning it you shall repose quietly on that couch while I sit down at my desk, and see if any important papers have come in my absence. For I will not disguise from you, dear Harriet, that there are great doings in this house to-day."

As he sat down he blew a kiss to where she lay glowing under the shadow of the room like an odalisque under her veil; and he squared his brow over the pile of papers he had found, as if he believed them to be much more important than he thought it in the least degree likely that they would be. Yet was there one which for a minute made him forget her, and what he might make her think of him. It was a letter from the family that (he had been credibly informed) deserved the deepest sympathy for having been under the curse of two warring infatuations; not one but had used his first moment of freedom from his nurse's arms to crawl towards an atlas, not one but had been instantly moved by his first and every subsequent sight of the sea to the agonising and dangerous upheavals of *mal de mer*. Whensoever he chanced to see the sight, so familiar to Londoners, of Thomas Cook and his sons riding down to their office in Ludgate Circus in the howdahs of elephants, wearing

Egyptian sun-helmets, and commanding Maori attendants, on their way to enable others to enjoy the
pleasures of foreign travel for which these poor
trappings could give themselves only the most insub-
stantial compensation, he had always admired them for
having turned to social uses a disappointment which
might have crushed lesser men to the depths of
misanthropy. A letter from them, therefore, made
strong claims on his attention; and indeed he grew
pale with the intensity of his interest as he read this one.
It confessed in simple and manly language that Thomas
Cook and his sons (even George, whose knowledge of
the globe till now had been considered exhaustive,
for he could differentiate between the towns in the
United States named Springfield without a fault)
had lately found themselves baffled by a certain
problem.

Five or six times in the last few years travellers had
requested them to arrange journeys to Mondh, but
they had found themselves unable to encompass this
succcessfully, even under the direction of the most
experienced guides. (With what heartrending irony
did the afflicted family express regret that they could
not undertake the search themselves!) Application
to the India Office had produced replies too official for
comprehension by plain Cooks. But they had thought
that since Mr. Condorex's Speech concerning his
Emotions on his First Visit to Mondh was not only an
acknowledged masterpiece of English prose but was
also within the sphere of children's intelligence, being

a favourite recitation on Empire Day, he could perhaps oblige them with more lucid directions.

Solemnly he gazed before him for a moment. Then with the austere benignity of one who yields a sacred torch to a younger hand, he laid aside the letter, to be dealt with by his secretary. Through such an episode had he risen ; through such episodes must others rise.

His butler stood before him. In such tones he ordered, " Tea," and wished he had had need to give a more exacting command in front of Harriet. "But she will come here again," he thought to himself, turning a doting look on her across his desk, " I must see to it that she comes often. Sweet tender gosling ! Was there ever anything so lacking in asperity save a dish of curds and whey ? I wonder if she knows how seductively so simple a gown exhibits the perfection of her form. Why, she is looking very smug just now. If she were a little puss she would sit up and wash her face. It would be very agreeable, now I come to think of it, were women to perform their ablutions in the manner of cats. Even now the rounder taper of Harriet's limbs might be pointing her black sandal to the ceiling while her sleek head bent to some recondite accomplishment of cleanliness. I fear I would not remain indifferent if it were so,—ah, she has changed her pose. Lying as she is now, with her delicate ankles crossed, and her hands disposed about her person as if to shield herself, is she not like one of the nymphs on my panels, abandoned yet not loose ? "

As he smiled across at Harriet, and she smiled back,

blushing a little, there came into his mind, and brought with it a sullenness as of November, what he had heard Ginevra say of her. The occasion had been not long after they were married, at a supper under Lady Ophidian's prepotent chandeliers. Someone was speaking of the young pianist who was also a great beauty, and he had sat dumb with his eyes on his plate, since he was still enraged with Harriet on account of that quarrel which he could not now re-collect. Suddenly he had heard Ginevra say : " But did you not tell us she was a pianist ? Then what you are saying about her cannot be true." " Why not ? " had enquired Harriet's advocate, fixing his monocle. " Why, if her hands were as small as you are pretend-ing, she would not be able to play the piano. So what you are saying about her cannot be true." Having uttered this defence of accuracy, Ginevra retrieved two or three peas that had fallen from her fork while it was suspended in mid-air and swallowed them as if they were the argument.

" Now, why," he mused, leaning his elbows on the desk, and cupping his chin in his hands, that he might the more comfortably look at Harriet on her couch, " is she tittering to herself ? " The part of his mind that was still gloomily occupying itself with Ginevra, as one bites on an aching tooth, reflected that he had so distinctly retained her comment on Harriet because it was certainly the most intelligent remark she had ever made. " But now the jade is looking sorry for me, and now she is looking very angry, and has twirled herself round on the pivot of her little hindquarters, and is sitting up ; and she is biting her lip, and wagging her head from side to side as if she would say something, and fears a nicer woman would not say it, but hopes that she will say it, ay, and in terms that will be remembered. Now she is looking down on her hands very intently. What a strange life of the mind she leads, playing catscradle with her own phantasies, like a kitten that has found a skein of wool ! Now she is rising. What an admirable energy keeps all her movements firm ! " His mind maliciously presented him with a picture of Ginevra as she would be lying at this moment on the sands of the Lido, golden and shapely and limp as an anchovy. There was no occasion in life when she was not limp ; no, not one. " Now she is advancing on me, and with an air of purpose, too. Is she going to upbraid me ? Well, it will be very curious, like watching a sweetmeat fly into a passion."

But Harriet was meek as a schoolgirl come to ask its teacher a question. Standing in front of his desk with her hands behind her back, she repeated him in a little voice, " You have not asked me about my music."

" Have I not, my dear ? " he answered. " Well, it was not indifference that prevented me from doing so, but confidence that you had fulfilled your early promise. I am sure that the faithful Bechstein still whinnies when it hears your step, and that you are a great woman, and I am right, am I not ? "

" I might be great, I might indeed be great," she

assured him eagerly. " Critics have said I might be remembered with the greatest, with Busoni, with Schnabel, were it not "—and she brought forward her hands and laid them on the desk that he might have the best view of them—" were it not for these ! "

" For these, my dear ? But they are perfect in every way."

" They are too small ! " she furiously mewed, and drummed them on the desk. " I cannot stretch an octave ! If you knew the exercises I have to drudge over to circumvent this defect ! "

" Yet I am sure, my dear," he told her, patting them kindly, " that they have caused you as much pleasure as a woman as they have caused you pain as an artist, for all of us love a pretty hand on a woman. I know I could as soon look at one as at a flower."

" Yes, but to be deprived of the credit for——! " she began tearfully, but checked herself.

He did not enquire why she should clap her fingers over her mouth, for he was thinking how odd it was that she should speak of her hands at this very moment. Idly he said, to prolong the pleasure of seeing her impassioned by talk of what seemed to her important : " And do you still give your famous recitals ? "

" Not so often now," she answered, and lost her petulance in gravity. " The great Karinthy and the great Martel have honoured me by letting me play with them in trio, and 'tis with them I make most of my appearances."

He thought, " This is surely much less glorious than

to have concerts dedicated to her sole performance, or to have whole orchestras dedicated to her accompaniment, as she used to do. Well, well! She has, I suppose, discovered herself not exempt from the iron laws which decree that a woman's frail form shall exhaust itself long before she attains the peak of supremacy in any art. Poor lass, I hope the discovery was not made too grimly!" He scanned her face for marks of failure which (since he feared it most of all earthly calamities) he conceived must be obvious and nearly as terrible as the scars of leprosy. But the creature held herself as confidently as an heiress; and while he scanned her the corners of her little mouth pricked up in a sly smile, and he was sure that had her eyes not been downcast they would have been jigging with merriment. " She seems very well with herself," he reflected, not without peevishness, " she is very near to smirking. Can it be that one of these foreign fellows is her lover ? For it cannot be denied that the little wench lacks principle. I have no doubt that did I ruffle her on yonder couch I would be infringing the rights of another; and let us be just, there is nothing to comminate in that, for it would be against nature if such loveliness were not enjoyed. Still, I could have wished it had not been a foreigner. But what is she after now ? "

For she had lifted the full skirt of her muslin gown, and was fumbling in her petticoat pocket, from which she presently brought forth a folded sheet of paper. With an air of being slightly offended, not so much by an affront to herself as by some failure to distinguish what was matter for jest and what was not, she pushed this across for him to examine; while she sank on her knees, laying her cheek on his desk, and playing with the fine toys he had gathered to pierce with holes his too solid hours of labour, such as his lapis lazuli seal, his Dutch brass tobacco-box scratched with a picture of Christ and the Woman of Samaria, and his French inkstand set in malachite.

"What is this?" Arnold Condorex asked himself. "Why, 'tis a programme of a concert she and her cronies have given, and it is ornamented with a photograph that shows them all. Well, I must take back all I said, for these are very old men, and though Harriet is a good girl she cannot work miracles." Aloud he said: "Your friends look very grave! You might think they had carried the cares of State on their shoulders all their days, instead of merely diverting themselves with musical instruments."

"You are teasing me," she answered comfortably, and stretched her white arm across the desk, pointing the lapis lazuli seal at the greybeard who held the violoncello on the glossy paper. "That is Karinthy, and he is the wisest man in the world, for he understands Mozart and Beethoven better than anyone else, and they were the wisest men who ever lived. I am fortunate beyond the earliest dreams of my ambition to be playing with him; and we play together, my love, because in the trio, the quartet, and the quintet, we have solutions of a problem that is, I fancy, not unlike the fundamental problem of government that vexes you politicians. Yes," she conceded, playing a game by chasing his fingers with the seal, " I shall say you statesmen, for you have been very civil to me, and have given me shelter from the heat of the day, and have promised me tea in cups so wide and shallow that I will have to beware lest I turn them over, as I drink, and so thin that I can see my fingers as shadows through them, and so old that the gold patterns on the white ground are as ghosts, for those," she said, her gaze climbing up and down the walls, " are the cups that go with the house."

" I will keep my title," he said complacently, " for my house is well filled." But because it had seemed to him that there was purpose in her wanderings, that so soon as she had mentioned his political work an unhappiness had come into her face and she had sought another subject to escape from pain, he pressed her, " Proceed with your attempts to lend importance to your art by comparing it with serious business."

She sighed, held her head for an instant between her hands, and said in a dragging way, " Are you not all occupied in finding a form of government which shall allow that invisible thing, the will of the people, to express its sense of the need for its own preservation, and its traditional knowledge of what subserves this or frustrates it; and which shall not be deflected from this end by the personal interests of any group ? So it seems I have heard Sir George declare, in such of his discourses as I have remained, awake to hear throughout!"

He nodded; but to himself, he said, "It is strange that this fundamental stuff of politics has never interested me. 'Tis the negotiation that has ever charmed me, and the struggle for eminence. This is the stuff that occupies poor Saltoun. Well, he must have something to occupy him, for he needs neither to negotiate nor to struggle for eminence. Shall I ever forgive God because I was not born with family and fortune?"

She let the seal roll clattering from her, and caressed his fingers with her own, while she cast down her eyes and went doggedly on: ". . . And so, you see, there is the same difficulty in finding a perfect form by which that invisible thing, the form of human wisdom known as music, can express itself. To sit alone at one's instrument is to be like an unlimited monarch. If one can so express one's personal genius without let or hindrance, why so we can express our personal follies too. For self-criticism is the weakest form of criticism save among the saints, and artists have not time to be saints as well. An orchestral performance, on the other hand, has the defects of a democracy. The conductor's task, in forcing so vast an organism to unify its conceptions of what it is rendering, is beyond the capacity of all but a few; and since the labour is parcelled out among so many it is inevitable that some should be given parts too small to hold their attention, and if so much as a grain of inattention lodge in the machinery of an artistic performance 'tis apt to throw it out of gear. But chamber-music! Ah, chamber-music!" She apparently felt strongly what she said, for she had begun to rock herself, and a stranger that looked at her through a glass window might have thought that she spoke in distress. "'Tis the ideal form of government for sound . . ."

He was saying to himself, ". . . I do not think I shall grieve overmuch because, after to-morrow, Saltoun and I shall be declared enemies. He has dared to despise me. I have felt him despising me. He has despised me for the meanest reason, that I was not born as fully advantaged as himself. He had made allegations against my solvency . . ." His eyes turned, without his bidding, to a file of papers that stood on the left-hand side of his desk under a small jade elephant, very fine, the gift of the infatuate Lord Ladyday. Sight of them made him feel as if this four-storeyed house were built not on the earth of Portland Place, but on a foundation stone lodged somewhere in the middle of his brow. That was mere feebleness. Had he not long ago discovered that the creditors of a Cabinet Minister would never make him bankrupt, since his fall from office would be a·final certificate that they would never see a penny of their money? Yet that discovery, true as it was, did not engender such comfortable feelings as the knowledge that there were receipts instead of bills under the small jade elephant could have done. He passed his hand across the brow and tried to dash the knowledge from him.

. . . " Saltoun," he said urgently, moving to a more favourable coign of the situation, " Saltoun has no power over the mob. He is a most frozen speaker." Contentedly he swung to and fro the monocle he wore suspended on a broad black ribbon, but never used. " His lack of animal magnetism makes them turn from him when he is arguing like an angel. How far from me is he in that ! Let me speak to a meeting for but three minutes, and then let a fellow stand up and ask what was the wisest question in the world, but one unfriendly to me, and I have but to turn on them my three-quarter face, let my eyes burn, use a chest-note, and they will lynch him. 'Tis such as me the party wants. Indeed 'tis me the party wants ! They will let Saltoun go. They will let Derrydown go too. Not a doubt of it. Integrity and his inheritance of tradition once gave him a kind of bleating majesty, that would make a meeting touch its forelock. But his years have worked for me. The brutal mob think him but a silly old bag of bones. And Ladyday ! Ha, poor Ladyday ! A touch of my ridicule will kill him. Ay, they will never dare to lay their finger on that weak point that I must leave in the manifesto, since I cannot see a way round it. I am of value, and the rest are not. 'Tis true, of course, that were there another war, we would have need of Saltoun. But he would then come back to office for the sake of his country ; and I could then better my credit by seeming to have cozened him into returning by the exercise of tact. What a verdant prospect lies before me !

But what have I been thinking about ? Why, nothing, nothing."

So talented a negotiator was he that in a trice it seemed to him he had in truth been thinking of nothing. But he was in none too easy a case even then, for he came to the knowledge that Harriet had ceased to speak, and now knelt in an attitude of utter desolation, with her arms cast down upon the desk and her face laid against them.

" Why, Harriet ! " he said.

But she did not answer, nor did she raise her head.

" Oh, Harriet ! " he cried, and rose from his seat, and went to her, and raised her in his arms. " Come, look at me ! " he begged ; but the face she turned to him was a blank white mask, on which there was no mark of laughter, or of love.

" My dear," he said very desperately, " I grieve to see how things come and go between us ! I told you when I came in that I thought I could see the tide of the heat rocking against these walls. I begin to think there is more in that than an image, for I feel as if I were a great stone on the bed of some flood, and you a lovely water-plant that grows near by. When the tide flows so, it is well, for that inclines your fair frondage to flow close by me ; but while the tide goes t'other way, your frondage flows far away from me. Indeed, if that tide flowed much more strongly, I think it would wash you from your place, and you would go sailing away, and I should never see you any more ! It is a great pity, my sweet, when I love

146

you so! Tell me, can I do nothing to set back this most unfavourable tide?"

She remained miserably blank; and said in a choked voice, "I would like to go home."

"No, that you cannot do, for very shame!" he protested, and lest he should weep with disappointment, tried to laugh. "Come, would you have that dark, decorous, oblate spheroid that is my butler hang himself from a beam (after having taken a deal of trouble on such a hot day to find one in the neighbourhood, for I fear there is none conveniently exposed in this house) because you scorn the tea he is even now bringing you down the passage? And I perceive, my love, that I have showed you far more than I promised when I ordered that tea. For I said, I think, that I would prove to you that it is not true that in a house where ten servants are kept orders are obeyed ten times more quickly than in a house where there is but one; and I think I have proved to you that they are obeyed just ten times more slowly. Will you not pay me for that overweight of instruction by sitting down in that great arm-chair on the hearth?"

She slipped down into it, her eyes very large; while he said firmly to the butler, "On the small table by the fireplace."

When they were alone again he enquired, "And where, my dear, is that very shameful little paper-bag? For when I have finished pouring out your tea, which I am doing as well as I may, considering I dare not ask you whether you take milk or sugar lest you burst into tears, I intend to sit beside you on the sofa (since it is more than big enough for two) and share some of your low street-bred cherries."

And so he did, looking sideways all the time for her favour; but got no more from her for doing so than a watery smile and a whimper of welcome.

" Oh, my love," he burst out, " we are acting as if we were not ourselves, but visions gliding from pose to pose of unreason across the iris of a fever patient! Why do you behave as if you loathed me? It is an aberration due to this stifling hour; for I admit that though the blinds are drawn this room is still a sirop of heat. Your hands prove that it is so and that I am really dear to you, for while your head moonishly plots treason against me your fingers have been burrowing in that paper-bag to find me the most splendid cherries and lay them in a plump red ring round my cup, and have kept only the wizened seniors for yourself."

" I did not think you would notice," she sobbed.

" I notice all things about you! " he cried. " Oh, Harriet, Harriet, admit that there is a tie between us so strong that on the Day of Judgment, should I be sent to Hell, you will lie on your stomach at the edge of the floor of Heaven, and let down your arm, which by a miracle will be protracted far past its perfect length, and haul me up beside you; and then you will go about very busily enquiring what the weaknesses of the angelic attendants may be that you may bribe them to let me stay. And if by the influence of my wife's family I were admitted to Heaven (for they tell me they have done everything for me) and you were not, because some angel that had passed your home late at night had not known how to keep his mouth shut, I will smuggle you in by folding your small bulk in my fitted dressing-case ; and I am sure a gentleman's dressing-case could not be better fitted. And if the fraud were detected, why we should go out together. Harriet, I am sure you know that it is so !—that there is a real and infrangible union between us. I will not say it comes from a mystical transfusion of our spirits, for indeed I do not know what spirit is, and this seems something as homely and natural as could be, ay, and very fixed and irrevocable. It is as if our finger-nails were cut from the same piece, or that there was confusion in the first distribution of our parts, and some of your hair is growing on my head, and you have some of mine. Oh, Harriet, admit we are not quite separate, and do not feign we are entirely so ! "

She met his gaze and nodded, though she did not seem as gay in assenting to his proposition as he was in making it. There came a lump in his throat, and as he swallowed it he closed his eyes ; and while he sat in this private darkness he felt, in the centre of his large mouth, her little mouth alighting like a butterfly.

When the kiss was accomplished she whispered, " No, we are not quite separate ! " and they regarded each other for a time in silence. Then, looking confused and rose-coloured, she spun in a very thin thread of sound the words, " Give me back one of my good cherries."

He did not, and when their mouths were met again he felt another stab of surprise, such as he had felt outside Boodles', when he had realised that his ambition to be counted among English gentlemen was in part an ambition to defend a noble way of living, and in this room when he had realised that his struggle to rise in the world had brought him a benefit that was neither base nor transient in letting him live in this house. He had won this woman back when her soul had gone from him ; and he had done it not out of joy in his power of negotiation, but because there was wholesome commerce between them which it did him good to desire, which it did him good to enjoy.

" Nevertheless," she murmured in the shelter of his arms, " I had better go home."

" I do not believe you," he said firmly. " You are not a person of importance. I doubt if you have many appointments. You had better stay with me in this very pretty room. It will not be for long, since I am sure to weary of you soon, and will kindly send you home in my magnificent new motor-car. So make the most of your time. And to tell you the truth, oh, my love, I find great joy in having you here among all my treasures ! " And he drew her further down into the great chair, and put back her cup of tea in her hand, and smiled at her in pleading ; and though she shook her head a little, she smiled back in complaisance.

" It is a joy for me to know that you are lodged with all these fine things around you ! " she purred. " I have always beauty around me, for I have but to go to my piano, and trace one of the million designs that have been made by my masters. But I believe you are as well off, with such things about as those rams' heads that ornament each side of your mantelpiece!"

"Yes, are they not charming!" said he, with his mouth full of cherries. "They concentrate in themselves all that air of submission which gives a bleating flock such power to affect the sympathies." His mind ran on to itself:

"How close a resemblance to a sheep runs through the Derrydown family! It will make my destruction of Ladyday a not difficult matter. He will himself attack me in the Commons, for he does not lack gallantry. That long face, those baaing accents, will win me my case before he sits down; and without exception he speaks too long. I will not have to use more than two barbs of ridicule to kill him." And then he had to cry, "My love, what ails you?"

Certainly a convulsion had shaken her as far from him as the way they sat made possible, and though he took her face between his hands, and she being occupied with the care of cup and saucer could do nothing against that action, she did not abandon herself to goodwill as he hoped, but stared tearfully over his shoulder. "It is a very odd thing," he thought, "but she looks as if she were listening to some sound I cannot hear. I wonder if she has some grounds for that pretension to occult gifts she used to make? Can it be that she is exercising them even now, and sees disaster impending over me? Much in this world goes wrong! That woman was dying in the street!" Terror made the hot room chill. "Harriet! Harriet!" he called to her remote, white, listening mask. Then he exclaimed to himself: "Why, how ghastly she has grown! I have always heard that the exercise of these gifts, if they exist, is very pernicious to the possessor. I would not learn my future at the cost of dear Harriet's health! I must hail her back to wholesome being. Ah, but she recovers of herself! Her colour is improved! She smiles!"

She did more, she leaned towards him and rubbed her head against his shoulder like a grateful cat. "My dear love, how the heat affects you!" he deplored; and dolefully thought to himself, "Maybe the kindest thing I could do for the sad wench is to ring for my car and have her driven home, but 'twill be a sacrifice. For the truth is I am fearful as if I were living on the brink of hell and a landslide expected at any moment, and shall be so till the messenger comes, and she has so many ways of beguiling my attention that she would make me clean forget my plight if she would but stay till then. But I cannot buy my peace at poor Harriet's expense. But what is this?"

For she had wound her arms about his neck and opened her eyes so that they looked very innocent, and was saying: "I have a friend who has a lodging in one of the meaner streets in this grand neighbourhood. And the sight of those rams' heads reminds me of a very singular experience which befel her early one morning."

She paused and primmed her mouth into an ingenuous shape. " Come, she cannot feel so badly," Condorex told himself in delight, " for she is about to tell one of her fairy-tales, the outrageous little liar."

" My friend had chanced to awaken early," Harriet continued in a cosy and circumstantial tone, " and she was lying as most of us do at such times, reflecting on her past life, and promising to make amends. But presently she was amazed at sounds as of a dry river flowing along the highway which betoken that a flock of sheep is passing the house. There could be no mistaking it. These minor sounds which suggest that the torrent of dust is leaping over boulders, but which are in fact caused by the silly creatures' collisions with each other, came clearly to her ears. To solve the mystery she rose lightly from her bed and leaned from her window, and there in the street below (believe me or not) was a flock of headless sheep, driven by three sober-looking young men. She cried out bidding them stop, and they obeyed ; and very civilly answered such questions as she put to them. It was as she had supposed. They were the Adam Brothers, and this was one of the trials to which they were exposed by their immortality. For you must know that the Romans, and especially their gods, have never liked the gifted Scotchmen. A cheerful and materialistic people, they do not admire the austerity of Adam architecture, greatly preferring the monument

153

to Vittorio Emmanuele in their own city or (if they must choose from London) the interior of Frascati's in Oxford Street. And the gods (and I cannot think altogether unreasonably) are annoyed at the use the Adam family has made of them for interior decoration. Apollo is particularly bitter at the time he has spent in an alcove in the dining-room of Syon House in Isleworth, watching the Percy family at meat. Ordinarily, however, the Adam Brothers are protected from their enemies by their genius. Indeed, 'tis they who by its force apply compulsion to the phantom of the antique world, which finds itself obliged to behave with a dignity that is Scottish rather than Mediterranean. But genius has its ebb and flow. Sometimes the Adam Brothers are less themselves than at other times, and then 'tis the antique world which forces them to contradictions against their nature, and finds them all sorts of ridiculous tasks, such as herding the ghosts of the sheep they decapitated in the course of their decorations. But that, they told my friend, they bear with equanimity. The Scottish are a pastoral nation ; and the decapitated sheep enjoy great happiness. All bodies would be glad to be rid of the rash captaincy of the head, and without it they can still partake of the supreme pleasure of gregariousness, which they are permitted by the gods to find in many other places than the parks and meadows. For disguised by a slight enchantment which makes them indistinguishable from other members of the public they attend theatres, concerts, political meetings——"

"Why, Harriet!" exclaimed Arnold, "now you mention it I realise that when I was a younger man I often addressed meetings crammed to the doors with them!"

"And I," mourned Harriet, "have played to them more often than I care to think."

"They will not fill up the front rows, that is how you know them," he said. "But tell me, Harriet, are the heads as happy at the separation from their bodies? For I have grown fond of these two here, and I would not like to think they moped?"

"They are overjoyed," she exclaimed. "Did you ever know a head that thought itself worthily mated with its body — that did not make grave charges against it for its failure to correspond with the fine form of its intelligence and to suggest the magnificence of its moral attainments?"

"I am a little too stout," he said despondently, "and in ten years' time I shall be much too stout."

"I do not look majestic enough," she grieved. "I am in my soul very majestic, but who would think it from my form?"

"Yet you do not need to think yourself entirely weightless," he rebuked her. "Indeed you have given me pins and needles by resting so long on my one shoulder. Will you not try the other one? For though I do not like the pain, I like acquiring it. Now, my dear, that we are more comfortably settled, will you not admit that your story is a thundering lie? For these are not real sheep that Robert Adam decapitated. They are imaginary beings, and I do not see how an imaginary being can have a ghost?"

"But since ghosts are admitted by all sensible men to be imaginary, is it not more appropriate that they should belong to imaginary beings than to real ones?" she enquired. "Though, indeed, it is hard enough to distinguish which of the multitudinous forms of the universe are ghosts and which are not. And that reminds me," she said, with her eye on the ceiling, where eight handsome sphinxes guarded four urns among a plaster treillage, "of another experience which befel this friend of mine; who is, by the way, a teacher of needlework under the London County Council, an occupation which I do not think gives sufficient scope to her peculiar talents. She has been ministering to a friend who had been stricken with fever at his lodgings in Jermyn Street; and having calmed him so that he need no longer toss upon his pallet and could enjoy some repose, she set forth to return on foot, since she thought the walk would soothe her excited nerves. She was proceeding northwards up Regent Street, which was completely empty, it then being an hour or two before dawn, when she saw two large bodies advancing down the street which she at first took to be motor-omnibuses moving with unusual abandonment. But as they came nearer she perceived many points of difference. These had loose hair, and proud yet passive faces, and wings, and had neglected—as the chaste children of the London

General Omnibus Company are always careful to do
—to enclose their bosoms within the decent motor-
bonnet. She at once perceived that they were Adam
sphinxes, and that they had observed her. Rigid with
horror, she leaned against an electric standard and
closed her eyes. Presently a hot and scented breath
licked her face and a voice at once like a woman's and
a lion's (say like an oratorio contralto's) enquired of
her from what museum or gallery or private collection
she had come for the Hour of Animation. She could
not answer, and with a terrifying gruffness the question was repeated. Then another voice, resembling
the first in kind, yet carrying a suggestion of greater
intelligence and timidity, cried out : " Why, can you
not see this is no wholesome work of art ! Look again !
She belongs to that abhorrent species which is subject
to time, which changes its form and colour after it is
made, and varies in vitality ! Fi, she is human ! "
And my friend assures me that from the cries of
loathing and dismay which the sphinxes uttered before
they threw off the petrifaction of their horror and lum-
bered on their soft paws down towards Piccadilly
Circus, it was obvious that works of art feel towards
human beings exactly as we do towards ghosts. The
transparency of spectres, the diffuseness in space
which lets them drift through doors and walls, and
their smell of death, disgust us not more than we
disgust works of art by our meaninglessness, our
diffuseness in time which lets us drift through three
score years and ten without a quarter as much

significance as a picture establishes instantaneously, and our smell of life. So you see how easily——"

At this moment the timepiece which the brass sea-horses on the mantelpiece supported between their wings and their tails, coolly pronounced that it was six. He thought: "The messenger should be here very soon. Dear God, what if he does not come, and all my plan has gone awry? I shall have all the dreariness of plotting afresh how to overthrow old Derrydown and capture the young rebels' vote. And I am tired, I have had to travel so far since my birth, and I have all those debts to pay, oh God, oh God. . . ." He perceived that on a sudden Harriet had formed a notion of rising, since she had slipped her little feet down on the ground, but he caught her back to him, crying, " Nay, you shall stay and tell me another of your fairy-tales ! " But at once he started away from her. " My darling ! What is it that torments you? I could not have conceived that any but a hunted beast could have so quick and desperate a heart-beat ! Come, you must tell me what ails you ! "

" 'Tis nothing," she faltered, " 'tis nothing at all."

" Nay, but there is something ! " he insisted, "and it grieves me very deeply not to know it ! For, as I tell you, you are so dear to me that it is as if our passion mysteriously made increase during the time we are apart ! " He gave her a fierce, loving little shake. "You hurt me so greatly by not telling me ! "

She moaned, " That I cannot do ! "

" But why, my child ? " he pressed her.

Not a word would she answer; and of a sudden a quiet and frightened gravity fell upon him. He was silent for a minute, and then said: " I think I know what is amiss. The occult gifts you possess have told you that something far from pleasant is going to happen to me; and since you are my loyal friend this distresses you. I understand it. But you need go to no pains to conceal from me what you have foreseen." He paused to dry the sweat on his brow. " I am stout-hearted enough to look into the face of fate without perturbation, no matter what it shows me. So speak away."

She began to rock about in his arms and laugh wildly though softly. " Oh, no ! " she cried. " I cannot read the future ! I have foreseen nothing of your fate ! "

Grown ghastly, he persisted: "I assure you that you need not fear to speak. I have as much courage as most men. And——" he drew a deep breath, as those who fear they are about to swoon, " —I would like to know, so that I can make due preparation."

" Ah, my poor love ! " she lamented in a whispering shriek. " I tell you I cannot look an inch ahead of time ! and that what has appalled me is not what is going to happen to you, but what has already happened ! "

He recoiled from her in amazement. " What has already happened to me ! " he exclaimed incredulously. " But nothing but good has happened to me, since I dare not say when ! " And his mind shrugged its shoulders and said to him behind its hand, " Did you not remember that the poor pretty thing was always a little mad? This second sight of hers was but a bee in her bonnet, and you yourself would never have lent credit to it, were it not such an infernally hot day that you are bedevilled with fever."

"Nothing but good!" sobbed Harriet, who had fished a handkerchief from her bosom and was turning it to a wet rag more expeditiously than could have been believed. "Do you call guilt, and shame, and treachery good things?"

"Guilt, and shame, and treachery!" he echoed. "But, Harriet, there is no need to use these names of my life!"

"Do not endeavour to dissemble," she damply begged, "I have known all ever since I entered your hall, and perceived Disgrace standing on your stairs, true master of this house."

He controlled his resentment because she was disordered in her intellects, and it was very hot, and he had always had a softness for her, and spoke with the restraint of an honest man sure of his honesty. "I can truthfully say, and I thank God I can do it, that there is no such wickedness in this house as you suspect. Ah, Harriet! There are secrets of State that I can divulge to none before it is deemed time for all to know them. If my lips were not thus sealed, I might prove to you that such a stand is to be made for principle in this house, before sunset, as would lift you as far above your ordinary spirits as those suspicions you entertain of me have cast you below them. To-day

of all days," he said solemnly wagging his finger,
" I can look into your eyes and avow that, whatever
evil may be vexing you, it does not proceed from me.
Perhaps," he suggested indulgently, giving the poor
dear's supernatural inclination a sop, " there are bad
men in the next house."

" Oh, poor old Derrydown ! " wept Harriet.
" Poor infatuate Ladydady ! "

He had dashed back to her and taken both her
wrists.

" Who told you ? "

" No one ! " she sighed.

" Nay, you must tell me ! " His grasp tightened.

" No one ! " she sighed again ; and in the faintest
whisper stated. " It was my gift that informed me."

" Your gift ! " he shouted. He let go her wrists,
throwing her from him so that the frail creature spun
like a top and came to rest against the bookcase with
her arms set wide along a shelf, looking very piteous.
" Your gift," he said, lowering his tones for fear of
the lackeys, but still very furiously. " I remember
now more about that gift. It was the heat and your
damnable disguise of amiability that drove it out of
my mind ; and had that not happened you would not
have found your way into my house. To give yourself consequence you claim to be able to pick the lock
of my soul, and to bolster up this claim you patch
together what gossip reaches your obscurity and what
scribblers hint in their low sheets, and make wild
guesses on it. So you practised on my marriage to

Ginevra and spoiled it from the first. I never could attend upon her loveliness without feeling like a thief, and since I felt no pride in the relationship there was nothing to keep me from noticing she was an idiot. Now you hope to use the same creeping mystic ways to foul my public life. How did the rumour reach you? Speak!"

She did but mop her eyes.

"Ah, I have it!" he exclaimed. "It is Sir George who has been talking to you, is it not?"

"Oh, no!" she murmured, "Sir George has not spoken of you for a long time."

He crossed the room and thrust his face close to her meekness. "And why not? He has not spoken of me for a long time—and why not? Oh, you need not tell me. These old men despise me because I have neither family nor future, and even pretend they cannot trust me! He would not talk of me to you, because he thinks ill of me, and is too gentlemanly to speak ill of a man to a woman who professes to be his friend. I am sure Sir George is full of such small points of honour," he sneered, "and thinks himself most chivalrous because of them. But if he did not tell you, then who did?" He set his clenched fist to his temple and tried to pluck the name out of the category of things unknown by speculation. "But no one can have told you!" he groaned. "Have I not burned my lamp night after night contriving there shall be none of us in this enterprise who is not in the same box as all the rest, who stands to lose as much as his fellows by betrayal of our cause. I mean," he explained stiffly and hastily, "that we are all good men and true, men of principle. No," and for a space he was lost again in consideration—"you have not heard this by any natural means." Shuddering, he drove the knowledge home into his heart; and admitted that he knew what he had known so long. "You have this gift you boast of, this infernal gift."

She had turned aside from him because she could not bear the force of his rage full-face; and rubbed her cheek against a fine edition of Catullus as if it were a pillow, and she tired to death.

"Ay, but that is not enough wickedness for you!" he shouted. "For, look you, these things you say that I have done I have not done! By these supernatural arts you spy out the bare bones of my life, but with a wickedness more personal to yourself you clothe those bones with the rotten flesh of malign interpretation. Last time you saw that I was going to marry the Lady Ginevra. There was no harm in that. I had some natural qualities to match her own that made it not an utter squandering of her hand; and my behaviour throughout was pronounced by those who might most easily have resented it to be most gentlemanly. There could have been no fullness read into the business save by your mind that wanted to decry me. And so it is to-day. It is most true that I am engaged in a conspiracy to overthrow my elders; but I am not moved by any base or mercenary motive. I would be culpable only if I had withheld my support

from those who, more truly than myself, are its promoters, for there is here something that must be done
for the country's sake. Listen, Harriet. Since you
know so much you had better know all. I will be
frank with you. I could not deny, nor would ever
wish to do so, that I am beholden to Lord Derrydown
and his family for a thousand benefits. But old men
grow foolish, and the sons of great men are sometimes
born so. Believe me, dear Harriet, the history of
empires that have passed, as, please God, ours never
shall, all show us that no year of famine nor visitation
of the plague can do more hurt to the people than
one fatuous counsellor. Therefore, if I allowed myself
to be influenced by my personal feelings. I should—"

His voice was soaring with the most comfortable
serenity, and he was thinking to himself as he spoke,
" It is very fortunate that this is what I really believe " ;
and he stretched out explanatory arms as if he were
presenting her with truth on a tray. It was into that
encircled space there seemed to crash the rat-tat-tat
from the knocker of the great front door. His arms
stiffened and dropped, he forgot Harriet Hume, he said
to himself, " That is the messenger ! " The swelling
passage of his life that should be heard over all the
countries of the earth and linger in the ears of men
long after his own sepulture, had now begun. This
moment would not go from him ; and everything
about it was very clear, clearer, perhaps, than any other
moment in his life. Almost he could see through the
doors and passages on to his doorstep, where the

messenger was waiting, the glint of bright metal on
the boy's tilted cap was all but present to his eyes.
While utterly visible to the eyes of his spirit, and
delectable as if they had been plaited of roses, were
the thousand strings that had been cast about the mario-
nette messenger's neck to bring him where he was.
What commendable shrewdness (though he should
not say it) had held the other ends of those strings!
Was it not clever of him that night, when the Government came so near defeat because of Derrydown's
speech at Uttoxeter and Saltoun's lack of suppleness
with the Press, to turn and see the narrowing eyes of
Grindlay, and guess that his failure to get the War
Office had done its work and he was now ready to
revolt? And had not Grindlay carried himself with
a marvellous discretion? He had so dissembled his
rebel spirit that to the end he had gone about the old
men's houses, and had been able to pick up much.
Why, he had ascertained beyond all doubt that Derrydown had committed the lapse on which they were to
justify their splitting of the party for a reason concerning which he had sworn silence and would be therefore (being what he was) unable to defend himself.
And nearly nothing had been done in words! Nearly
nothing had been done in thoughts! It could therefore so trimly turn to anything one wished to
consider it!

For very ecstasy he closed his eyes, snuffed in the
wind of fortune, and puffed out his chest. He could
taste success as if he had a piece of it in his mouth.

As the tension of his ecstasy grew less he opened his eyes and looked into the face of Harriet Hume. If what she claimed was true, then the image of his enterprise which shone so clearly before his spiritual vision was shining before hers only with such diminution of brilliance as marks the difference between an object and its reflexion. And what she claimed was true.

He made a gesture towards her as if her mind were indeed a mirror and he could break it; and sent out a cry of hatred, which hurt his lungs and throat as it rushed upward from his bowels. That pain also he counted among the harms she had done him. Since there was blackness humming all about him he staggered to his chair and had laid his head down on his desk.

"But why," his spirit asked itself, "is this more terrible than the other two discoveries she has made regarding me?"

Detestably, since he had not spoken aloud, she answered; "Because then you were outwitting women, and there has been such an immense deal of propaganda in favour of regarding this as a proof of high spirits in a gentleman, that it is neither here nor there. But now that you have turned against your own sex, where the obligation of honour is recognized, then perhaps things are going not so well with you." Her voice grew fainter. "If it is so I would not be thought to blame you. In the composition of every truly female there is much of the

poacher's dog. We pick up the game our masters steal.
To all you have done I consent in my soul."

Then she said in a voice like the bleating of a new-
born lamb, so small that he was not sure if she was
speaking or if he was overhearing her thoughts,
" And to-day is terrible because it has shown we are
still concerned with one another. Each of us has
always hoped that a stranger would come who would
scatter holy water on the image of the other and lay
it for ever, but time goes on, and that stranger does
not come."

He murmured, "Ay, so it is, so it is," and the
darkness round him became as absolute as if it were
the womb, the grave.

He sat up sharply because he had heard one come
into the room ; and found that his butler stood beside
him, holding out a letter on a tray. It was the letter.
He could recognise the superscription. But he did
not take it. It had become a toil and trouble to him.

But he could not send it away. That choice was
not open to him. Summoning his rage to him he
cried in his mind " Well, what do you want me to
do ? I must go on with my public duties, I suppose ! "
and rolled his eyes fiercely round the room, but did
not find her. He snarled at the butler, " Where is the
lady gone ? " and the voice of those qualities which had
till then protected him said within him, " This was no
time to assert your mastership, he had caught you at
a disadvantage, you should have won him over to
your side by revealing that you were a pitiful and

suffering man." But it spoke with detachment as if it would not go to any pains to combat that wild portion of himself which replied, " Nothing is so important at this moment as my need for fury." A bell seemed to toll in him, as if to mark the first of something.

The butler's eye was too obedient to its oyster quality to flash ; but the letter shook on the tray as he answered, " The lady went past me when I opened the door to the messsenger, sir."

Arnold Condorex's hand could not instantly grasp the letter so crooked was his arm with the cramp of rage. But his lips were drawn back from his teeth by exultation as he thought that when Harriet Hume left his house she had not gone into a wooded garden to lie by a lily-pond, not she ! She would now be walking along that charred street he had seen, and the fire of the day would be burning the soles of her feet with heat from below, and would consume her marrow with light from above. So passionately that his stiff fingers could hardly rip up the envelope, he wished that the Saharan presence hovering about the housetops might find a slit among the houses to thrust its vague sultry arm towards her, and would cover her up for a while with its yellow sleeve. He longed to see all that would be left when it withdrew again. He would be pleased wherever they were lying, whether in the hot blue shadow, or in the rock-hard sunlight ; that heap of tiny bones, shining like grey glass.

IV

Rampound had done far worse than this. Had he not! He had obtained the vile George Filiaepandarus a baronetcy to help him dupe the simpletons of England with prospectuses promising much gold to those who would lay out their money in such enterprises as the London Hills Exploitation Company, Ltd. (which had for objects, to send to Covent Garden the prim-roses of Primrose Hill and the lavender of Lavender Hill, and to market to cooks and chemists the saffron from the crocuses on Saffron Hill, with as side issue the felling of the tall redwoods of Westbourne Grove.) " For services rendered during the Great War," the patent of nobility had run, and there had been this and that of questioning in the House concerning the right gloss of that phrase ; and it had been stated (and the Speaker, whom we all know to be impartial, had quashed all ribaldry) that what England owed Sir George was *per contra* that foresight which had made him, through the early years of the War, push on in despite of Dora's building regulation with those orchid-houses which were later mistaken by the Zep-pelin crews for the Crystal Palace. But "Forty thousand pounds," the lobby had said, " Forty thousand pounds," Fleet Street had said, "Forty thousand pounds," the City had said, and (it seemed likely) "Forty thousand pounds," God had said, who had seen the affair from beginning to end. Oh, Rampound had done far worse than this, and he was still the admired, the popular Rampound, fawned on by the great and small.

Fawned on by greater than gave their good fellowship to Arnold Condorex. There was an ill-atmosphere about this drawing-room to-night. It was in part an emanation of the room itself, the damnable room. Odd it was to think that this house had ever soothed him by its beauty, instead of irritating him as the fair setting of an indifferent play. It looked very grim in the half-light he had made when, that he might think over Scorchington's proposition in not too much brightness, he had switched out all the lamps save the alabaster urn on the chimney piece. The fluted pilasters, their grooves black with shadow, looked like claw-nails drawn down the walls, and the gold convoluted capitols might have been the claws that traced them. The painted lunettes on the panels and ceiling were black oily smears from which shone only the whiter details of a universe lackadaisically falsified, swan necks bent by angelic meekness to re-entrant curves, profiles so tense with nobility that the breath must rush forth from the nostrils like the shriek of a police whistle, forearms like fins with languishment. As always, when there was not full light in the room, a shadow fell in one croner of the gold damask settee

in the recessed alcove and took the shape of a woman,
lying on the cushions in the attitude of Madame
Récamier in her picture. Oh, he would like to sell the
place and go. But it was not only the room, seen two
thousand times at least, loathed a thousand times at
least, that gave the evening an ill-flavour. He pushed
out a glowering lower lip at the three chairs which
still stood about at odd angles as if they talked together
in the way chairs have that have been pushed back and
left to their own device which still bore on their
cushions the moulding of his late guests' posteriors.
Three second-rate men, his guests had been. And
Faycequonpeut had left early to " go on," the climbing
pup.

There was something wrong. He was Lord Mondh
and held high office, but the great did not frequent
him, they denied him intimacy, they would not come
to his house save on those occasions where the inter-
secting rays of chandeliers and tiaras form a *chevaux
de frise* between the souls of all present. Had he done
well or ill to fall to Grindlay's blandishments, and
join in that rebellion of five years ago ? God knew,
God knew. Certainly the rebellion had been successful,
and he attained his peerage and his high office long
before he would have done had he been disagreeable
with the conspirators. But had he not lost more than
he had gained ? " And heaven bear witness," he
groaned, " I wished myself out of the business before
I was in." He shuddered, and drew the back of his
hand across his eyes, as was his way when he wished

to expunge a thought; and he looked sharply at the shadow woman where she lay propped on her cushions in the alcove, as though to see if she had moved. "Is there any position so pitiful," he burst out, "as that of the men whose steps irresistibly lead them to greatness, but who have neither family nor fortune? Every man's hand is against us, it would be a miracle if we did not sometimes fall!" And one fall, God knows, leads to another in this damned unreasonable world: a diminution of political credit means a diminution of financial credit. Since his participation in the Grindlay rebellion his creditors had been on him like a pack of wolves, though he had not been less solvent after than before, nor could have been, indeed. The confession of these matters he had had to make to his leaders had, again, impaired his political credit; and when he felt himself about to think of what this had done to his financial credit, he put his hands to his temples and cried out aloud, "My head, my head!" There was nothing to be done save restore financial credit by making that future with which he ought to have been born if there had not been cruelty in Heaven. Why it might be said that refusal of Scorchington's proposition was no longer open to him, for it must already have been accepted on its behalf by the abstract principle of prudence. After all, Rampound had done far worse than this.

Yes, Rampound had done far worse than this. Some four years ago he had done incomparably worse than this. 'Twas then that the Government had decided to use naught but Bongoleum for the snouts of submarines, scorning Zongoleum, Longoleum, Tongoleum, and Rongoleum, cheaper though those were, alleging that craft snouted with them could not comport themselves with that degree of defiance proper to His Majesty's Navy. ('Twas Scorchington, by the way, had made the speech announcing that decision, and when it had been attacked there had appeared a most noble ingenuity in all its parts, which gave its enemies not a piece of cloth they could pick holes in but a skein of wool they had to unravel; that was a heartening memory to-night.) But free-moving merit cannot have its way these days without stirring the spleen of those who come up to St. Stephen's from the Midlands, soured by nourishment on high tea and the Congregational Word; and these had discovered a lesser Rampound, a younger Rampound, that was not so far separated in the scheme of things from Bongoleum as one would have wished for the party's sake. This younger Rampound, the exhausted gametes of his parents, had not shaped in the great-man mould of their elder son; he could not stand on a platform looking so oaken thick and tall that an audience would believe England must fall if he did. But seeing him built on whippet lines his resourceful parents had exclaimed, " What might our darling not do in the City?" Speed is often lent to shareholders by the compulsory liquidation of the company for years after, but they would never be able to catch

Reginald's sponge-bag trousers as they twinkled along Fenchurch Avenue, up the side street, into the new building, past the door painted with the new and aureate-promising name, into the office where the staff was new, all save the red-haired man with the wen on his neck. The optimism of these good people (nothing was ever proved against them) was justified. At first he had not been rewarded by any conspicuous success. Indeed, there were some years when things went very ill, and would have gone worse had it not been for the loyal devotion of his wife, Perpetua Virginia, blonde and well-educated daughter of Mr. and Mrs. Badger-Gayme of Bray-on-Thames. But now the lad was on the right track, the foolish inventor of Bongoleum (whose improvidence could be judged from his failure to bring more than one of his legs home from the war) having sold him seventy-five per cent of his rights but an hour after the expert's report in its favour had been accepted by the Lords of the Admiralty in private conclave.

Oh, it had looked nasty when the Midland creatures dragged it out, four years ago. But Rampound still throws open his French windows of a Sunday morning and strolls on the terrace of his great house in Wiltshire; leans down to his spaniel and pinches his ear, with that air of doing it to gain time which willynilly infuses all his innocent actions; and rises and outfaces the grave brows of the Lebanon cedars, the avenue that runs straight as integrity from the Corinthian Arch on the crest of the hill, the belvedere in the beech grove that Vanbrugh built to ancient virtue. It is most true that Rampound had done far worse than this, and prospered on it.

The shadow woman on the sofa commented on his argument no more than shadows do ; but it appeared she had sat up a little, and one could fancy that her brows were knit and her lips pressed tight, and her silence no consequence of immateriality but a pause to find critical words. Certainly the gold rams' heads at the base of the mirrors between the windows looked down their noses like one's father's friends when one has told them all one has done since setting up in business and they are about to say, ' Chk ! Chk ! I wish you had come first and had a chat with me. . . ." Condorex began to speak aloud, not in his platform manner, but as if he were settling some local difficulty with a small committee of supporters. " I do not know," he owned persuasively, " that I have ever before known an occasion when a politician could so well serve the interest of himself, his country, and his party at one and the same time, as those will who collaborate with Lord Scorchington in his proposal. For, do you see, this is a very expert piece of statecraft . . ."

Ay, so it was, a transcendent piece of statecraft. Notoriously Prince Camaralzaman of Mangostan was anxious to make close friends in the British Government. None deplored more than himself that destiny of insolent appearance which dogged him everywhere. He could not ride out to make the salute at a Durbar, correctly robed upon a horse correctly geared, keeping within the forms of ceremony as within his own skin, eyes downcast, mouth sealed, features moulded flatly as in sleep, without the Viceroy paling and starting back and crying that spears had been rattled in his face, a naked sword offered at his breast, and a huge flag unfurled that for an instant covered all the sky with rebel emblems. 'Twas an embarrassment for the monarch of a Protectorate. If the unfortunate young prince should be admitted to a comradeship of financial adventure with which (it would be understood) the junior and more brilliant members of the Government were not wholly unconnected, how it might sweeten his sense of security, and thus set on his shoulders such a cool head, disordered neither by apprehension nor defiance, as one would wish for in a ruler. "Why, this is true Empire building!" he exclaimed to himself, greatly impressed. And it would not do the young potentate an atom of financial harm, nay the reverse. All six of the experts that had reported on the mine had said that there was every chance it would not happen the catastrophe which would set at naught the hopes of the investors; the possibility of which one could not regret, since it made the speculation a good gamble, and what gentleman does not love to lay out his money on a good gamble? Oh, Rampound had done far worse than this.

He rose to his feet, looking impatiently towards the sofa. "I will turn on some other of the lamps," he thought. "Nay, I remember that that does not

disperse the figure. In brighter light she grows more
aery but remains. 'Tis like the tedious character of
this house to have a ghost without a name or nature,
a mere eavesdropping patch of darkness on a cushion.
Well, there is no reason why I should cabin myself
with this insignificant slip of gloom. There is no
reason why I should not go to bed and sleep. I have
made up my mind. I will write to Scorchington with
my own hand as soon as I rise in the morning. Heigh-
ho ! " He rubbed his eyes, and yawned, and stretched,
and looked around at the rams' heads and said in-
solently, " I will pay all ! " Before his mind crowded
his mob of creditors ; among which, curiously enough,
since he owed her no money, he saw the Lady Ginevra
as she would be at this hour, dancing at the Embassy,
limp in the limp arms of one of her own kind, like
two anchovies side by side in a bottle. But she and
the rest of them now appeared to him as if discom-
fited. " God, this is good," he breathed, " to feel
the sap of success rise in my veins again ! "

But the door opened before he reached it ; and that
pallid sphere, his butler, stood before him.

For an instant he did not speak, and Condorex
knew. " He is thinking something ill of me. He
brings news, and is holding it back so that he may
consider the worst effect it may have on me, and
thus exercise the greatest art and distil the greatest joy
in telling it. How I would love to put him to the
door ! But I dare not, knowing what he knows."
Then his preoccupation tugged him, and he cried

aloud, "Is there a message from Lord Scorchington?"

"No, my lord," said the butler, and stopped to smile at his master's disappointment. "But there is a lady who says she must speak to you, and will not give her name"

"A lady!" cried Condorex. Nay, Nancy of Palace Street would never dare. "Is it not very late?"

"Past midnight," answered the butler, "and I have told her so, but she will take no denial. She says she must speak to you before morning."

"And did you not put her to the door?" raged Condorex. "You know how night and morning we are beseiged by the witless, that were kept seven years in Nottingham Asylum for no reason, that have recognised in Ivor Novello their only son stolen from them in infancy by a plot of the Pope, or (and the most afflicted of all are these) that have discovered a new alternative to the gold standard. To which class, pray, belongs this lady?"

"That I cannot say," replied the butler, with a kind of composed pleasure, "and I did not like to put her to the door, for though I do not know her name I remember that she visited your lordship once before."

"And when was that?"

"It was about five years ago," said the butler, "on a very hot day."

Condorex slipped his hand between his neck and his neckcloth.

"Is it Miss Harriet Hume?" he asked.

"I do not know her name," replied the butler.

His breath gave a leap in his throat. "Is she of low stature and not richly dressed?"

"The lady is very beautiful," said the butler.

One end of his neckcloth had come loose: the hand that pulled it was damp with sweat. "Do you think she has come here for money?" he snarled.

The butler leaned forward sharply, his face more alive than usual; but checked himself, and stood upright again. "Ah, he thought then of something shrewd to say to me!" knew Condorex, fuming. "And I can guess what it was! 'What—come for money, here, to this house? It is as likely that she brings it!' How he hates me, and hates me more than when he framed that phrase, for that our positions make it impossible for him to speak it!" And he noticed with sick fear that the man's dull eye looked past him at the room behind, seeming to plumb how many cubic feet of misery the house could hold if tightly packed with it, while he said, "The lady said that she had come to speak with you on a matter of the gravest importance, my lord."

Nonchalantly, as if fear were the note omitted from his range, as if condescension were the only not awful relationship he could have with other human beings, Condorex grumbled "Oh, I will see her! I will see her!" With long-legged strides he strolled past the butler and down the staircase. From a niche the scent of a honeysuckle plant set in a fine jardinière plucked at him like a hand on his sleeve.

"So it is Spring," he mused, "I had forgotten! How ironical is a Spring that brings no hope of renewal save of flowers and trees, that lets the branches of fortune be bare as ever! For I feel this woman's visit is a most sickly omen for my future. Ah, how softly that villain pads behind me! Is it not monstrous that I, who am counted a great man, cannot turn round in my own house, and go to my room, and shut the door, and sleep, but am marched down to this Cassandra by my most detested lackey. Well, it must end. I will put her to the door, and will go forward with my plans to-morrow, and will grow rich, and being rich I can send him away, for having had debts is no discredit when one has paid them off. Nay, it gives a favourable impression, as of a good man struggling with adversity." Now he had his fingers on the door knob; and fortified himself before he entered by turning and hissing to his butler as urgently as if he were sincere in his imputation of squalor to the situation, "Do not go to bed! Stand by, lest I need you!"

At the back of his mind he had promised himself some gratification in being shocked when he saw Harriet Hume at the ravages wrought by time on her appearance, and for that reason he laid his hand on the switch that turned on the sconces as well as the table-lamps. But when the downward draught of pure light fell strongly on the sofa where she sat, it revealed nothing shocking. Though she had come to an age when a day of weeping will forever take away a woman's beauty, she had not shed those tears as yet. She was still exquisite, though no longer as flowers are, but rather in the manner of ivory, or pearls, or alabaster. Neither did she look to be poor. Her cloak was not such as a woman of fashion would wear by night, since its stuff was merely a fine black cloth, but it was rich and new and clean. " 'Tis not that she could not buy herself a proper mantle," he thought with disgust, " but that, unstabilised by social duties as she is, if she goes out by sunlight she is as like as not to come home by starlight, ay, and as like as not to come home by sunlight if she has gone by starlight, for she is loose, I am sure she is loose. Therefore she must have some garment that will not betray her too grossly as she gipsies among the hours." Nor was she disordered. Indeed there was spread smoothy on the oval of her face such a deliberate composure as many persons assume on the approach of a thunderstorm.

He could not despise her for anything it seemed, certainly not for malevolence. That she was feeling neither that nor any other mean emotion was proven by the accord between her appearance and the study where they sat. " Ay ! " he said aloud, noting it, and stared very fixedly at her. In this quiet green temple of a room she was as proper as a swan on a lake. Though the vexation of his spirit had long prevented him from taking pleasure in the place, he was still sensible of its benignant quality, and knew that when he recognised it in her eyes, her mouth, her bearing,

he was pronouncing her not base. Why had she
come? More of this damnable quality! She had
come to be kind. Ah, God, was he never to rise above
the subject of kindness, was he never to be in a position
of power!

He put out his hand. When her fingers touched his
he made a slight grimace, because he had caught
himself being aware a second before that they would
feel as no other woman's fingers do, having the texture
of coolness and the temperature of warmth. But he
said to himself, " Well, at any rate I have forgotten
her voice!" and groaned as she spoke, for nothing
in the world, not even his right thumb-nail, at
which all his life long he had stared whenever he
had need to collect his thoughts, was more familiar
to him than her meek, ingenuous, and tinkling
tones.

He backed from her, halted and decided to make for
the authoritative chair behind his desk, where he could
look at her across the gear of his important business.
He sat back on the cushions and tried to swell a little,
and thrust out his chin so that he might stare at her
under dropped lids. What she had said to him had not
penetrated to his intelligence. Perhaps it had de-
manded an answer. His jaw dropped, his eyes ceased
to hector her face and fell to his desk, and there became
fixed on his ink-bottle. " There are those," his
mind told him with an idiot emphasis, " that can see
strange things in a pool of ink poured on their palms."
He twitched his head erect again, and made belief

there was not sweat upon his brow. "This is be-witchment," he murmured in his soul, "'tis I, not she, who am behaving as if I were a midnight visitor to an unwelcome house. Oh, God, wilt Thou not absolve me from the hideousness of circumstances that I anticipate comes to its climax in this hour?"

Harriet said in a little voice, "I suppose you think me greatly wanting in discretion to pester you at this time of night?"

In irony he answered, "It is an honour, it is an honour." His voice humbled him by wavering, but mercifully her cloak had slipped from her shoulders and exposed her form closely moulded in a white gown of a Greek fashion. He was therefore able to enjoy that sense of being at an advantage which he always derived from admiring a woman's beauty in detail; until it struck him that she was as still as though she sat for her picture, and his heart cried out, "She knows what I am thinking! She is letting the poor fool find what solace he can in the ridiculous position of being an open book which another can read at will!" Each of the three occasions when she had mortified him by her accursed gift flashed before him, and he recognised wearily that he was remembering them exactly as they had happened, without any disguises that would make them less wounding to his pride. "I have lost power to negotiate even with my-self!" he thought bitterly.

Harriet said quickly, "I must explain to you that I come so very late because I have been playing with my comrades at a rout given by the Countess of Pavane and Schottische."

" I am not asked then," he said with a sneer.

" You are fortunate," she told him with a trilling placidity like a canary's. " One would not consort with any of the women there unless one had brought some article of furniture that claimed Queen Anne's as its period, for if any remembered having seen it in her girlhood one would know it for a very early specimen ; and they have wisely married husbands somewhat older than themselves, so that many of the men clapped each other on the back and swore they had not met since Agincourt. Even . . ." She ceased for an instant and turned on him a gaze like porcelain in its shining quietude : but he marked that the left globe of her bosom was sensibly shaken by her heart-beat, and was afraid, for he knew what fear she felt would be on his account. " Even Sir George looked not so old among this decrepit assemblage."

" Oh, the Lord help us, Sir George ! Sir George ! " he cried, wriggling in his seat and rolling his head from side to side. " That croaking raven, that un-buried corpse that eats its cake and has it, that has assumed the ghastliness of spectrehood without for-feiting the opportunities of tiresomeness which belong to a living old man ! Well death never removes what has been his own for more than a decade ! So you are still friends ? What delectable evenings you must spend discussing me, or what news of me you can scrape together, you with your high occult kind of eavesdropping, he with his ear to the ground eager to catch the steps of young men marching towards disaster quicker than he crawls to his grave! Faugh! I wonder at you, Harriet!"

"As for Sir George being my friend," she replied mildly, "I am not sure that he is so to-day. My place in his heart has been taken by one of those counterfeits which old men's minds invent, and often prefer to the reality. I will sometimes go and spend an afternoon playing to him the Scottish airs, the Songs Without Words, the melodies from Balfe and Donizetti, which he dotes on, and yet draw from him few thanks enough; and the very next day I will hear he has been striking the parquet with his stick and vowing I am the same heartless flibberty-gibbet as all the other young people (for he is so old he thinks me young), and have not been near him for a month. Whereas when I am far away, making music in Barcelona or Warsaw, he will tell his friends that I have taken tea with him that very day, and have never been more lovely and gracious, nor better gowned. He has already travelled as far away from life as that; and this is why——" She laid two fingers across her throat as if to still a pulse, breathed deeply, and said steadily, "he gave me no more explicit warning than he did this evening."

"Can you not tell me more directly?" he said coldly, as if she were detected in doing him a mischief instead of a service. "I have recovered my self-command, which I lost at the sight of you, remember-

ing how ill an omen I have always found each of your
visits. I understand that you have something disagreeable to tell me. Pray say it as expeditiously as
possible."

"I cannot tell you as expeditiously as we would
either of us wish," answered poor Harriet, "because
I am describing something that happened in the ruins
of a man's mind, and was much influenced by its
setting. It is necessary that I should tell you I was
late in arriving at Pavane House, and found Sir George
in the vestibule, preparing to leave. Among the immense marble columns which support its dome, the
tall young footmen full of blood that stand against
them, the stout candles in the lustres which carried
plump and steady flames that will not be burned out
till morning, he looked creaking and transparent like
the cast skin of a snake. I went to him with both my
hands outstretched, but he greeted me with no great
favour, since I was my real self and not the graceful
phantom he has made my surrogate. Nay, he faced
me very grimly and pointed back his stock to two
pictures in the anti-chamber and bade me tell whether,
for all the boastings of my generation, there were
artists who could paint like that to-day. One was an
unmistakably female figure from the rich brush of
Mr. Etty; the other was a complete census of an
occasion of public rejoicing undertaken by Mr.
Frith. I confessed the default of my generation, but
he was not appeased. He went on to grumble, very
inconsistently, that the women of this age were, on

the other hand, furious renouncers of their femininity, who had sacrificed all, even to their bosoms, to ape the men, and on the other hand wantons who made the whole earth their mattresses. There was no health anywhere, it seemed. As for politics . . ."

She turned the white arch of her neck aside and spoke to the parquet, as if nothing else were there. ". . . Why, they were now a filthy business, and he blushed to think that he had spent his life tinkering with them. Ay, and they were like to grow filthier still when this pother with that friend of mine was finished. God, what would the mob think of the governors at the end of that." I asked him, what friend of mine he meant? He rolled his old eye, blue and dilute like soapsuds, and weakly clicked his tongue against his palate, and made sounds drier than the rustling of dead leaves by snapping his worn fingers, yet could not call the name to mind. But it was the tall fellow he spoke of, the very well-built young man, who was a close friend of mine. Why, only the other day, the old man said, he had come into my house and found a man's black silk scarf on the table, and had rallied me, and I had cried, ' Oh, this belongs to—— ' oh, plague on him, he could not call to mind whose I had said it was, but I had named this man he thought of now ; and I had picked up the scarf and tied it round my neck with a neat bow under the chin, like a cat's. Then, Arnold, I was sure it was of you he spoke, for that I did, fifteen years ago, with a scarf of yours."

" Did you do that ? " he asked drowsily. He saw, stretching his right hand across the desk, palm upward, as if he would have liked another hand slipped into it, and he was faintly smiling. " I wish I had seen you so," he said. But a fit of shuddering convulsed him. " Go on ! Go on ! "

" Lest we should be overheard by any lackey I led him to a seat in the adjoining room, where chaperones dozed in their corsets like jellies left overnight in their moulds, and there I questioned him. I did not thrust his poor dissolving wits with your name, but I begged him to tell me what pother threatened this tall young friend of mine. It was difficult to keep his attention on the matter, for he kept on looking round at the chaperones and blaming them very censoriously for being old, a state into which (he seemed to think) it was disgraceful for any but himself to fall. But this I got from him : and when he spoke of it he was more nearly recalled to life than I have seen him in a year. Though he himself is not quite a living man, his faltered words and shaken gestures reflected, like an old and clouded mirror, the speech and carriage of a living man. He affected turns of phrase and tricks of bearing, which I have never known him use before, and which I concluded were borrowed from his recent companions. Again and again he swore ' by thunder,' and as he said it raised his right hand with the wrist held far forward——"

Condorex rose to his feet and swayed backwards on his heels, his fingers busy with his neckcloth, " It is

the Duke of Allsouls to the life!" he groaned.
"Derrydown's brother-in-law, Saltoun's associate!
Gad, the conspiracy that is between all those who were
born with family and fortune!" The chair caught
him, and he sank in a hunchback heap, glowering at
Harriet. "Oh, if she would only speak too loud,"
he thought, "so that I might tell her not to shout!"
With satisfaction he watched her mouth forming a
little O until it occurred to one that she had read his
mind and was giving him what he wanted. "Oh, is
your accursed kindness inexhaustible!" he shouted.
"Go on! go on! Tell me what your old crony
has discovered." "Why," she continued patiently,
"that your party feels its honour something compromised by the presence in its Cabinet of Lord Rampound, the peculiar odour of whose reputation has
spread to all parts of the country, and they would
welcome an occasion to demonstrate their integrity.
The older members of the Party do not love you,
no, nor Scorchington, nor Grindlay, since the rebellion you engaged in that shipwrecked the fortunes
of Lord Derrydown. Grindlay is so sensible of this
that he has turned King's Evidence, and has slipped
away to them by night with news of a scheme in
which, he says, you and Lord Scorchington have
designed to demand a loan from Prince Camaralzaman
of Mangostan under the pretence of an investment,
the understood consideration being your friendship
in the Cabinet."

She paused, but not to look at him : to pass a tiny

handkerchief across her lips. Timidly she continued.
"You are to be allowed to proceed far enough for
your guilt to be established, and then the Government,
with much sanctimoniousness of the Roman father
kind, will cut you off as rotten branches. I tell you
with more coherence than Sir George imparted to his
story, but not more certainty. The disgrace your
enemies plan, it seems, is final——"

They sat in silence, until she cried out, "Arnold!
This is a great peril, like a flood or fire, that must be
fled!"

He did not answer. He had rested his elbows on
the desk and covered his eyes with his hands. On
the dark screen of his lids appeared, with a dreadful
distinctness, the mob of his creditors. There had not
gone from them Ginevra, whom he saw just as she
would be at this moment, dancing at the Embassy,
her jaw slightly dropped although she spoke, as if
conversation were a ball she must hold in her mouth
as a boar's head holds its apple. It was unfortunate
that success was one of the few ideas the creature
entertained. There is surely no hell like living with
a mate whom one despises, yet who presumes to despise one. God! It could not be that the universe
was framed to leave him in this trap! Nay, it was this
Cassandra who was jockeying to ruin, and not destiny!
His fists crashed down on the desk. Of course, she
had put a malign interpretation, in her old way!
He did not care whether the butler were listening at
the door. This thing must be blown out of the house

by the most forcible explosion spirit and lungs could produce. Therefore he blustered across the seal and inkstand and dispatch box, striking the desk so that they danced and danced again, " Busy as I am need you have brought me this old man's tattle ! "

" Ever since I supported the old man in his automobile I have been hoping that I need not," said Harriet wearily. " And because I debated it so keenly it was not I who played my part in Mozart's Water Music, but my fingers that found their way home like dogs whose masters have fallen dead by the wayside. And I have been standing half an hour opposite this house, looking up at the room where I knew you sat alone, before I could bring myself to knock on your door. Believe me, I take no pleasure in bringing you bad news."

He cut into her words to ask quickly and softly as one actor might speak to another as they waited in the wings : " You knew I sat alone ? What, can you exercise your gift at such a range ? In the same tone she answered, " Yes, and further," and he immediately flung himself into his set speech and was about to say, " So you persuade yourself ! But I will have you know——" when he noted that she had closed her eyes, courteously forebearing to screw them up, but resolutely lowering smooth lids to protect herself from what she might of his Boreas manner. " Is it not odd," he wondered, " that I feel as if we had lived together for a triple lustre or so, and had our first boy at Eton, and a girl ready for Heathfield in September, and a brace more doing well with a black-gowned Swiss governess, and as if I had treated Harriet not too well a thousand times, and a thousand times she had devised some bland and patient way that ended all in merriment? It is very odd?" But the bridge of his sentence hung an unfinished span in mid-air. It had been begun, it must continue. " —That this is the most nasty libel ever framed on a business enterprise of gentlemen, and has not one atom of truth to excuse its ugliness! Nor need you have believed it otherwise, were it not your desire that it should be thus and so with me! You say yourself the old man's wits have died before him. Why then if you are not moved by malice, do you believe what he says of me to be other than his senile ravings?"

Harriet did not reply, but sat with her gaze bent on her lap where she pressed her long white hands palm to palm. So might appear a gazelle with an iron will.

Again he thumped his desk. " There is nothing in this imbroglio! I do not doubt that your foolish old crony heard all that he reported, but there is nothing in it! This business is clear of all dishonesty! I would not care if to-morrow every newspaper in the kingdom carried full news of every step in the affair! Let these senile mischief-makers plot as they will, publication cannot harm us!"

She raised her head. On the death-white oval of her face her eyes and mouth made three dark signs of alarm.

"There is nothing in it," he roared.

She did not move at all.

He modulated his voice to something very pleasant and conciliatory. "Look you," he said, "ladies do not often like to hear the sordid details of the ways which garner up the wealth they like to spend, and I would not weary you. But I can assure you that this scheme in which I and my good friend Scorchington have taken an interest (for we are in no sense its promoters) might have been framed for the market by an incarnation of that virtue which public men like myself must value above all others, Integrity. Ay, it is the very cream of legitimacy! And as for the invitation to Prince Camaralzaman, why, that was a piece of political finesse, that when all should be known, would not be considered at all to my discredit. So, though I am very grateful to you for running to me with this gossip, I think I will not be foolhardy if I smile at your silly old men, and wish them good luck in their malevolence, and go on my way armed in my honesty."

He pushed his chair back, so that she might take the hint and rise to go. But still she did not move.

"Oh, I beg of you, do not look sibylline!" he burst out. "You cannot think how much a man dislikes a woman to look sibylline."

She had to lick her lips before she could speak. "Does it really seem so to you?" she asked in a harsh and creaking tone. "That you are honest?"

"It does," he answered pat.

She rose to her feet, but not to go. She cast herself down on her knees on the other side of his desk, with desperation though not with vehemence, and regarded him with a fear that was white as a snowflake. At the back of his mind he saw snow falling on a grave. She shuddered and drew back on her haunches, shielding her bosom with her hands. For an instant he thought she was about to fly and made a contemptuous gesture, as if to advertise that he had no wish to stop her. But she swayed forward with a floating motion, so that he thought again of snowflakes. Her eyes grew vast in their intention on him; and whispered, in a voice dry as the cricket's call with fear, " Oh, look within ! look within ! "

Panting, he put his clenched fist to his brow, while the interior self rolled back the cover of his mind. " Ah, how you frighten me," he sobbed, till up from his belly came a shout of victory. " Nay, you are a witch, a lying witch! There's nothing here but honesty ! All's honesty in my mind, and more than honest, honourable ! In the past I have done this and that which was not clean-mouthed, but now to-day I can lay my hand on my heart and swear that it is inhabited by not one motive but would pass the scrutiny of law, and equity, and the custom of gentlemen ! " At that she uttered a deep sigh and rested her head face downwards on the desk. He felt very superior to her, and cast himself back in his chair, laughing very heartily and tapping his chest with his fist. " All's well within," he cried, " and I think I compliment you more than your merits when I called you a witch, for if you had the gift you pretend you would have stepped into my mind and seen that, so far as these matters are concerned, it is a church."

"I am there already," she answered with a melancholy kind of tartness, "and it is much more like a masked ball. Oh, Arnold! This is the midnight of your destiny. Bid all your principles and motives doff their masks and sever all connection with this scheme!"

Roughly he told her, "I do not know what you mean. I am honest. This is an honest business enterprise. The reports of the mining engineers, I do assure you, are such as make the mouth water. Upon my soul, if I knew a poor widow, I would advise her to invest her all in it." A piteousness came on him, and he cried, "I am sincere. Do you not see I am sincere?"

She groaned, resting her brow again on the cool wood, "Then I must tell all!" Unshed tears shook her for a minute only, and she rose neatly to her feet. "It is strange," he thought, not altogether in the mode of hatred though he was hating her very much, "she bears herself as if the tide of fate had invaded a dancing academy where she happened to be taking a lesson at the time, and she felt it her duty to keep her feet prim and not be washed away." In an abashed voice, as though she owned a fault, she said, "You were not at the rout given by the Countess of Pavane and Schottische to-night. But last night, I think, you were among the guests of Mrs. Chutzpe-Ponem, the South African millionairess."

" That is true," he said ; and again he felt fear.

" And so was I," she said, " and stood at your elbow in the doorway of the Golden Room, while an Italian singer in the further salon sang an aria from Gluck. At first I did not know you were my neighbour and approached only that I might better partake of the manna of that music. But there came at once the feeling in my brow which means I am going to share in your thoughts. It must resemble, I fancy, the tremor felt by a water-diviner when his rod twitches in his hand."

" You must excuse me interrupting you, my dear," he said, laughing very loudly, " but have you ever had this remarkable gift with any other man ? "

" No," she answered.

" Why, that is very strange," he cried, choking with merriment. " Surely you will admit that it is very strange you should not have had it with at least one or two other men as well as my poor self."

She held her head high and agreed serenely. " Yes, I think it very strange " ; and then continued, " At that I instantly recognised you, though you were standing with your back to me. You are very well made. Had there been no company pressing around us, I would have liked to run my hands down your broad shoulders, which always make me think of a fine horse. I have never seen you without taking great pleasure in you. But I was sorry to find your thoughts very uneasy. You were not listening to the music."

Malignly he told her, "You cannot think how I dislike music."

"I do not suppose your mind has ever been free enough from affairs to listen to it," she said, without ill-temper. "Certainly it was not so last night. You were noting a youngish man with hair the colour of the May fox, who stood at the back of our hostess and whispered in her ear with very anxious affability. I think you called him Mr. Faycequonpeut, and you were wondering if you had got so far and known so many people when you were his age—oh, what have I said?"

"Will you never weary of spying on my naked-ness?" he groaned, rocking his head in his hands.

"I am indelicate," she said, and at last she wept. "But indeed I think the same as that over every young female pianist, and I am not ashamed. Do we not all long to have set an unprecedented standard of personal glory that our juniors shall find it impos-sible to outstrip? Why should you be ashamed of *that?*"

He turned an awful face on her. "Now, in the name of Christ, be careful. For I think you are going to father a lie on me. Ashamed of that, you say, as though there was something else of which I had good reason to be ashamed. But I tell you there is nothing disgraceful in my life. I will not give up my scheme. My scheme is honest. I can outwit the old men. I am honest. I can look the whole world in the face."

The tears ran fast down her face, though it remained calm as any marble. "Yet from eavesdropping on your thoughts last night, I know the core of your mind thinks otherwise."

"You lie," he said, "you read nothing in my thoughts but honesty."

"Yet though my brows there beat the words that beat through yours," she said, "and they were there : *Rampound has done far worse than this.*"

He stood up slowly. "Now," he pronounced in measured accents, "I know you for the reptile thing you are, who creeps into the houses of those who are rising in the world and injects them with phantasies that make them snap short their budding greatness. I will not deny those words have a certain evil magic. Hearing them disturbs me, I must admit it. Yet I never used them. Never in my life. Yet if I did, what then? This is *miching mallecho.* What do they signify?"

She shivered as if in superstitious awe. "Why, they have a dangerous cadence," she said. "Do you not hear it? And as you said them you saw a felon's cell and a felon in his hideous livery, and the one was Rampound's residence and the other was Rampound had he not been lucky, and would be your residence and yourself, were you not as lucky in this business as he had been in his like venture. So it was plainly written on your mind."

" You lie," he told her, " oh, how you lie ! You
are a very wicked liar ! " His eyes were set on the
wall somewhere above her left shoulder, and one
watching him would have thought there hung there
a very hideous picture.

In a flat and hopeless tone she repeated, " *Rampound has done far worse than this.*"

He screamed, " Why, I have said nothing else all
evening ! " and crashed down in a heap across his
desk.

She went and stood beside him, tucking her hands
into her bodice, as if her bosom felt a need to warm
something and must use what material it could obtain.

After a long while he muttered, " Am I insane that
I could so delude myself, and swear, and believe I
swore truly, that I had never thought what I have been
thinking over and over again those three days ? "

In a mouse squeak she answered, " Nay, 'twas but
an excessive development of the habit of negotiation
which you have acquired during your political life.
I am sure, my love, it is of no consequence."

He said coldly into his hands : " That was a rhe-
torical question, and required no answer. I do not
think it is of any use for you to comfort me. You
cannot conceive how difficult a man finds it to be
comforted by a woman who has just discovered to
him that he is a cheat."

He sat and stared over his clasped fingers for a time.
" It makes your offence much greater, Harriet, that
you are a pretty woman. A man very intensely

dislikes to have his faults pointed out by a pretty woman. Such things should be done by the thick-ankled aunts of the world who still, whatever may happen in the particular debate, get the worst of it."

The mob of creditors stood close round him now. Ginevra's face, blindish-looking though her eyes were clear, as if she suffered from a severe cataract of the spirit, was so near that it seemed much larger than life-size. " I suppose you know," he said, " that though you have saved me from disgrace you have left me without hope."

There was silence. Then he asked. " Are you crying, Harriet ? "

" Yes," she mewed.

" That pleases me a little, for I am very cruel, and would like to hurt you. See how I trust you, for I tell you that, and ask you to kneel down beside me, and lay your cheek on my sleeve. Ay, like that. I knew you would obey me."

After he had stared his full in front of him, " Now will you not be kind and take a glass of wine and a biscuit with me, to show you forgive me ? There is no reason why you should, but, you see, I trust you. Look, they are all set out on that tray in the corner. There are soda-water, whiskey, lemonade, Madeira, port. None of them is paid for. Which will you have have ? "

" I will take some port, if I may," she murmured.

" Then get back to your sofa and I will pour it out," he told her, and pulled her to him and squeezed her, as if he had been a ploughboy and she his doxy, and they had been sitting under a hedge. She rubbed against him in the way of a pleased cat, and nimbly had herself curled up on the cushions of the sofa when he came back with her glass. But she kept her eyes steadfastly on him, as if she could not be sure she were forgiven.

" You are no Christian," he said, watching her while he poured out some wine for himself, " you are an animal, and cannot be saved. For you dip your lips to your glass as a cat dips its muzzle to a saucer, and do not raise your glass to your lips, as houseled ladies do." He made himself a place on the sofa by her side, and sat flourishing his drink with one hand, while with the other he stroked her forearm. " You astonish me always with the perfection of your person ! " he exclaimed. " How I should like to have a plaster cast of you in all your purity ! How I should like to have it in my room, extended on a couch, so white and still ! Why, your little hand is trembling, and too cold ! Ah, my love, were you chilled to the exquisite bone while you waited under the lamp opposite this house ? "

She smiled up at him and shook her head.

" But it must be so ! " he cried remorsefully. " My darling, what have you not suffered for me ! "

" Nay, you forget," said Harriet, " it is the Spring."

" So it is, so it is," he assented. " I noted as much this evening, as I came down my stairs and was halted by a very agreeable scent of honeysuckle ; although

I am sure that as I drove along the Mall this afternoon there were no leaves on the trees."

" Oh, there are no flowers yet save in the conservatories of the rich, and no leaves either. Yet," said Harriet with assurance, " the Spring has come."

" How can that be, foolish one ? " he asked indulgently, putting his glass to his lips and his other hand on her waist.

" There is a wind that brings the Spring, however obdurate the leaves and flowers," said Harriet, " and it has blown."

" Why, you are right, my pet," he agreed. " I remember how when one was coming home late from a party in the days of one's youth, a wind would blow on one from the end of the street where the dawn was presently to be, and one's young blood leapt to know that the winter was gone." He held out his glass to her that she might sip from it, and motioned her to give him hers that he might exchange the courtesy. " You are the cosiest of company," he told her, and passed his hand up and down the pipestem of her waist. " Ah, youth was good ! " he sighed : and let himself muse as if his young days had been more pleasant than they were, and had been spent far more in Harriet's society than was the case. He sipped his wine again, and said, " My love, this is a very strange, transparent, and bloodless contentment that comes on one in the condemned cell."

At that she set down her glass and turned towards him, and put her arms about him and rubbed her face against his neck, making soft sounds such as a cat makes to its kitten.

"Oh, do not distress yourself," he told her nonchalantly. "It were better, even as you calculated, that I feel this emotion than the thousand times sharper pang of disgrace. Or is it so? Have you done anything for my good by saving me? It may perhaps seem ungracious of me to mention these doubts, but I am now perfectly convinced that you are aware of them whether I tell them or not, so I might as well afford myself the relief of self-expression." Turning his empty glass between his finger and thumb, he meditated for a while; then asked. "How do you account for this gift of yours?"

She answered timidly, "You yourself once explained that there was a mystical confusion of substance in us."

"Oh, my lords and gentlemen," he bayed in travesty of his own deep-mouthed platform manner, "what are we to think of a universe in which there is a mystical confusion of substance in opposites!" He laughed idly. "What an unseemly chaos!" He swung the wineglass round a few times more, and asked, "You would agree, would you not, my dear, that we are opposites?"

"Ay, we are opposites," said Harriet, putting her hands under her cloak as if she feared they might be slapped. "But surely that is no great harm. There is the North, and there is the South, and there is no war between them."

" They have their position, however," he instructed her, " in extended space where there is room for everything. In the world of the spirit it is not the same. Look, I have spilt a drop of wine upon your gown ! "

" It is of no consequence," she said, " this was the gown's last wearing."

" I do not believe you," he said, keeping his eye upon the spot, " you are too inveterately agreeable. I am sure it causes you trouble. Yet I cannot be sorry I have spilt it, it looks so pretty. How like a drop of blood it is, there below your breast ! As I was saying, my love, there is no room in the world of spirits for opposites. It is as vast as the universe, but it is small as a pin-point. Believe me, it has room for only one will. There is not a particle of accommodation for opposites. I have been defeated, I perceive, not by Saltoun, nor by Allsouls, nor by Grindlay, nor even as the moralists would pretend, by myself, but by the odd and unstable Immortal who made us, and at the moments of our ingeminations forgot this important principle in the technique of creation. Well, well, the milk is spilt." He glowered before him, and presently her fingers worked their way into his palm. " Why, how kind you are," he said, " how amenable, how you cling ! Will you not concede a little to your opposite and compromise with my principle of negotiation ? "

Her eyes met his very tenderly, but she shook her head.

" No ? " he pressed her. " Well, you are right.

To concede to one's opposite, in the most infinitesimal degree, is to die."

She said in a low voice, " I have always felt it my one duty not to die."

A silence fell and endured until a coal fell from the fire, and he exclaimed, " How long have we been sitting here? How long is it since those last words you spoke? I have a sense that my spirit has travelled a long distance in the time. I have the dry feeling at the back of my eyes that one gets when one has stayed up all night. I have been far away, I have resolved something massive, if I could but remember what it was. Why, my love, how blanched you have grown! And you are trembling! You are riding softly down the moments as a snowflake rides down the airs, white, oh, so white, and weightless as anything in this ponderous universe, and you are trembling, trembling, trembling! You are afraid. My love, what do you fear?"

She whispered, " Do you not know?"

" What you fear? I have no notion." He recoiled from her steady gaze, and cried very piteously, " What, have I thought something I have already lied out of my knowledge? Need I unmask more children of my mind?"

She shook her head, and he sank back relieved. " I fear it is no use," she said wearily. " I see I have done you no real service by coming here to-night."

Putting his hands behind his head and lolling back on the cushions, he laughed. " Well, that is my trouble, and not yours ! Go home, sweet little fool, and sleep, and rise refreshed, and make real troubles for yourself, by swaying your full skirts round your garden in the morning, so that the young man who takes his bath late in the house opposite is reminded of a rose ; and by reminding another, in the afternoon when you spread these skirts behind your tea-equipage, of a dove that preens and coos ; and by making yet a third man wait a long time in your drawing-room, while your sewing-maid pops her head round the door and says (the lying mopsy) you will not be above a minute more, and then swimming in with your white arms bare and a display of the lovely line which runs from your chin to your bosom, you will make him think as tenderly of swans on a lake as ever Leda did. Oh, you will have troubles of your own ! "

Harriet had her lace rag at her eyes again. " Oh, I know well I have not yet come to the painful age of serenity, she sobbed, " but if I have been of no service to you, then the world is not good music."

" I have not the slightest notion what you mean," he said, " since the only usefulness I have ever seen in music is that it affords employment. But whatever you meant I am in a position to assure you that you are raising irrelevant matters. The world is but material created to afford the separate race of creditors scope to gratify their curious appetites ; and from their point of view it is an excellent world. Upon my soul, I do not see how it could be better." He rose to help her with the adjustment of her cloak, and after gave her a friendly hug. "You are a good girl for coming, and I am very grateful to you, and I wish this were an hour when I could send you home in one of my automobiles. For I would take some pride in showing you that, though I shall not have enough to buy myself a crust of bread when all is over, I have three as handsome automobiles as anyone could wish to see. Well, well, another time. How shall my butler telephone for a taxi. No? Ah, I presume the broomstick waits without. I would not keep you from it, indeed it excites some envy in me. What should I not give to step out of this house and rise up into the air, and rise, and rise, and rise, until I would not be able to tell my roof from any other. Yet I believe I would know it from any height, for the smoke it would wear as a feather in its cap would be coloured the peculiar tint of burned bills, which might dye the product of other chimneys here and there, but never to the same degree. Well, there is no use dreaming. I must stay at home and face my ruin. Give me a farewell kiss, sweet enemy, who has at last proved to me that it is absolute."

"Then will you not forgive me?" she whimpered, and raised doe's eyes while proffering her mouth.

But when their lips met he twitched sharply, hissing in his breath, as if an excruciating ecstasy had laid hold on him like a twinge of gout. "But this is an extraordinary pleasure!" he drawled gloating. "You know, my dear, that I have felt for you always the extreme of love, as well as the extreme of lasciviousness. But there was a third emotion always present, which I cannot name even in this moment when it possesses me. Ah, you nod your head? Then you always knew it? Will you not name it? No? How you tease to-night! You knew where my soul was wandering, in that period which lasted either a second or an hour, yet you would not tell; and I think it had some relevance to the point we now debate." He folded his arms round her, and rocked her fragility to and fro, tenderly smiling down on her, who looked submissive yet big-eyed and vigilant, like a little cat who fears that the petting she receives may yet turn to tail-pulling and rough usage.

"Ah, it wells up in me, stronger and stronger, this unknown emotion I feel for you!" he breathed voluptuously. "It is perhaps nameless because unprecedented, and unprecedented because evoked by your beauty, which has no parallel, and now upsets the standards it has established for itself by entering upon a new phase. For you are different in my eyes to-night. How sculptural you appear in this metamorphosis, with your marble pallor, and the close flutings of your gown disposed about your classically perfect form! You remind me of a painted lunette in one of my own upper rooms, in which the artist depicts a young man lion-ruddy with the hues of health, stretching out his arms in eternal desire towards a young woman that stands in the recesses of a cave, all black and white, and bloodless and perfect, like yourself. 'Tis Orpheus mourning for his Eurydice, gone from him to death. Oh, without question, you are beautiful ! "

He hugged her like a bear, he rocked her to and fro till she could hardly keep her feet.

" Now you look like a woman who dies the little death of pleasure, with your lips parted and your eyes fixed in a stare ! I fed the strongest disposition to interfere with your fate. I do not want you to recall a rose to that lad, a dove to that man in his thirties, a swan to that grave signor with the pointed silver beard and order in his button-hole. Why, what a universe this is ! One cannot mention any of its details without being shocked by its confusion ! For do not a rose and a dove resemble each other more closely than a dove and a swan, though those last two are birds ? I would transport you to a purer world where things sit more stably in their categories. I would clang an iron gate on you, and shut you in a garden, where there are no coloured flowers, but only tall lilies standing in wet black earth, and no trees save the decent cypress. Ah, my love ! " he said, clasping her very amorously, " What pleasure it would give me to shut you away from all the heat of living ! "

She wrenched herself away from him, and scuttered to the door, where she stood and looked back at him with immense eyes. " Am I rough ? " he enquired, but very absently, for his mob of creditors was pressing in on him again. " You must pardon me, my dear. A man has an inveterate disposition to deal freely

with what has once been given him freely." He
waved away the phantoms. "You must discuss this
with my secretary," he drawled, "ay, even you,
though you are my wife." Then he stalked leisurely
to Harriet's side and took the door-knob from her
hand, saying, "What, you must go? Well, so you
shall." He tucked his arm in hers and walked her out
through his hall, strutting as if they marched to a band,
and were under an obligation to amuse. "Now, who
could have expected," he remarked airily, "that the
mood induced by utter hopelessness should be so
exceedingly like the effect of laughing gas? Not,
God knows, that I want to laugh. But there is the
same sense of an expanding emptiness inside the skull,
the same sense of being a balloon and trying to find
a resting-place on the slipperiness of another balloon,
all being within another balloon that has escaped the
fingers of its holder. Write down this curious coincidence in that little book you keep for things it is
useful to know. You have given over far too many
pages in it to the addresses of manicurists, considering
you have but two hands."

He had to take his arm away from her to fling open
the door, and when it was wide he stood in forgetful-
ness of her, legs far apart, surveying the empty cradle
of the traffic. "Oh, I am thoroughly persuaded of
the truth of magic," he said. "What is waiting here?
Not these dark houses. Not these lamps nor the white
porcupines of light they radiate. Not the causeway,
nor the pavements, that are the gay colour of the

put-upon. Not the stars. These are inanimate. There is nothing else. Yet there is something waiting. Why, what is this ? Your hand, of course. You are offering to say good-bye to me. Well, if you must, you must. But you need not be so hasty about it. Time was when I should have felt shame at being seen to let a wench out of my house at this hour, but now I do not care. Nay, it is of service to me, for those who see it will know that the hearse which (my mind's eye shows me) is halted round the corner cannot be for me. But do not think I have lost all objection to irregular behaviour. I shall be annoyed beyond bearing if you turn into a black cat the minute I close the door. You must wait to do that till you get to the area-railings of the next house at least. I cannot have this mansion given a bad name, particularly as, in consequence of what you have told me, I shall now have to sell it."

She slipped away from him, looking back at him over her shoulder as she descended the steps. Very genially he cried after her, " Well, you must come back some afternoon ! You and I, and my wife Ginevra, and the bailiff's men, shall take a dish of tea together and laugh very heartily over the evening when you called on me and broke the news that I was a cheat and a bankrupt."

She had passed beyond the trench of sooty shadow cast by the house on the silver pavement, and was in full moonlight when she turned ; so that the tail of her gown, dropping beneath her cloak, shone like an

angel's robe, and the hands with which she covered
her trembling mouth seemed luminous, and the tears
in her eyes might have been taken by experts for
diamonds.

"Oh, you need not look penitent," he called to
her merrily, "for I have enjoyed every minute of your
stay. You are lovelier than ever, and you have kept
your fine shape. Even your shadow, squat though it
falls because the moon is at its zenith, has the lines of
a Greek vase. Pervasively attractive Harriet! My
sole complaint is that you have talked too little. You
have not made as many as I expected of those remarks
I love to pick up and wear in my button-hole for a
day or two and sniff now and then to keep up my
spirits. Why have you failed me thus, Harriet?"

She murmured in broken accents, "You mock me,
I am never witty. But I own I have been stilted in
my speech with you, and I beg pardon for it. But
what you have said to me to-night has for the most
part been so peculiar to your world, which is not mine,
that I have had the greatest difficulty in finding any
answers."

With sudden panic he cried out, "Yes, that is
what it was! And why was it so?" He pointed a
stiff finger at her, "It is because you are my opposite!"
He made motions with his hands as if to beat her away
from his home, stepped backwards over the threshold,
and slammed the door. He hung on to the handle,
breathing hard, and not letting his features loosen
from the harsh grimace of hate, till a look of cunning

came on him, and he claimed jauntily, "Well, I have excluded her!" He turned about and strolled back through the hall, swaggering like an actor in a costume play, and humming aloud, save when he stopped and shook his fist at the ceiling, whispering, "My opposite! My opposite!" When he had returned to his library he poured out a glass of wine, and overfilled it saying to himself, "No wonder she can read my thoughts! There is no need to suppose magic there. She need but look in her own mind, record what she sees, imagine its opposite, and she has all of me."

He had not drunk above two or three more glasses of wine before a dizziness came on him, and he had to feel his way across the room and stretch himself on the sofa. "What, am I ill? No, I am drunk! Now that I come to think of it I have been swilling ever since the morning. And it was the same yesterday, and the day before that. For long I have been unable to perform the duties attaching to my eminence without putting that into my mouth which whips my nerves to deal with them and at the same time dulls my sense of how much I am in debt. My body, believing that my mind would some day crown it with the bays of empire, protected it in the taking of its medicine by refusing to suffer the effects of alcohol, and by neither retching nor staggering. No one has ever seen me drunk. But now my body is no longer buoyed up by the hope of power no doubt it will betray me to the people's scorn; and I shall be known from to-day as a drunkard as well as a bankrupt.

That, however, belongs to to-morrow." He lay quiet for a little, then put out his hand among the cushions. "I am lying among the imprints of her form," he thought. He rolled one cushion on to the floor but found it too much effort to do more. "That, however, belongs to to-morrow," he repeated. "To-night I had better fix my attention on how I am to get to my bed. But do I want to go to bed? It is a terribly defenceless attitude, lying in bed; and even I discomfit the darkness by leaving on my light, I shall not like it when it is the morning, and they come in and find me sleeping and see me before I see them. For I shall sleep, I am so drunk that I shall certainly sleep. What must I do?"

He stared up at the ceiling and asked himself the question many times, until he became aware that his butler was leaning over him. His white face seemed curiously dewed with excitement.

"Will you not come out into the hall, my lord?" he asked.

"Why should I do that?" asked Condorex. "I think you are attempting to make me rise before I am able, that you may mock at me."

"Oh, no, my lord," said the butler. "I had observed nothing about your lordship's condition. But I have heard your lordship say at dinner that you do not truly know how many men and maids you keep in this house, and you could inform yourself of that at a glance if you would but rise and go out into the hall, for they are all out there."

"But what are they doing up and about at such an hour?" asked Condorex.

"Why, since an hour ago they have none of them been able to sleep in their beds for a feeling that something prodigious was about to happen in the house. For you must know," said the butler with a very sly leer, " that nothing can come to pass in a household without the servants getting wind of it instanter. And now they are all gathered in the hall in their nightgowns and nightcaps, holding their candlesticks to their bosoms with such shaking hands that several of the maids have had their curl-papers singed."

"Well, I do want to see them," yawned Condorex. "I doubt that they will be looking their best, and if they were I should not want to cast my eyes on them, since that would only the more vivdly remind me that there is not one of them whose wages are less than six weeks in arrears."

"If you would but go out into the hall," said the butler, "you would not think of that, nor would they. For the prodigy they expected is happening."

"I could wish that the Almighty did not fancy himself as a conjuror and treat this house as a hat," grumbled his master. "What is the new white rabbit?"

"Why, your lordship, there are three strange ladies descending the staircase, with a rope of flowers in their hands."

"Oh, those three trulls. I should not trouble my head about them," said Condorex. "They are but persons out of a fairy-tale that was once told me by a woman in a garden. Not but what they have their importance, of course. The ancients called them the Parcæ and respected them greatly. They are leaving the house because I have omitted to make obeisance to some antique religion. It all seems fiddle-faddle to me, but apparently the ladies have influence, for the upshot of the business is that I am ruined, ay, absolutely ruined!"

The butler's face bent lower over him, it began to change in texture; and when the change was completed it was apparent that it had taken place because a curtain of dream stuff that had hung between them was lifted. This real face bore a lustrous expression, as of one who has obtained by stealth information which greatly pleases him, and though he must cancel his pleasure for a time does not mind, since he will laugh over it so very loudly when he is by himself. Words came from this face that were harmonious with its mood : " My lord, I think you are not yet awake ! I said nothing of ladies. I did but ask if there was anything more I could do for your lordship to-night. Tee-hee ! Tee-hee !"

Condorex kept his eyes fixed on him, thinking, " It is extraordinary that I do not mind having made a fool of myself, but of course it does not matter now. I do not mind conduct that might lead to loss, for I have lost all I can." Aloud he said, " No, there is nothing more." In a cool and airy way, as if this were the path by which his thoughts mounted when they were inspired, he told himself, " This man did not hate me till my brow-beating of him that hot afternoon when I was confused by Harriet's knowledge of my plans. 'Tis her doing. Yet I do not blame the poor slut. She cannot help it. Such things must happen because she is my opposite. Ay, they will happen, so long as she lives."

V

He spoke to his image in the mirror above the mantel-piece, as he was apt to do nowadays when he was alone; for otherwise a feeling came upon him that there was nobody in the room, not even himself.

"It is a strange thing," he began, and broke off to wonder, "Is this mirror my own or have I sold it? I know there have been great transactions of late to which I am a party, but at the moment I cannot remember whether they are concluded. At any rate my reflection is my own. Ha! That is an asset they cannot rive from me." He picked up the broken thread again. "It is a strange thing, the pleasure one can draw, in the most disadvantageous circumstances, from knowing what is a secret to the vulgar. I will own that on going down to the Cabinet meeting this early afternoon, and passing the posters which cried out again and again, 'Fall of Mondh,' I felt a certain gratification because I was aware that they announced the piece of news quite other than that the consternated city imagined. When I tipped my hat to the crowd which had gathered round Downing Street to give me that dreadful croaking which betokens loyalty to the unfortunate (I am a sinking ship) I had much

ado not to point my stick at the newsboy who hawked
his wares on its fringe, and explain, "Ladies and
gentlemen, you have misread that notice. You think
it means that the pearl of Asian hill-towns, Mondh,
has been invested by the enemy. Believe me, you are
wrong. That town enjoys, and ever shall enjoy, the
supreme impregnability of a cloud. As soon shall the
twilight he stormed, as soon shall the governor of sunset give up his keys. The placard concerns only myself,
who am the first Baron Mondh, and who am fallen.
'Good day, ladies. Good day, gentlemen. If you do
not pray the Lord to have mercy on my soul, I shall
pray Him to let you rise in the world, for I am not so
genial as has been claimed in the public prints of my
own party.' And I preened myself again, on passing
back to my house in the late afternoon, at knowing
the catch behind the placards which announced ' Relief
of Mondh.' I lolled back on my cushions of my
Chimborazi-Mecklenburgh, which is, so far as I can
see, the last automobile I shall ever own, and which I
own, indeed, in a highly technical sense of the word,
since I have never paid for it, and laughed to realise
that those placards referred to another subject than
their fellows shown earlier in the day. The Mondh
that had been relieved was not myself but the city,
which had never been in peril. I am most certainly
still fallen. Without a doubt I shall soon go from the
Cabinet. It is a most disagreeable law of human affairs
that only those things can be saved which have never
been lost. Only those who have been born to family

and fortune can ever raise themselves above the danger of obscurity and pain."

He gloomed into the mirror, and his thought, swinging clear of its groove, noted: "I am very sallow. It is as if the blood did not reach my skin by half an inch, which is possible enough, since the ambition that was the engine of my heart is broken down. I perceive I am no longer very handsome, and I have a look of failure. I do not believe I could vanquish a woman casually encountered, now. Ah, what a delicious satisfaction must be reigning in the breast of Prince Camaralzaman, who is fighting an enemy whose womenkind he so freely dishonoured before ever the campaign began! How silent are the Duchesses who, till the news came three months ago that the Mangoes had risen, were delighted to have it supposed that all had happened that could happen on the yacht at Deauville, in the cottage at Marlow, under the night-blue flag printed with the vermilion lotus-flower!" He tittered scornfully at them and all women, and felt more of a man. His mind ran in its groove again. "'Tis a jest that I should have been proud to make myself, this announcement of Mondh's fall! What artistry to go through Eton, Oxford, and the Embassy, and let none of his playmates or instructors know that he doubted the India Office explanation that Mondh is the name which, by a curious obstinacy, the British give to some unspecified fortress in Mangostan! For truly, so had I watered the fame of Mondh with my oratory, its

reported fall spread as profound a consternation over
the spirit of England as the loss of the *Royal George*
or the death of Nelson. It was an excellent jest!
I remember that when I met the young prince I seemed
to see a dark eye smiling through a curiously shaped
cut in a palm-leaf. Well, well, what should we have
said, I wonder, had I known that he was to play this
prank at my expense, and had he known that I alone
of all men was to play a rather better one at his! For
I have bested him! Oh, no question about that!"

He and his image laughed together like the old
friends they were. "Gad, they had none of them a
word to say, sitting round like whitings at a loss
because they have come into one of their sacred places
where it is not manners to swallow their tails. 'We
cannot contradict the news,' said Grindlay, 'because
such contradictions are not believed. If the Mangoes
go on feeding the Soviet wireless service with details
of the Fall of Mondh, to which the Russians give
their honest homespun touch and spread and spread
and spread with their passion for spawning the
unpleasant, we shall not be believed if we say in our
flat Island way, "Mondh has not fallen"' And sour
Saltoun grumbled, his eyes downcast on his blotting-
pad, 'This is a most loathsome business.' 'Ay,' said I,
'but not unmendable.' 'What?' said they. 'Not unmendable?' Not one of them had it, not one." He
bent towards his image and wished it had a solid
forearm on which he might rest his hand while he
laughed out his story. "'Why,' said I, 'I cannot

imagine a matter more easily mendable. For cannot Mondh be retaken as well as taken?' They stirred their bottoms doubtfully on their seats. ''Tis a flat announcement to make,' our Grindlay moped. ' " Mondh was taken, Mondh is retaken." Against the subtleties of the Mangoes, and the filthy directness of the Bolshevists, we shall perform no great feat of conviction.' 'Can we not give such details of the city's rescue as shall swell the hearts of England at least, and with reasonable luck excite the rest of Europe favourably?' said I. 'We are not an inartistic people. The contrary is proved by Shakespeare, Milton and my Lord Byron.' 'Details?' snarled Grindlay. How I love to torment that little drysalting kind of man with my nonchalance! 'How can we give details,' snarls he, ' without giving the names of generals and regiments that performed this great feat of arms, and you know there is none. And if we say those are there who are not, how shall we procure their silence, or keep their confidence in our government if we approached them to that end?'

"It was strange that it was I who kept my head through it all, though it was my reputation that was in most desperate case.. 'Not so fast,' said I. 'I think you have overlooked a regiment we may draw on here. We all know that Mondh, although lacking in certain attributes common to other cities, is for all that a very good city. I do not know of one anywhere that has better served the purpose of its founders. Does it not occur to you that a city of that sort may well have inhabitants that would develop the same quality of usefulness? Ay, Mondh was defended by a regiment raised from its own citizens, which was temporarily overpowered two days ago by some monstrous treachery of the rebels relating, I think, to its womenfolk. But between two and three this morning they came to their own again, and there is a very useful little man I have in my office who could write as stirring an account as anyone could wish of the dauntless courage which gave them back their city. He is a very useful little man, this Maurice Tarnishwing, who came down from Oxford with great gifts which he has diluted with the juice of the grape till the mixture is out of keeping save in a place set apart for the consumption of liquor. But he is a very useful little man, for his pen strikes flame from the paper, and he does what he is bid and keeps silent, ever since there was some trouble with the accounts in the Ministry of Munitions; and he is a great patriot. Why, if you will let me go to good Tarnishwing and say the word, you will have by noon to-morrow the whole of Europe without a doubt in his head but that Mondh is retaken.' Why, they had not a word to say, stirred their bottoms about again for a second or two, out of reluctance to give me credit, and then grunted assent. Even Saltoun did but draw a seventieth triangle on his blotting-pad and croaked again like an old grey parrot, ' This is a loathsome business.' Oh, I drew them and my party out of adversity as deftly as a seamstress threads a needle."

He lurched towards his image so heavily that his outstretched fingers stubbed themselves against the glass. " Ah, if it had been a real man, and they could have got drunk together and staggered weeping down some street of wavering lights, clutching each other's necks and weeping, but feeling very warm within ! " They hate me so ! " he mourned. " I have saved them, but they hate me so ! When all was sealed and settled, and I had seen to it that good Tarnishwing had been set down at his patriotic task in a sitting-room at the Cavendish with Rosie Lewis to bring him the champagne and orange juice that are as mother's milk to him, and we could all go home, there came a moment when good-byes should have been said, but were not, they were all so poured out in the work of hating me. They do not send their hatred wringing towards me as candid hostility, for I have arrows of my own that are more sharply pointed, and I shoot them straight. They send them downwards grey and hissing like rain, to make the earth sodden so that I cannot stand on it ; and there is none can stop the rain. Why do they hate me thus ? I have rescued them to-day, and I do not believe there was ever a yesterday when I harmed them. It is in part, I know, because I spoke honestly though craftily, and brought to light that we all knew there is no Mondh : but I do not think that is a large part of it. 'Tis independent of my separate actions. I am sure that if they were wakened suddenly from sleep and could not remember anything that had happened in the last twelve months, they would hate me. Oh, why is it? For I have qualities, I have a good heart, I am kind, I cannot help feeling that in some recondite sense I have always been a good man. It is because of the savage that survives in all men, and is magically minded, and believes all conditions to be infectious, that they shun me. They are aware that I am wasting away with a disease of the future, and they fear but that the germ may be carried on the breath. Oh, the case against me is strong! I am financially sick, I was never one of their sort, I was poor and had to struggle, and maybe there is contagion in that lowness too. And in any case all men rejoice in the ruin of others, and most of all if it be one like me, in whom the desire to rise was a social impertinence; and I have baulked them once of the consummation of their rejoicing, for they were certain they had me trapped with Scorchington. Which they had not."

His eyes met his image's, and looked away. They both grew pale. "Which they had not. . . ."

"Lord knows, Lord knows, I have confused the ground to my own disadvantage, and given those that hated me from sheer malice a chance to pretend they hate me from love of the virtue I have discarded, and much evidence by which they can win the public to their side. I am afraid I must admit that I am a rogue in a much less recondite sense that I am a good man. Why, I have all the hallmarks of a rogue, even to the follies, though I am so shrewd. This afternoon, did not my heart leap up in amazement and fury when

I stood in the lobby and saw them all penguin-flapping their arms back to the arm-holes the lackeys proffered, and fussing the scarves round their squat necks, and taking care during all processes to keep their heads turned so that I was north-north-west to their straight gaze. 'Twas an almost insectine uniformity of movement; such as one has observed when walking in the country with a naturalist friend who stops and cries with a rapture hard for a man of more liberal interests to understand. What! Do you pass by the smaller yittlewiffer at its wondrous work! Ay, those small specks proceeding towards that rottenness in the plank! See how the pretty dears carry on their backs a grain of dung to some safe place where they may eat it and thus by excrement procure a plastic material for their hive! Do you not regret your lack of learning in natural history, which would enhance your enjoyment of the country by revealing to you customs as dainty as those? But these still smaller yittlewiffers that stood with me in the lobby of Downing Street, surely the smallest yittlewiffers that ever God with His talent for minute creation could make, had for their communal task the building not of a hive for the living but of a tomb for a corpse; and that corpse was my fame. And not one stood aloof from it, not even Scorchington. Why, he was worse than all the rest, for when I sought him out with my eyes he was full north-west of me. Scorchington, who has so often laid his head close against mine to our mutual advantage! But my fury

died as soon as it was born, for I remembered that
I had myself often noted that it is the special weakness
of rogues (and the most common cause of their ruin)
to expect from one another a degree of loyalty that
it would be rare to find among honest men.

" Well, since a rogue never realises his roguehood
till it has grown common knowledge to all the world,
I suppose my quality has been notorious for years.
And the deuce of it is, I am come the wrong time to
win success with my peculiar quality, for in each
generation there is but one rogue and no more who is
allowed to be great. One of the kind the common man
is willing to pamper and adore for sometimes he himself tires of respectability, and then it is a comfort to
him to see a rogue sitting in comfortable grossness
with his ration of eight bottles of champagne and two
wenches a day, all earned by cheating, and coming to
no harm, nay, on the contrary, rising to power, wearing
red robes at the Opening of Parliament, talking to
kings with but the faintest inclination of the head.
For if a rogue can triumph so, the universe is not
such a closed prison as they say, and one might find
a road yet out of Surbiton. But, mark you, there
must be only one of us, for if there are more, why, this
ceases to be a heartening dream but another certificate
that life is intolerable ; since that it would be, if
there were an army of scoundrels that had to be fed
on earth's first fruits before the virtuous might eat.
Oh, there is reason in it. And the rogue's single
seat is occupied. Rampound took it ten years before

I came. There is no place for me, I shall be turned away."

An image is but an appearance on glass that has been mercuried. It cannot be a friend. It cannot say "But, look you, none of this matters. Have you considered . . ." Oh, if it would but say, "But you are far too tired to think of this to-night. Listen when I tell you some pleasant news that resolves the imbroglio!" But it does not, it keeps mum. So there is no reason why one should not lay one's head on the mantelpiece and sob it out. But soon he jerked himself erect and cried to himself, "And do you see nothing in all this, you fool? Do you conceive that all this happened by accident? Why, wake up, man! How came it that you came after Rampound instead of before, or at the same time, which would have suited you, for on equal terms you could have bested him? How came it that you were born with genius of a sort that demands wealth as its setting as imperatively as diamonds demand an aristocracy to wear them, and there was not one thing in your native estate that did not stink of poverty and try to hold you to it?" He paused, agape, scanning the background shadows of the mirror. He could not be sure but that the door had opened, and there had hung in the crack the blank sugar-almond of his wife's face, to which age had done nothing but turn it from pink to white, as if Time had held it too long in his cheek. But no interruption came, there was but the drip-drip-drip of his own misery. "No, it was nothing," he murmured. " But it might well have been nothing, and yet been my wife." He broke out into more of his screaming-fit. " Have you no eyes ? Do you think all those were pure mischances ? Why should you not have had the luck of other men and have a beautiful wife who was no idiot, or have been unhappily married on terms so free from obligation that infidelity was not a mean welshing ? And other men's creditors are devils only within reason. They do not prod and prod one's vitals with hot pitchforks, and give a man no time to rest and get the brain-pan cool, and think how he might pay. This cannot all be accident.

" Do you not see, you fool," he told his image, pointing his forefinger professionally, " the influence of your opposite ? If one is sealed within a globe, and is a candle, and must burn, how shall one survive if the globe is flooded with water ? I will not be a limp fish, I am a candle. Yet nothing is more sure than that so long as one's opposite survives one will be liable to be plunged into conditions utterly con-trary to one's being, which are an attack on one's essence ; ay, which condemn one to death. I have told you already, in this matter the spiritual world is not as the physical world. The gross air of the physical world offers resistance to waves of hate, it will not carry them very far. The lion can live in safety with the lamb cropping the lawns not half a mile away, until the mawkish smell of her herbivorousness seeks him down the wind and draws him to her by its insult to his difference; and her terrible meek breath on his fierce muzzle posits a relationship and makes him her murderer. But if the wind sit in the right quarter and he be not hungry they need not meet, he can remain innocent. But in the spiritual world, alas! it is not so! The medium is too volatile, it can be stained in a second all one colour: if one part is stained, it must all be stained. Why, its headstrong alchemies, the confusion of substances it not only permits but procures with delight, are most dangerous. They prevent a man from standing upright, they cut out his most vital parts, they yield him utterly to his opposite, who by necessity must wish his death. That is why the lot of man is so fruitful. 'Tis the reason why he must bind on himself the torment which is consciousness, the heavy burden which is the will, and thus deprive himself of rest. One cannot tell from minute to minute what one's opposite may do! Great God, what is my opposite doing to me now? My face is shining more brightly from the mirror, and I had hoped it was a good omen, but I perceive the effect is but an illusion due to contrast, for the walls behind me are dripping with darkness. See, the shadows have advanced till they are looking over my shoulder. Ah, give me strength to turn and face this new appalment!"

With his hands out before him, shielding his face and breast, he spun round on his tottering legs; but let fall his hands and sighed. "There is no fighting

an impalpable foe. I surrender. And how it is gaining
on me ! Not half an hour ago I could see each plaster
wheat-ear on the treillage of my ceiling ; but now there
is a new ceiling to my room, and it is made of blackness.
How is the malign power of my opposite demon-
strated, that can take light away from me, which is
as freely given man as air ! Or is this not a transformation of the external world, but has my sight been
blasted ? Oh, I will not be blind, I will not be blind ! "
He flung himself towards the windows and cast himself on his knees beside it, gripping the sash, and staring
out and up, his mouth wide open. " No, 'tis a general
wreckage, not a private malady ! Look, how the dark
lies like a great cat in the yard behind my house, and
how darkness sits on the clouds that were as good and
grey when I came in ! Something is swallowing up
the world ! "

Two windows high up in the house behind his
leaped suddenly to brightness ; and it could be seen
they had bars. " What, a secret prison in a house
like this ! " he thought, and was appalled by the
wickedness of man. But a white figure, not such as
prisons see, showed now before the one and now before the other, opening and shutting cupboards, trailing
armfuls of softness. It seemed to be a woman. She
opened a door and passed through it, and was not
seen for a few seconds : then came back with a bundle,
which, when she had seated herself, she began to
unwrap ; and though it beat at her, she lifted it high
and kissed it. Arnold Condorex stood up and stepped

back into the room and looked across at his distant image in the mirror. "That was a nurse and a child she put to bed, and it is evening. See how my opposite wrought in me, to form fears of such simple, natural things as these! For dusk is a sign of rest even to me, since bills are not delivered in the middle of the night, nor does the Cabinet meet, and I sleep, sometimes." He sank down into the chair at his desk, and sat with his head in his hands. "The power of the opposite!" he grumbled. "If it takes away a man's power to recognise the night and day, it is time something was done."

His left hand had pulled out the wide drawer in the middle and his other hand was very busily groping at the back of it. "What are you doing? You are half asleep!" he told himself. "Why, I am indulging a whim," he explained to himself clearly and loudly, "I am indulging a whim. I have ever heard that when a man has fallen to the depth of ruin, his wife and his friends tiptoe into his room, and steal away his revolver, lest he should escape that way. In this matter I have no fear of my good Ginevra. The idea is a little too complicated for her grasp. But I think that is very much the sort of action that might come natural to my poor dolt of a secretary, who loves me, but is such a dolt that I sometimes feel he will never rise in the world, and enjoy such felicity as mine. Ay, 'tis very likely he would slip in and take my revolver, and then I should find it gone, and for the first time be convinced that my mind knows but will not believe, that my ruin is now complete. So I will put it in my pocket."

But first he broke it, and saw that it was loaded. "What, all chambers full? It would be prudent to unload it. But no, I am too tired. I do not think another body in the world can be as tired as I am now." He turned it over and over, admiring its forthright look; and felt a sharp pang in his brow. Indignant with his pain, he cried, "What has made you tired, what gave your head that pain, except your opposite?" and slipped the revolver in his pocket. He began to rub his eyes and yawned, "Oh, yes, you seem tired enough, but I am not sure that you would sleep if I gave you a chance. I think you are too tired. I believe I would be better to go out. Why should I not? I have had no fresh air all day. It is perhaps the very medicine that I need."

The butler and the footman started apart when he went out into the hall. It could be seen they had been whispering in each other's ears, their eyes set on his door.

The butler said, "My lord?"

Condorex thought: "When your white face sways in the shadow, it is very difficult not to believe that you are something lying among the weed in that part of the harbour between the breakwater which the tides never truly clean, but only disturb, so that a scum rides on the surf. I perceive I have been constrained to have you always about my house by the influence of my opposite, which would have loved to suspend myself in some such place. I must take steps to end all this injury." Aloud he said, "My hat and coat."

For an instant the butler did not move. "Are you going out, my lord?"

The footman, too, was waiting for the answer as if he gaped at a street accident. "Oh, Christ, have mercy on me," mourned Condorex's heart. "What have I done that has betrayed my state of vanquishment to those, the lowest of my enemies? The fathomless ill-will that brings me to this plight! There is nothing I can do now save but be haughty!" He nodded stiffly, and said, "Ay, and I do not want the car."

While he was being nursed into his sleeves the footman moved across the hall and stood by the front door. His dark livery melted into the shadows, his face was pale as a mushroom. He looked to be a tall, thin stalk. "Can he open the door by himself, do you think?" asked Condorex.

The butler's anger grew stiff upon his collar. "Why should he not, my lord?"

Condorex thought, "What am I at? I cannot tell him that, ever since the night when the lackeys and the maidservants stood in the hall and watched the shining women carry their ropes of flowers down the stairs and out into the street, it has seemed to me as if an invisible rock had been rolled against the door and must be rolled away again before I can go out or come in. For my reason tells me that my lackeys and my maidservants saw no such sight in my hall at any occasion and that two of the properties of rocks

are to be visible and not to be in Portland Place, and
that all this is a dream instilled into me by my opposite
for my embarrassment. Well, there is nothing to be
done ; and after to-night all will be different. Ay, I
have a curious confidence they will be gone after
to-night." He stared into the crown of his hat before
he put it on, thinking, " I do not know why, but I
have such respect for to-night that it shames me to
be covered in its presence. Night, what do I hope you
will bring forth that I respect you so ? I could almost
believe that you might rid me of my opposite, though I
have no idea how that might come about. Oh no, there
is no way of ridding me of my opposite, none at all."

He paused at the head of the steps, to puff out his
chest at the violet grandeur of the twilight street lest
it should perceive he was not good enough or rich
enough to live in it ; and started back because a grey-
ness slipped between his legs. But in a trice he was
straight again, and laughing loud after the habit of
royalties and all the overlooked (for he was not sure
if he had heard the door close behind him) and had the
twisting rag of fur and sinews caught to his bosom.
" You are the cook's cat, I think," he told it. " And
how that woman loves you ! For I have complained,
and no one would call me unreasonable, of the infernal
yowling you raise by nights under my window, and
have been told that if I will not have cat I shall not
have cook. Ah, for all the pretensions to race that
are made by the length of your coat and its orgulous
references to Persia, what a vulgar animal you are in

your craving for publicity, and, in considerateness, how inferior to man! For have you never reflected that if we men and women managed our business as inconveniently as you do yours, and showed such lack of self-control in lamenting and inconveniency, the world would be pandemonium and no puss could get its nap? What, you wriggle, you ask to be put down? Well, I am sure it is not due to embarrassment, for I have far too often had evidence of your lack of that. What, your pink muzzle throbs in the direction of the area? Ah, I have come between you and your dinner, which is also mine." He let the cat drop from his arms and stood confronting the twilight with a little more pallor than he had done at first. "How utterly am I lost among the ordinary landmarks of life! So that is why my butler was surprised at my going, since I had told him I would dine at home. Shall I go back? I do not think I shall. They will chatter as much if I sit at my board and do not eat as if I do not sit there. And, believe me, I will eat well after." He put an enquiring forefinger to his brow. "After what? I fear I am raving."

He descended the steps, and paused, and shuddered to see the pompous regalia of street-lamps worn by that thoroughfare. "It was well decreed by the Synod of Elvira that lights should not be lit by daylight in places where there are the dead; for the effect is very ghastly, and would depress the spirit of one newly dead, or indeed undergoing any such ordeal, such as having to dispense death." He shook himself as if to throw off a thought that clung to him, and walked briskly for some yards, then checked himself. " I vow I have not the least idea which way I should turn, no, not the least. Since I am out but to cool my head with fresh air there is no reason why I should go one way rather than the other, and I am like Buridan's ass between two bundles of hay. Why, I must toss for it, I suppose." He drew a coin from his pocket, and let it slap his palm. "Heads—did I not say that was towards Oxford Street?" He turned that way, and peace fell on him.

" 'Tis the fresh air which is an incomparable medicine," he mused. " Did I not fear to be recognised and attacked for taking the misfortune of my country lightly, I would buy a stick and twirl it as I walked, and hum. I have the strongest feeling as if I were headed for a successful achievement. I could do more than hum, I could sing. ' *There is a tavern in the town, in the town, where my true lover sits him down, sits him down . . .*' Why, I remember the words and the air to perfection. I must close my lips tightly lest I disgrace myself. Really, I feel very easy, very comfortable. This rebellion put down, I must go for a holiday, and build myself up to wrestle another round with fortune. Shall I go North to the fjords? I am told there are great white mountains that stare up to the sky, and great white women that can do that too, and an air that makes one feel lively, and very noble, so that one's liveliness excuses itself on high grounds. Or shall I be faithful to the Duchess's villa, on the hill

behind Cannes, which she always lends me, because
she believes all leaders of my party to be good men
who protect her from being ravished by a boilermaker
from the Clyde, and has been deaf for ten years, so
that she has not heard the spreading news that I am
a villain? Well, the choice must depend on what
time of year it is . . ."

He came to a standstill so sudden that he swayed,
and wished he had a stick to lean on, not to twirl.
" Why," his spirit said in a thin voice, " I am now lost
in the year as a little while ago I was lost in the day. I
do not know whether it is the spring, or the summer,
or the autumn, or the winter. A year is a far vaster
space than a day. I do not like being lost in this great
desert ! How shall I find my way out of it ? "

When he stared ahead of him he saw the grey curve
of Regent Street, for he was not a little distance from
Oxford Circus. "Dear God, I wish this had not
happened to me here, in view of this architecture that
bears the stamp of no age at all. I feel I am lost
among the centuries as well, and if all time is my laby-
rinth, then I must be lost forever ! It was a woman
and child set me on my right road through the day.
Surely some such fellow-creatures will appear now to
save me ? " He had almost rushed across the street
to a crowd of people, doubtless concert-goers, that
hurried along towards the Queen's Hall, but he caught
himself back. " Who do you know for certain is
not the instrument of your opposite ? " he warned
himself gravely. " In this matter you dare not depend

on any other than yourself. Use that supreme part of you, your reason, to discover what season it may be." He had begun to stroll majestically again, and at a leisurely pace.

"Let us examine the evidence. It is not a cold day, it is not hot. It might be spring, or it might be autumn. Yet who is to be sure of that? I have known weather as mild as this in December, and I have known a midsummer sky wrap itself in just such an old grey flannel dressing-gown of clouds as this. We flimsy-minded English cast off our heavy garments at the least alleviation of our winter, and our climate is at all times so uncertain that we keep our thick coats by us in the prime of the year; therefore it means nothing that the women are slipping past me not encumbered yet not wholly free. I cannot tell where I am in the seasons. I cannot tell! But I am a fool. I can tell with assurance that it is neither midsummer nor Christmas. For it is growing dark, and it is a little before the hour when my dinner is served. It must therefore be late spring or the early autumn. See how the right use of the intellect will reveal all we need to know of this world!"

Though he tried to walk springily on the balls of his feet his gait soon flagged. "God forgive me for talking like an idiot when He did not make me one! Is this all a man needs to know of his position in time, that he is in spring or else in autumn? Would a traveller be at ease if he knew he were somewhere in North America, or if not there somewhere in Africa?

I am still lost. I am profoundly lost, and I feel the panic that comes on those who are lost in a vast desert! Oh, but I am indeed an idiot!" He burst out laughing. "That is very amusing, to cry out in misery when I am faced on all sides with salvation!" By now he had reached Oxford Circus; and all round that cold bowl of glass and stone, in which the dust was rising like smoke from the butt of extinguished day, he could see figures that lolled against the shuttered portals of the shop, clad from hip to toe in terse renderings of the world's affairs. "I have always suspected that money was of more service than intellect," he said, smiling at his own shrewdness, " and now I have proved it! For by the expenditure of one penny I shall buy a newspaper and read at the top of every page the knowledge that my opposite took from me and my intellect has failed to restore!"

But when he slipped his hand into his pocket his face fell, nor did it light up again when he tried any of the others. "It is a most incredible circumstance," he thought with awe, "that there is at last a breach to the rôle which has held good with me for years, that the same way of living which ensures that I am in truth unable to meet my debts as the poorest bankrupt shopkeeper, also ensures that I should never go out without having in my pockets as much money as a prosperous shopkeeper's till would take in a day. My wallet is gone, and I have not a copper in my pocket. It is a pity, for I do not wish to go back to my house till I have achieved my purpose!" Again he laughed aloud. "How pompously I speak! For that is a very Sunday-go-to-meeting way of saying that I mean to take a walk!"

Full misery came on him once more when he turned the corner into Oxford Street. "What an antipathy there is between money and myself!" his soul groaned. "When it sees that it may do me a service, how it flees! When it might have bought me the solid pedestal on which English statesmen must stand or not exist, how the gold ran from me, as if it had heard news that Danaë was in town! When a trifle of the basest form of wealth would have led me out of this huge desert that is three hundred and sixty-five days long by three hundred and sixty-five nights broad, the coin escaped me and my valet as if it had been on the end of a string! And the hard, hating metal wins the final victory. For I am really lost, I did not know a human being could be as lost as this! Time, I had thought, stayed by one always. Oh, but if one's opposite starts playing tricks with the order of things, reading one's mind before one speaks it, making one see through closed doors, bringing to light those parts of me that should stay in darkness if one is not to fall to pieces with discomfiture, why, all must come to chaos! And no one cares! Why, look, this crowd is very gay! It might be carnival!"

So, indeed, it seemed. There was still so much daylight in the air that the lamplight could not penetrate it, and the unspent rays clotted into soft yellow blossoms on the standards, which gave the street the appearance of being decorated : and twilight masked the faces of all the passing people so that their eyes and teeth flashed brilliantly, and they were hurrying out of the evening into the night as if they were sure the deeper the shadow the greater the pleasure. "They are slipping past my misery as callously as my cat when she went on her way to her dinner," he thought bitterly. "And they have not her excuse in being different in kind. But I must walk among them wherever they are, for I am not treading this road by accident, I am on my way to Hyde Park, to frustrate my opposite. For I will be no longer lost when I am there, I will look at the trees, and if dead leaves drift to my feet I shall know that we are in the autumn of the year as well as in the autumn of my fate, and if the sight of buds makes me weep by its irony then I shall know it is spring. This plot of my opposite will not succeed. Oh, but how horrible ! " he cried, and came to a standstill.

He was passing a florist's shop, that had not drawn its blinds and was as a wall of dark, shining water, in which, it seemed, a nymph had drowned ; for in its depths there stood alone a vase of very white flowers. "Is it not fatuous," he mused, putting his face close to the glass and letting his teeth leave his lips in a sneer, "that the lily should be held as an emblem of purity ? I do not know any flower that is better fitted to symbolise the most perverse confusion. Look at its shape that suggests a mineral substance that has been cut and carved and is immortal ! What

a lie that is, when it is made of stuff corruptible as
cabbage, that a rude finger-nail can bruise as brown as
dung. Oh, I would like to break this window, and
then rush in and break the vase and snap the lily
stems and stamp on the flowers until no one could tell
there had been anything here but something vegetable
that had the capacity to rot and stink. To snap those
stems would give one such delight. . . ." Panting,
he stayed and planned the crime until a deepening
of the darkness in the glass, a heartening of the mir-
rored lights, made him aware that the world had
sprung on him another change, and he spun about,
looking very cunning.

But it was only that night was now achieved, and
artificial light had come into its own. The electric
standards laid their will of white brilliance on the
streets, and the smiling faces had been unmasked and
streaked with luminous paint, and the hurrying bodies
subdued to the colour of grey cats. Such of the shops
that had remained unshuttered lit up their goods and
threw over the passers-by pailfuls of harsh illumina-
tions. " Oh, it is far too bright ! " breathed Condorex,
putting his head down as he hastened on his way.
" To-night I would like darkness. I do not want to
be lit to bed by these strangers. Why do they say to
me : ' Here is a candle to light you to bed. Here is
a chopper to chop off your head. . . .' God, what
a sinister rhythm those words tread out on the ear !
It is the very gait of a murderer, stealing behind his
victim ! To think that is part of a nursery rhyme,

that tender infants are instructed to move in such a measure! Yet I do not know that that is so very shameful. Is it not perhaps the subterfuge of some pagan force of wisdom, long persecuted by this new mewling Christian affectation, yet too concerned with man's survival to leave him without instruction in his necessity to defend himself from ruin by his enemies, his opposites . . ."

He had to stop and master himself, for he had now before him the task of crossing that open space which is dominated by the embarrassment of the Marble Arch, who, good dumpy widow that she is, knows she will drop dead if the tall picture-palace pressing so close behind her should accost her. At night she is quite blue with fear, for it is notorious what bad men think of with increasing boldness after sundown. And no one cares! The traffic goes on its godless way and not one item of it stops to say how good it is in these days to see a woman who is not loose. "How I wish," he said, laughing aloud again, and balancing on his heels, at the edge of the curb, "that my fantasy were true! I should like some place in London where there are great outgoings and incomings to be dominated by a vast figure of a woman who had once been beautiful but was now made ill-favoured by age, and who was ridiculous as ageing women are, perpetually set against the sky in some grotesque state of discomfiture. Then one could look out from one's automobile and be refreshed. That would be better than all these statues of statesmen, who (though I have no

desire to foul my own nest) have no particular message
to give in marble terms. How curious to think there
will never be a statue of me now in any square! Oh,
the malignity of my opposite, which saw to it that
when I fixed a deed to happen on the stroke of midnight all clocks in the world would strike thirteen!
Oh, I must go on!"

Without caution he ran across the road. Swords
struck at him, but they were not made of steel, being
beams from the headlights of automobiles. Shouts
were raised, but not by armies, nor by mass meetings
of the Primrose League, or by the boys at the Mill Hill
prizegiving, or any crowd such as he was accustomed
to review. He waved at the unseen people whose
swords and shouts these were, to show that the
matter was too low for him to be concerned with it,
and passed into the Park. The road stretched from
the Park Gates widely as if it were meant for several
kings to ride abreast, the traffic spun gold lines to it
and from it with the smooth, slow rhythm of a
capital. Pleased by the scene, he crossed the road with
a swinging, monarchic gait, saying, "Now shall I
defeat my opposite by looking at the trees. If it is
a dead leaf that I find, it shall have a finer funeral
oration than any Cæsar, and if it be a bud, how shall
it overestimate its importance in the world through
hearing my wild pæan of its being! But—what is
this? There are trees here! An avenue of them
lining the road! I need go no further to read my
riddle!" He was discomposed. He had thought of

other trees that would give him the news, trees in the centre of the Park. But as he gazed towards these which he increasingly wished were not here, he saw that beneath them were built flat cairns of mankind, the summit of which swayed, let its hands sing out, and emitted sounds. "Why, these tub-thumpers and their followers are juſt the very dabblers in public matters who would be the quickeſt to recognise me! Decidedly," said he, pulling his hat down over his brow and turning up his collar, "I cannot ſtray among such as these to get news. Come, I muſt visit the chaſter groves that have chosen a more secluded ſtation."

Very robuſtly he ſtepped along an asphalt walk that left behind the Marble Arch, the road, the orators, and waved his hand across the grass to a row of lights that on his left marched more directly south-ward. "I shall meet you later!" he said cheerily. "This is a short-cut. Ah, how I love a ſtraight road. It has the beauty (of a peculiar kind, I grant you, yet I maintain a true beauty, that endures when smoother kinds have failed) of a weapon pointed at the heart of its due victim." At that moment there came towards him out of the darkness a couple of policemen, ſteadily lurching from foot to foot, grave-bodied like great dogs. He went down into his collar, and did not have the spirit to come out of it and laugh at himself till the slow creaking tattoo of their tread had long passed from him. "Why are you afraid?" he asked himself. "To take a walk, to look at a tree, are these ends not harmless enough ? And I perceive that so far as one end is concerned you have nearly attained it, for the plantations that were but delicate islands against the skyline when you took this path are revolving themselves into their component parts, any one of which will answer your riddle. Indeed, you need not go so far, for hardly a hundred yards away I see a modest grove of trees, spread out on either side of the path, that should serve your purpose as well as a forest. Try yonder tree, that I am not country enough to name, but is very upstanding and looks as if it would answer a civil question."

He left the path, and strolled along very easily, looking downward and letting his breath hiss through his teeth. " Oh, it is good," he said, " to feel earth, slightly wet, and grass, under one's feet ! I suppose the pleasure that it gives is not unlike that which those horrible ruffians, the Eastern tyrants (how necessary it was that Mangostan should become a British Protectorate !), devise from walking on the throbbing bodies of their victims. I thank whatever powers there be which implanted in me the capacity to enjoy the more innocent delight. I am, indeed, surprised at my own innocence to-night. For I do not know when I have enjoyed a carouse as much as I have enjoyed this purposeless ramble." He swung around and looked back at the meek, crouching darkness of the grassy flats, over which the lighted walks marched militantly like soldiers sent out from the emblazoning city, that pressed its frontier of giant electric standards up to the plumy edges of the park like a victorious power closing in on a beaten people, and varnished the clouds above with its own glow. " How sweet it is," he said, " to see the sky all tinged with red! 'Tis nearly impossible not to believe that there is a conflagration raging which shall turn every man and every woman in London to ashes by morning." He watched awhile, sighed " Hey-ho! " and turned about again, saying briskly, " Now for the tree."

For the last ten paces he kept his eyes on the grass, then raised his eyes to the tree-trunk. " I must tell you it is my salvation that you are lifting to the skies," he said gratefully. He smiled at the bark as if it were the face of a friend. " Ay," he said, " Here is Nature, which is neutral and cannot be suborned by my opposite. The spiritual world is infected against me, that I know, but here is good hearty matter which is not permeable by hate, and will tell me honestly how the land lies." Still smiling, and laying his hands on each side of the tree-trunk as if he would have taken it by the coat-lapels had it been a man, he looked up at the branches.

When the drumming of the blood in his ears grew too loud, he cried pitifully, " Wait, do not hurry me! " and staggered for an instant.

He steadied his weight against the tree-trunk, thrusting out his stomach as old men do, and dropped his jaw so that his strength might have as little to take care of as might be; and he looked up again. A part of him grumbled, " Ah, you poor dog, your eye must climb branch by branch, and take a census of each twig. If you were a poet, now, you would be endowed with a knack of apprehension that would make the tree grow within your knowledge instantly you saw it." "Ay," said another part of him, "but poets are worthless folk, I would not be a poet." "That is no excuse for the universe," answered the part that spoke at first, "why should worthless folk be dowered with so useful a gift? You might as well put your head down against the tree-trunk and weep. Weeping is the apposite act to this dispensation." But the rest of him kept his neck stiffly uplifted. Then he drew back and cried, "It is not possible that I cannot see anything up there save some stars that have caught in your branches! Is it conceivable that you have not one dead leaf to show me, and not one bud! Then I am lost, I am lost!" He kicked the bole that curved down to the ground. "Do you think it is enough for me to know that it is not summer! For I know more than that, since a ferocious autumn or a dilatory spring might leave you bare like this. I am lost in a desert the size of half a year!"

"I told you," said a part of him, "that you had better lay your head against the tree-trunk and weep."

"But what is this?" cried the other parts of him. "I had forgotten how profoundly infected is the spiritual world! Do you not see that it would be the first device of your opposite to make you seek out the tree in this grove that had been blighted! Try another one!"

He ran to another, grasped it, and looked up : and did so with another one, and with another one, and with another one. The asphalt path was hard under his heels. But the half of the grove that was on its other side gave him no more fresh news.

"There is not one of you that has more about you than the stars which have caught on your long hair ! " he groaned. "Oh, I am utterly lost ! And it is worse to be lost in time than in space, for it is not known what happens ! If I were wandering on the desert I should presently die and become a heap of bones to appal the later traveller ; but for all I know I may be wandering as irretrievably away from death as towards it. And am I perhaps moving in a circle ? Am I perhaps even now entering the same moment where I was ten minutes ago ! Oh, my opposite, my obscene opposite ! "

He began to run along the asphalt path, and did not stop until he had come to a junction of several such paths, at a place where there was a thicker grove, and a large house that was full of lights and had a lamp-post beside it marked, " POLICE." At that he scowled and said, " There is interference everywhere " ; and walked with a more furtive gait down a slight hill that was before him. On each side of him incommunicative tree-trunks held high branches that were always bare. " There are thousands of them," he thought furiously, " they drive avenues into the darkness every way, and they are all my enemies. Oh, I see what is happening ! " He stood still and shook his

head at them. " Matter, did I call you neutral ? I
had then overlooked one little aspect of you. There
is an element in all matter subject to growth and decay
which cannot be accounted for by its own properties.
At any given moment an object is as it is, and if it
is as it is, then it is not changing. Since this is true of
all moments in its life, then it should never change,
should never grow, never decay. Yet change and
growth and decay so permeate life that some say they
are all of it. How are they achieved ? Why, by the
will of the spiritual world that pushes matter here and
there out of its disposition to stockishness." He flung
out his arm at the immobile trees. " And that will
has ceased to work ! Look at them ! Is there a
movement stirs a twig ! And see, does not the rising
moon show those trunks strangely carven-looking,
have they not a cold appearance as if they had slipped
backwards from the state of being wood which knows
the rise and fall of sap, into the state of being stone,
which knows nothing but its own even being ? Do
they not look as if change had ceased to work on them ?
And that man and woman on those two seats over
there, is it not evident from the sack-like way they sit
that they will never move again ? I tell you, the will
of the spiritual world is paralysed. And it has become
so by the pull of two strong opposites ! Oh, I must
instantly relieve humanity of its sufferings, which
must be immense ! " He began to run towards the
road he saw at the end of his path. " Think of the
lovers," he panted, " stretched taut on the rack of their

own delight for ever ! Think of the child, exempt
from this curse by its non-being, threshing about
within its mother and never being shown the road to
freedom ! Think of these that perpetually live who
should long have been lanced out of the sound body of
life by the surgeon Death ! Oh, I muſt act ! "

He was walking along the road by now. Automobiles spun by him, but that did not dismay his
sureness of his case. " Ay, they are moving," he
admitted, " but do you not see how this paralysis of
the spiritual will would operate ? All would continue
as it was at the moment the curse fell. The trees that
were bare and had been jilted by the wind at that
moment shall ſtand ſtripped and forsaken forever.
That man and woman who sat so heavily pondering
whether it could not be put out to nurse with Aunt
Emmy at Portsmouth and none be the wiser shall
squat there till eternity be sent down to the butler's
pantry to be cleaned. And that which was moving
shall perpetually be confined to its notion. See how
that poor sentinel walks up and down in front of the
classic colonnade of the Powder Magazine across the
road ! Without cease he shall trot up and down that
moonlit oblong, his fur busby covered with a second
fur of moonbeams, with not a chance to ſtop and use
his good bayonet to kill. (Oh, I muſt hurry, I muſt
hurry !) And these automobiles run by me because
they were so doing when change was annulled and
therefore cannot ſtop. No doubt they were in Leeds
or Salisbury when the devilish work began, and before

it is done with drive down into the sea in search of rest; and when they have done that, poor souls, they will not find peace, for they will find themselves obliged to drive and drive under the waves, and those ground swells will make bumpy roads. Oh, the infernal pull of opposites! I must end it without an instant's delay."

He set himself to a trot, and had but time to bend his neck over the Serpentine Bridge; but what he saw made him shake his head gravely enough as he jogged on. "Ay, there has been abolished order. That is shown by the destruction of that division between human beings, which confined one to little fiddling activities which are but one disguise worn by obscurity, and exalting another of more grandiose make to appropriate grandeur; for I, even I, am threatened with obscurity. And here I see there is setting in a further confusion of substance. That was not water underneath the bridge. It was black and hard. It was marble, or agate, or onyx. Those images of trees, those smeared replicas of light, they are very different from reflections on water that has not been tampered with; they were as markings on rare minerals. Oh, have I not seen man-high vases of such stones in the palaces of Italy and fatuously admired the cities and lakes and forests in their depths," he groaned, " and never guessed that these commemorated times when the lovely living earth was petrified by the foul action of opposites! For so it must have been. Yet, God knows such horrors are exceptional.

Water is for the most part truly water, and reflections have behaved gracefully like ladies dancing. The spell sometimes breaks: though doubtless not of itself. Oh, I will not be dismayed though the moonlight looks far more like rime than itself on the grass beneath yonder groves. There are victories to be gained," he panted, " if the hand is but steady enough." He went on at a jog-trot until he saw the lights that march along the southern border of the Park, and waved to them gaily, crying, " I told you we should meet later ! For I have had a curious notion all the evening," he said, wagging his head, as he came out of the Park gates, " that my walk would in the end bring me to Kensington." And certainly he stood on the earth of the Royal Borough. Some of these poor doomed automobiles that would before long spin their wheels among the fishes had to go by before he could cross the road; and while he waited he eyed with a sneer the stiff snake of light opposite that marked the street down which he meant to go. " It descends a considerable hill," he said grimly, " Kensington lies very low, for all its gentility. Its boasted squares have indeed the quality of a lilac-bush bursting from a grave." He laughed aloud.

" Lights, lights, there are too many lights in this street," he grumbled as he trudged, getting down into his collar. " And for all the vastyness of these houses, how little true majesty they have ! They are quite comically without the importance of my own part of the world, where we are all statesmen. Owing to

this accursed confusion of substance they look in this
moonlight very like enamelled tinware, and that with
their design gives them an exact resemblance to mag-
nified jelly-moulds. I do not think that persons of the
highest consequence would ever live here. Yet Sir
George had his residence here, I seem to remember.
Ay, that is what I mean," he gibed. "It is just the place
where Sir George would live. But does he live anywhere, or is he dead? Oh, I should have known if
he had died," he told himself bitterly, "from the long
and fulsome obituaries. Everyone would speak well
of him, for he was high-born and exceedingly rich
from the beginning." He tramped on, thinking no
thought in particular, but blanketing his mind with
a general hot close-weaved disposition of hatred
against his fellows, when at his elbows he heard a
gentle scuffling sound, and wheeled about. There in
the coign of a porch and an area-railing he saw a meanly
dressed boy and girl who, perceiving how the night
permitted nothing to stand sharp and separate but
fused all in darkness, were so doing with their lips
and arms and bosoms. "Faugh!" said he. "Faugh!"
But they did not hear him, and though they drew
apart it was not to pay him attention, but to confirm
the wonder that, God knows why, they felt at the
sight of each other's very ordinary round eyes and
snub noses as amazed at life as puppies' muzzles are.
"Tck! Tck!" he said, as one who sees a practice
that, persisted in, will wreck the State, and strode
along, till suddenly he plumped down on the steps

of a great house as if he had been a gipsy and cared not a thing for appearances. "My feet hurt," he whined. "It is years since I walked so long a way on pavements ! And ought I not to run back and tell these two young people that they are opposites, and what the end of it will be ? But they will not believe me. The beginning of the business is very enjoyable. Ah, is it not, is it not ! Oh, I must go on if ever I am to save us all ! " Up he picked himself, though he seemed to weight half a ton and to be another person, and he set off on his jog-trot again.

But soon he gasped, "This street, I do not trust it ! It is very long. Good God, it is unnaturally long ! I am afraid it has swung loose into the ether, and that I am walking not along the earth but at right angles to it, and presently shall come to a thin knife-edge of macadam, and shall thereafter find myself floundering up a rungless ladder in the skies. I shall go on scrambling up it for ever and ever, and shall not come to anything. Oh, I am going to be lost in space as well as time if I cannot find my opposite and put an end to these schemings ! Do you not see how the aspect of this place confirms my intuition ? The Sir Georges and their like can live in these great houses because they have family and fortune which act like weights to keep them down to earth, so that they shall never fly off into space, no, not if they so wanted. But these lights that stretch down the street show what will happen to one who is not weighted down by these convenient leaden pellets, if he stray

here; for they go on and on and on, and are very low
and of a very ignoble degree of radiance as if they would
lead him into infinity and obscurity! Infinity and
obscurity! That shall not be the lot that falls to me!"
At that he struck his bosom very violently. "Where
is my opposite! I must find my opposite! For that is
the road I must tread, if I do not deal with my opposite! But hold! Is that not a very familiar corner
over there? Is that the side-street I must take?"

He ran across the street hotfoot. "Ay, this has
a look of it," he muttered, and rubbed his nose
against first one pillar of a porch and then the other
to see what number was painted there; and when it
appeared there was a one craned his neck backward
to read it on the fanlight. "Eighty-three," said he.
"Eighty-three. 'Tis odd that I cannot remember
if it was at Eighty-three I used to turn off the damnable
street; and odd that I should forget so relevant a
number, when I have had at my finger-tips the figures
of population that the last two India Office papers
on the subject have ascribed to Mondh. And I fear
that nothing regarding the City is likely to be of much
service to me henceforward." He loitered about the
pavement, biting his nails and looking up and down
the street, not knowing what to do; and presently,
looking from the corner down the side-street, caught
sight of a small white dog sitting on its hunkers in
the gutter under a lamp-post, very busy with what it
was doing. From further along the street came the
voices of a man and a woman, crying together, "Tray!

Tray ! What are you doing ? " to which the dog looked up with a leer that said very plainly, " For two pins I will tell them, if they do not hold their peace " ; for he was a very low kind of dog, a fox-terrier such as seems to be wearing a cloth cap, and to be at home in gin palaces and wherever the fancy are found.

" Why, little dog, you look to me very much like an omen," said Condorex, and waited.

The man and the woman who were calling the dog stood side by side, stockish and alike as brother and sister might be, at the foot of steps leading from a house of less pretensions than those in the broader thoroughfare but of respectable appearance : and from the open door behind them an old voice creaked, " Andrew ! Phœbe ! Will you not come in and get your father Paris on the wireless ? For there is Dean Inge at London and one imitating the noises of little children and farmyard animals at Daventry, and you know your father has the gout." And the two turned and cried, " Yes, when we have found our little dog ! We must not lose him the very first day."

" Ay," said Condorex. " The pieces are fitting together at last. I am sure that I am where I wish to be ; for these people inhabit the same dream of the Creator as my opposite." He walked past them as they stood calling in their clipped honest voices, " Tray ! Tray ! What are you doing ? " and with a slanting look saw them knitting their simple sandy brows as they stared through the darkness. "That such guileless things," he jeered, " should be a guide to truly important business! Not that I am there yet. It is round the corner. Dragons and dangerous things have twisted passages to their lairs. Ay, see where we are!"

For there, across the road, was the long wall of Blennerhassett House. The bare strands of creeper waved from it like the fleshless arms of the long dead ; and the moon shone bright on the brass handle of the door.

" Is this not peace?" he sighed, crossing the road at a leisurely pace, since there was now no need to hurry any more. " What peace is like an accomplished ambition! But what is this?" He stopped in the middle of the highway.

For though there was now, owing to a rising wind, a marble screen of moonlight clouds pierced here and there with windows giving on to the pure stuff of night, and though the macadam beneath his feet shone like dark glass, there were other things than these and the stucco fronts of Kensington before his eyes. It seemed as if a high hill lifted its shoulder against a sky that was diamond hard and dazzling as Northern skies are in the night, and did so a second time in a round lake at its feet, whose smoothness was ringed by circles fine as the lines about a woman's neck. The waters of the lake lapped and sobbed among the sedges at its rim ; and a sound of bells came from the darkness at the side of the hill. They were all saying one thing, the sky and the hill and the lake and the bells. They were saying, " Harriet Hume is here, she is ours, she is here."

But he shook his head. "Nay," he told the lot of them very resolutely, "You are wrong. For she said to me I had the gift to have supernatural knowledge of her as strongly as she had the gift to have it of me, would I but exert myself; and in such a universal crisis as this (for indeed I consider it no less) I do not scruple to use it. And it tells me very plainly that she is here in Blennerhassett House. I would wager the fortune I hope to have if all goes well to-night that when I open that door I will see the light shining through her sitting-room jalousies. The rest of the house will be dark, I grant you, for society has long lost the freak of resorting to this dismal suburb for its amusement: but Harriet will be where I wish to have her. Wait."

He laid his hand on the door-knob; but before he turned it he had to stand still and laugh into his fingers for a second. "I cannot help but be entertained," he chuckled, "when I think how she herself instructed me in the plaguy secret of this loose knob, and bade me never forget it. Well, she cannot say that I have not obeyed her." He held back for an instant to make another matter clear. "The light will be coming through the slits in the jalousies," he predicted, with his forefinger on his brow, "and in a great beam at their middle, for the jade has left them a little open. Now for it."

It was exactly as he had foretold.

"I have hitherto disdained to use your resource of magic," he said coldly towards the yellow window, "but you see I am nearly your equal in it. Well, I need not hurry. I have you trapped. You cannot leave your house save by this garden. I will see you the minute you show yourself at the window, and if you turn down the light and run for it you will perhaps regret the ardour with which you have confused all substances you can lay your will to, for against the white sand you have made of the moonlight on your lawn, your floating form will show with an admirable distinctness. Since all the cards are in my hands I can afford to take my time and arrange to enjoy the play better by taking a thorough survey of the setting, which upon my soul is uncommonly pretty for such a factory of mischief as this has been for me." He cast his eyes about the neat groves and parterres, the wrought-iron gate that threw its lyre-like shadow on the grass beyond, the shrubbery that was so gracefully disposed about the foot of the iron steps to the house. "This ingenious garden has still its air of being a park," he owned in grudging accents, "of being genteel and harmonious no matter how meanly it is partitioned and surrounded. And there, I perceive, stand the ladies Frances, Arabella, and Georgina Dudley. Hold now, I would look into their state." He strode hastily across the green to them, glancing over his shoulder to see that no advantage was taken of his distraction; she must not get away. He inspected them as carefully as the trees in the Park. "I had thought," he murmured, "that she might have left one dead leaf or one bud in her own garden. But I see that her carefulness has taken no chances. Heigh-ho!" He turned away, though not before he had said icily to them, "You do not seem to have greatly bettered your estate by leaving my house, your ladyships. But you are doubtless under just such an enchantment as myself. Well, that will be soon broken, I can promise you."

He strolled down the lawn towards the house, a gloating smirk on his face. "Now is a mystery explained," mused he. "I have heard salesmen in shops holding out goods to their customers and saying, 'This is all silk,' or, 'This is all wool,' and have wondered at the voluptuousness in their tone. But indeed there is a delicious quality in a state of wholeness. I am deriving a most exquisite satisfaction from being all hate, as I am now."

At the foot of the steps he paused. "Did ever bridegroom go to his wedding-chamber with so intense an emotion as fills my bosom now?" he breathed. "Nay, why should he? For what he is about to do he had probably done before and will certainly do a thousand times after. But my occupation is unique. Since, having but one self, I can have but one opposite, I can never again have the pleasure of destroying it. And what profit I shall derive from it! After to-night all tides shall flow my way."

Softly he climbed the steps to the little terrace outside the French window; and said into his pocket: "Come forth, my friend, my deliverer." His lips blubbered on his pistol, his eyes rolled upwards. "Oh,

God! Oh, Jesus! Oh, all angels! Pour down your blessings on my friend, my deliverer! And now," said he, getting down on his knees by the window, "we shall send our message to our opposite through one of these slits in the shutters. There is nothing to prevent me from going into the room and doing justice straight and without falderals, but I am feeling fantastical, and it will entertain me to sight the source of my ruin through this narrow space and send my bullet winging through it on a mission. Come, friend, deliverer, advise me! Is this the most admirable slit for our purpose?" Yet when he had fixed his weapon there, a fit of shuddering shook him from head to foot, and for an instant he could not proceed with his enterprise. "What agonies of apprehension the poor wretch must be enduring through her gift of foreknowledge!" he muttered through his teeth; but steeled himself. "And why should she not suffer as I have suffered in my ruin?" he asked wildly; and set his eye askew against the slit, to take his aim and save his life.

But then it was that two heavy hands came down on his shoulders. His pistol crashed to the ground; and as he swung about and tumbled back on his haunches against the shutter, he saw that two tall men were standing over him.

He shrieked with fear.

The two men swayed backwards as his shriek rushed up into the night as if to let it pass, and then bent over him again.

"Oh, God above!" he muttered, squirming and looking from the face of one to another and seeing nothing but patches of white dimness between a helmet and a chin-strap. "Has my opposite not only done me all this spiritual mischief, but has raised up a material army against me also! How very strange you look! Those are very ridiculous, those brass buttons that go down your chest like the buttons on a child's bodice, and the leather strappings on your helmets are as foolish a device as I have ever seen. But how now! Is it poseible that you look strange only because you are so excessively familiar? Are you policemen?"

The two looked at each other with a gentlemanly kind of diffidence. "Ay," said one, who was the taller and the older of the two. "We are W Division men; and the lady telephoned to the station for us about half an hour ago."

"I said that the world was chockful of interference," groaned Condorex; and fell right back against the shutter.

A creak announced that the French window in the middle was being opened further, and they all turned their heads. Into the widened beam of light two hands fluttered like a brace of doves much under standard size, and from within a silly tinkling voice cried through sobs: "Did I not tell you that I knew everything in your mind? And did I not tell you, too, that 'tis my one duty not to die?"

"So," said Condorex.

He was sitting on the stone now, with his legs sticking out in front of him and his chin digging down on his chest. " And yet I do not understand ! " he sighed. " Surely I wrapped up the thought in enough coverings ? For I will swear to you that, what with dark talk about opposites and the like, I had completely disguised my intention from myself. I had no notion that I meant to kill you till I saw the moonlight shining on the brass knob of your door."

" God forgive me," wept Harriet Hume, " I mastered that trick of yours so long ago."

He sat for a while so motionless that even himself almost believed he was dozing. The wide beam narrowed and widened a little as her quivering frailty swayed between the windows. The dark garden waited.

At length he jerked up his head and said imperiously to the two policemen : " Officers, do your duty ! I will not resist you, or claim any privileges I might obtain by my rank. For bad as I am, and mad as I am, I have never disputed but that you must reign supreme. I know well enough that if you had not been practising that vigilance which has enabled you to prevent me from dealing as I wished with Harriet Hume, I would myself long ago have fallen a victim to some footpad, or perhaps a more exalted enemy, since the old men would have loved to send a grandson against me any day. Hail, law, exercise your functions ! Bring out your gyves ! I have enough love of order to find a curious bittersweet pleasure

in wearing them, since I muſt admit I am disorder
personified. Besides," he continued, in a more shame-
faced manner, " I am that from which a community
would in any case, however catch-as-catch-can its
ſtandards regarding murder might be, want to purge
itself. For I am an ass. If killing were as permissible
as eating butter, I ſtill had no need to kill poor Harriet.
Now that I have heard her bland though not very
intelligent voice I know that she has done me no mischief. It is I who have contrived my own ruin by
my own qualities. She was but conscious of them.
She did not manufaðure either them, or the external
circumſtances againſt which they dashed themselves to
pieces. Yet," said he, rubbing his chin and looking
before him pensively, " I ſtill feel I have a case againſt
her."

" Ay, and you have ! " faltered poor Harriet, who
was so shaken by her emotion that her parchment-
coloured skirts kept bobbing back and forth from the
window, in and out of the light. " The ſtrongeſt
in the world ! "

" I believe," said Condorex, " that you are generous
enough to reveal it to me."

" Why, what was the use of me being so innocent
in this g-g-garden," she bleated into her handkerchief,
" when I had no power to impose my ſtate on the reſt
of society ? I may have been innocent, but I was also
impotent. If I had derived a comprehension of harmony from my art, it was a grave lack in me that I
could not inſtil it into others and eſtablish it as the

accepted order of life : and I should be churlish if
I blamed those who have the power I lacked, and went
out into the world, and did what they could or what
they knew to govern it. Humanity would be unbearably lackadaisical if there were none but my kind alive.
'Tis the sturdy desire you have to shape the random
elements of our existence into coherent patterns that
is the very pith and marrow of mankind. Think,
my love ! You must admit that when you were not
pursuing the chimera of greatness, you performed
many very worthy achievements that enabled our
species to establish itself on this globe more firmly.
Did you not see to the building of bridges, the teaching
of children, the suppression of riot and bloodshed ?
Is that so small a thing ? "

" True, I was an excellent administrator," he agreed
gloomily. " But all the same I feel guilty beside you
and your life spent in contemplation of the eternal
beauties. Do not forget that I found it impossible
to work without surrendering to the principle of
negotiation ; and that it led me to murder, and logically so. For that principle forbids one ever to let
the simple essences of things react on each other and
so produce a real and inevitable event ; it prefers
that one should perpetually tamper with the materials
of life, picking this way with the finger-nail, flattening
that with the thumb, and scraping that off with one's
knife and stamping it on the ground at one's feet ;
and the most ambitious performance in that line, ay,
and the most effective and——" he drew his hand

across his brow, looked down on it with repugnance, and with a shuddering wiped it on his coat—" as I now know with every sweating pore of my body, the most horrible, is murder."

"Ay, but the end of contemplating the eternal beauties, and doing nothing to yoke them with time," mewed Harriet, " is smugness, and stagnation, and sterility ! "

He stared before him into the dark garden, tapping his forefinger against his upper lip. " You put an astonishing good face upon my destiny," he said. " And what is as important, I feel as if the quarrel between us was over. I feel soothed already ; and I have no doubt you could put me right about the universe did I but have the time to hear your exigesis complete. But these gentlemen will be growing impatient." He rose to his feet and extended his wrists towards the policemen. " Come, officers ! Take your prisoner ! "

They showed, however, not the least eagerness to obey. They looked towards the window and hesitated ; and one of them said, " Do you wish to give him in charge, madam ? "

" It is for him to say that," replied Harriet.

" There you are wrong," said Condorex sadly. " An attempt upon the life of another with firearms is not such a small matter that the assailant himself is allowed to say whether or not he shall pay for it. I fear that our two friends here will regard the matter in a very different spirit."

"Oh no, sir," said the taller of the two policemen. "The lady is right. We will leave it to you to decide whether or not you shall be arrested."

"What," exclaimed Condorex. "Do I hear that from the custodians of the law themselves! This is a very disorderly plot of ground, where that which keeps our Constitution rigid shows flagrant signsof laxity!"

"Well," said the same policeman, "You are the first prisoner I ever saw who was shocked because he was dealt out mercy instead of justice."

Harriet put her head out of the window so far that the light gleamed on her sleek parting. "Does it not show that there is something fine and unbendable in him?" she fondly enquired of the constables.

"Oh, he is a leader," agreed the taller one. "If I had to take part in a charge on a battlefield I would as soon follow him as anyone. And when one says that, one says so much that one is a fool if one does not leave a great many other things unsaid, no matter how just they may be. I hope the gentleman will understand that we are feeling nothing uncivil against him, whether he comes with us or not."

"What happens if I go with you?" he asked.

"Why, we will go to a police-station, in a street off the Fulham Road, and there we will find a white-washed room with a harsh light under a white porcelain shade, and a man writing at a high desk; and after all that goes by routine."

"And I have ever found routine dull work," said Condore dolefully.

They all stood in silence for a moment, looking on the ground.

The younger policeman, who had a very simple face, cleared his throat and spoke. " You would find a calendar standing on the desk where the man is writing," he said helpfully. " It will tell you the day and the month, ay, and the year."

" True enough," said the elder, " but it is the only thing he would learn quickly. Routine is the most roundabout stuff."

" I do not think I wish to go with you," said Condorex, and he looked in a mortified way round the garden, which a nymph-flight of clouds across the moon was filling with graceful and volatile shadows. " But the truth is, I must dispose of myself somehow. I suppose I could walk the streets for a time."

" What ! " blurted out the younger policeman. " A gentleman of your condition ! And have the children scream at you, and be sprinkled with holy water ! "

" Why would they do that ? " asked Condorex.

No one answered him. Harriet drew back in the doorway. The two policemen had had their eyes fixed on him, but now they looked once more on the ground.

" And I could, of course, go back to Portland Place," he reflected.

Harriet leaned forth into the light again. " I do not think I should do that," she said quickly. " There is one there who has had an accident with a pistol as he sat at his desk, and they have carried him up to your room and laid him on your bed, and there is a great running to and fro of doctors and secretaries and messengers and such. Oh, no, I would not go back to Portland Place, if I were you. I think," she ventured, timidly, "that you had better stay here."

"But surely you understand," he answered, "that I am ashamed to do that? I should like nothing better. But you are well aware in what spiteful follies I have been engaged regarding yourself. I clean forgot your pretty image about the North and the South, which would have kept me from identifying difference with enmity, and I most maliciously pretended that the spiritual world had been infected by you with a condition of hatred that was entirely of my own making, and you know well what I was at when these two good fellows found me."

"What is a little matter of murder between friends?" responded Harriet. "Had all gone conveniently with us at the beginning no doubt you would have left me, and I would have had to write you that well-worn letter they read in court, which contains the phrase, 'I will let bygones be bygones.' But things being as they are, I have the words by me still for use, and I will use them now. And I hope you will give them in your turn to me."

She leaned so far forward from the step of the French window that he could see the swan line of her neck and shoulders.

"Dear Harriet," said Condorex. "If you will let me, I will stay."

She swayed backwards with the languor of contentment. "There is an end to my anxiety!" she breathed. "For I was not sure but you would find some reason for wandering from me in some new form of stately discomfort, and I am certain that what you want at the moment is some of the quietness we have here. But," she said, her voice rising to the jesting firmness and her hands bringing the windows close together, so that the beam narrowed to a pointer, "I will not let you in at once, for I must tidy the house, which is something disordered, since I myself have returned only a little while from a long journey."

He felt so far easier in his spirit that he could feel in his pocket for his cigarette case. Why, it was now nearly as if it all had not happened. "You have been to your home in Cumberland, have you not?" he said, not wanting her to go so soon, and liking to have a little casual talk with her, as they used to have before all these upsets.

"I was obliged to go there to assist at a religious ceremony," replied Harriet, "since they informed me they could not well have it without me."

"I hope your mother was well," he said, remembering the photograph behind the turtleshell box.

Harriet popped her head far out of the window, and though he could not see her face through the night he felt that she was regarding him with some severity. "My mother is still very handsome," she told him tartly,

" but will you never learn to think of only one thing at a time ? " With a snap she closed the window ; but opened it again to call to the policemen, " I will bring you some refreshment, officers, in a few minutes."

" Would you not rather we went ? " asked the elder.

" I would much rather you kept my friend here company," said Harriet, " for I think he has been too much alone of late. Here ! " She flipped three cushions out into the darkness. " Sit on these and wait until I am ready."

They ranged themselves in a line on the stone flags, some little way from the window, and scrambled down on their haunches. It was easy to settle down very comfortably, with their backs against the wall.

" An excellent lady," said the elder policeman, " and manysided, for I can see that she is full of poetry and fancy and whatnot, and yet not unmindful of the consequences which may follow if the poor weak sons of Adam sit themselves down on cold stone."

" I have thought her perfection on and off these many years," said Condorex, in the offhand manner of proud proprietorship, feeling again for his cigarette case. " Will you smoke ? "

" Thank you, sir, I do not mind if I do," said the other. " Have you known this district long ? The lady has lived here for many a year."

" It was the summer of the Great Comet I first came here," said Condorex. " I remember we used to watch it trailing its diamond coat-tails over these tree-tops most nights."

"Why, that was twenty years ago," said the other. "It was the very same year that I caught my pneumonia."

The younger policeman looked at the elder with respect. "Is it so long ago as that? It is but two years since I dived in to rescue that boy in Blackwall Reach."

"And a good job you did," said the other, "for that is a likely boy. Is he about here to-night?"

"He is waiting for me on the shadowed side of the wall," said his junior; and he put his two thumbs in the corners of his mouth, and let out a kind of hooting whistle, to which there came instantly an answer from outside the garden.

"Ah, these events make good faithful comrades," pronounced the elder, and he turned towards Condorex. "That is what you will be finding out now, sir."

"I do not know what events you mean," replied Condorex, "but I am sure you are right. And for that very reason I beg you to excuse me, for I cannot rest till I have said something to her that has just come into my mind." He pushed to his feet, and ran to the middle window, which he tried to open. But it was secured by a chain which, he remembered, she used in the past to let down when she wished to make sure who stood at the door before she gave them entrance.

"Harriet!" he called softly. "Will you not let me in? Of old, you would always take down this chain when you saw it was me that had come! Harriet, be kind!"

"Nay, Condorex, I beg of you!" she whispered. Her voice sounded close to his ear, but he could see her nowhere, until he perceived that she had wrapped herself in the right-hand window curtain. "On this occasion it is appropriate that I should come to you with a clean new face, wearing a clean new gown, in a clean new house; and till I find myself in that condition I beg you to excuse me."

"You misread what I want," said Condorex, "so grossly that I must suppose you have lost the power to read my thoughts."

"That I have! That I have!" she crowed happily. "'Twas part of my gross pretensions to innocency, and 'tis gone! Decent veils hang between our minds to-day, for I lost the plaguy gift at the moment you pointed your pistol at me, and spurred me to consider our true positions in the universe."

"Had you not lost it, my pet," said Condorex, "you would have seen that I do not care a fig how or when I see you. Have not my eyes had their fill o you time after time? All I wanted was to tell you tha I have heard a certain noise, to wit, the rustling of the newspaper you have been picking off the floor, and that I perfectly comprehend what it means."

The curtain swayed, and she tittered in a guilty fashion.

"You poor blind bat, you have been reading," he told her in compassionate tones. "You came from your journey, whatever trivial pilgrimage to superstitious festival that may have been——"

275

"Do not speak ill of it," she bade him gravely, "for there were some there who were deeply affected, and the singing was very pretty for a village choir."

"Have it your own way," he said, "but do not avoid the issue. When you came back from your journey you bought all the newspapers there are, since they were so full of my speeches and my doings and you spread them all over your house. And because you are so devoted you have run from room to room, and at each newspaper you have squatted down on your gazelle-like hams, and supported yourself on the poor little makeshift you have for a hand, so that your arm was curved like a scythe; and you have pored down to see what of my adventures your infirm irids could convey to your infirm intelligence—why, you poor winking, blinking, purblind thing, you dote on me, you dote on me!"

She giggled. "So I do! So I do!" she confessed. "And because of this occasion I have opened three pots of jelly—the quince, the apple flavoured with orange-juice, and the bramble as well—though before you thought it the height of extravagance when I opened but two! And the dressing for the salad we are to have with the cold beef does not come out of a bottle, for I made it myself!" She began to whirl about on her columbine toes, with exultation, so that the curtain she hid behind dragged at its rings, and she stopped in great compunction. "But at this rate I will ruin my house instead of furbishing it. Go you back to your companions while I pursue my housewifery!"

"So I will," he agreed, and trotted away; but was back again at once, crying wistfully, "Harriet! Harriet! Give me but another word!"

"What is it, my love?" she enquired, peering round the curtain.

"I am flattered that you should be interested enough to read all that was written of me in the public prints," he said sadly, "but did not what you read seem very discreditable to me? Have I not made a sorry fool of myself over the Mangostan affair?"

"Oh, run along, run along, and think no more of it," she told him. "You showed traces of a certain confusion, I admit. Throughout the whole business you applied to statecraft methods that are more appropriate to banking. The whole idea of Mondh, my love, was not at all unanalogous to the conception of credit which still prevails in Threadneedle Street. But run along! We will talk of this afterwards."

He made his way back to his seat between the two policemen, stepping over the sturdy legs of the younger. "I beg pardon for leaving you," he said shyly, "but I had something important to say to the lady."

"Ay, now that one has no longer a game to play and points to score," said the elder, "one can talk fair and above board. You will find you have never known such pleasure as this honest conversation with one's dear ones."

A block of light stood out in the darkness, high up on their right-hand side. It showed the bare boughs of a lilac-tree glistening like the lean hands and arms of some iron-black native.

"She has lit the lamp on the landing," said Condorex, "it shines out too from the staircase window."

"Has she got up there so quickly?" marvelled the younger policeman.

"She moves as quick as a mouse," boasted Condorex, "and though she ran so quickly up the stairs, I dare swear they hardly creaked under her. Aha!" He shut his eyes and snuffed in the air. The wind that had been disposing the clouds very fantastically about the moon for some time past had now come to earth, and was fresh in his face. 'Ay!' he said, opening his eyes. "This is the wind that Harriet was talking about the other day, that bears the Spring, no matter how aloof the trees and plants may keep themselves. Well, I am relieved of all uncertainty about the season; and I am glad to find it is the best of all seasons that is going to have its way with us."

"There is something a deal more dulcet about the aspect of the heavens than there has been of late," said the elder policeman, pointing his cigarette towards the sky.

All three stared above their heads, where a well in the clouds showed an æther not so black as it had been earlier in the night, and stars not so biting brilliant. Indeed their brightness seemed to soften, to swim, to melt.

There was the sound of a casement being lifted above them. They tilted their heads still further back and saw a beam of light projecting from the right-hand window of the upper storey, with Harriet's head and shoulders black against it.

"Harriet! Harriet!" cried Condorex. "This is very irregular! There is a kind of sweetness dripping from the stars!"

"Put out your tongue and taste it, please," Harriet called down to him, "for I have always wanted to know what the flavour of starlight might be. In my youth I would have vowed it would be very sweet, but now I would be more inclined to wager that it tasted something like salted pineapple. But do you deal with the matter! I must put my house in order."

She withdrew from the window: but Condorex cried out, "Harriet! Harriet! There is the strangest sound in this garden, like rain hissing upwards."

"Oh, that," said Harriet nonchalantly. "It is the grass and the flowers pressing up through the earth. This is the Spring."

"But Harriet! Harriet! do not go! There is another strange sound, that is like kissing, though it comes from the branches of the trees, the boughs of the bushes, where no lovers can be?"

"It is the buds that are opening," said Harriet. "This is the Spring, I tell you, it is Spring." As she turned away they could hear her singing to herself.

Growth was working in the garden like yeast. There was a pattering like an inverted hailstorm, and it was the snowdrops that had come. Like slow lightning the cherry-blossom drew its white design

279

along the wall. Closer at hand the black fingers of the lilac-bush clutched close together as if they had to part with a penny and knew the pain of avarice; grew gnarled and sticky with a disorder of buds; and suddenly spread wide gifts of green leaves and white blossom. They had not been stingy, they had been conjuring. At the far end the Ladies Frances, Georgiana, and Arabella Dudley were shaken with a sharp tremor of quickening twigs, and lo! had their leaf bodies full and well-fleshed, and a cable of foliage to which the moonlight gave an appearance of flowers. In the dark spaces behind them chestnuts upheld candles, that shone vaguely as though they were guttering, yet were steadfast.

" 'Tis better than the Park in May," said the elder policeman.

" Why, 'tis as good as one of those flower shows where we sometimes had to do duty," said his junior, " and I always liked that better than anything. I am sure we are very grateful to you, sir, for giving us such a fine show."

" I had nothing to do with it," said Condorex. " You must thank the lady."

" Oh, no, sir," chuckled the elder policeman, " you need not disclaim all credit. For do you think it would have entered her head to do it had it not been for you ? "

Condorex did not continue with his modesty, for just then there was the sound of another casement being lifted, and on looking up they saw that the left-hand window in the upper storey was now bright and open, and had Harriet leaning from it.

" Harriet ! Harriet ! " he cried. " This is a very lovely seedsman's catalogue you are showing us, but I must confess there is one item that defies my knowledge. What is this very pretty blue flower that grows in the parterre by the foot of your steps, and carries its bells on its sprays with such remarkably aery grace ? "

" That ? " said Harriet, craning her neck. " Oh, that ! It is other things as well as a flower. It is a phrase in a sonata by Mozart, which I like to think he has given me for a keepsake because I have taken such pleasure in playing it. It is also the feeling that was in your heart when you wished to give me a ring, and tenderly reflected how small it would have to be to fit my finger. And it is something I felt about you once, but what that was I will not tell until we are having supper together. If you wish to know why it is growing just where it is, I will remind you that that is the spot where you used to bury your stick very deeply when we stood and enjoyed those protracted partings, which were all long silences, and lookings down, and bursts of speech, and then long silences, and so on, for God knows how long, in the days of our first friendship. But I must attend to my orchestra ! " And she flicked a feather duster from under her arm and began to lean forth as from a conductor's desk and use it as a baton. " Here, you almond trees, can you show no more spirit in dealing

with those fine pizzicato passages of your blossom?
Fi, you make very feeble second violins! But,
daffodils, I beg of you remember that it was ever the
fault of brasses to blare!" And indeed they were
ranged a little too militantly at the foot of the Ladies
Frances, Georgiana and Arabella Dudley, and swung
trumpets a thought too superb. "Pray do not drown
the scillas too indelicately! Bring out the theme,
please, the wood winds there. Yes, I mean you, my
hawthorn trees! But I perceive you are doing what
I demand most excellently already, both with the sober
crimson of your blossom, the rich yet not cloying
accumulation of your scent. Oh, this is all vanity, for
never could orchestra look of itself so well." She
held out the feather duster and shook it with a great
promise of housemaidship. "I will go put this to its
proper uses. Yet I would have liked," she said wistfully, "to be a conductor once in my life. I have no
special pianistic gift—I could not," said she, and
proved by her accents that if she believed herself
cured of her smugness she was wrong, "for my hands
are too small. But I am a sound musician, and I am
sure I could have bred perfection by a masterpiece
out of an orchestra once in a way had I been given the
chance. Heigh-ho!" But again, when she turned
from the window, they heard her singing.

For a time all three smoked in silence while what-
nots of flowers and leaves completed the design;
till the elder policeman took his cigarette from his
mouth and declared, "Ah, say what you like, there

is nothing can beat the good old lilac! It does not surfeit with its scent; it preserves a very seemly proportion between leaf and flower. And it is not fickle. It lasts, it does not rush downward to try what the earth can do for it before it has fairly sweetened the air."

"I am very fond of a flowering currant-bush," said the younger policeman. "There was one at each corner of my father's kitchen garden. Do you think there is one here?"

"Why, Albert, I am sure nobody will think you are taking a liberty if you look about for one," said his senior.

"I would like to do that," answered the other, hoisting himself up; and was presently a stumbling darkness down on the lawn, sending the white proboscis of his lantern among the shrubs and plants.

"What takes my breath away," said Condorex, as he and the other continued to smoke, "is that the show we are seeing in this garden, which empties pell-mell on it all the resources of Spring, is nothing to the revelation that will be showered upon me in the house."

The older man made no answer, but he knit his brows, and set to puffing very sturdily at his cigarette.

"Ay," said Condorex, waxing in enthusiasm, "this does but exhibit the plentitude of nature, but when I go into this house I shall learn that which shall reconcile me to nature, in its poverty as well as its wealth."

The older man showed signs of embarrassment.

"I hope you will not be disappointed, sir," he said, gruffly, "for indeed I do not believe there is anything in the house except the lady!"

"Innocent old man!" exclaimed Condorex. "Now I see that you have led a good life, and have never been infected with the desire to rise in the world, nor sold your soul to the abominable principle of negotiation. Else you would know that there is no more delicious knowledge for me than that there is nothing in the house but a lady, and that I need not be at pains to make the one a palace and the other an empress, and turn both to my profit. Why, I do not think I would be dismayed if you told me that there was nothing to the universe but the universe, and there was an end on it."

At that moment the French windows swung very wide, and a silly tinkling voice cried, "Gentlemen! Gentlemen!" and the two less than dove-sized hands held out a tray with two glasses on it in the beam of light.

"This is for you, I think?" said Condorex.

"The lady is very polite," mumbled his companion, and they rose to their feet. He took his glass with modest grunts of courtesy, and cried to the darkness of the garden, "Albert! Albert!" Then he turned to the others and shook his head, saying, "He is a good lad, is Albert, but he is the sort that is ever wandering when the beer is handed out. But I will take it to him," and with a glass in each hand he went very gingerly down the steps.

To the windows, which Harriet's hands had drawn together, and curtained more closely than ever, Condorex remarked, " You would not have performed these final courtesies had you not been really ready, I am glad to think. But even so you have been a very long time. Were you never taught that since you are a woman it is your duty to please men, and that men hate to be kept waiting ? "

" Nevertheless I cannot let you in," said Harriet, in firm and prudent tones.

" Oh, I know well enough what you are at," he told her. " You have not lost your habit of picking up your clean clothes hot from the kitchen where they have been airing on the clothes horse, and bringing them straight into the sitting-room to save you the trouble of running upstairs to your bedroom. Lord, it is a low habit ! I have never known a lady who had her residence in Berkeley Square that did it, no, nor Grosvenor Square, neither."

She giggled very foolishly.

" I am perfectly informed of what you are doing at this very instant," he insisted, " for I have just heard a sound like a whisper, and it was not a mouth that made it but crumpled silk ; and from that I know your dress is now a circle on the floor. Ay, and your petticoat has gone now. Fi ! Harriet ! You are as you would not dare to go to church, shameless hussy that you are. Modest women, I believe, manage so that they are never thus."

" Why, how do they do that ? " wondered Harriet.

285

"It is, my love, one of those phenomena which confound the scientist by ceasing to be true once they are ascertained," said he. "And now, my dear, you had better know that I am fully aware you are powdering your prettiness before you put it away again."

"Would it not be better if you employed some method to distract your mind?" she begged. "Could you not perhaps recite the dates of the Kings and Queens of England, or the names of the Derby winners since 1890?"

"Oh, no need for that," he assured her, "for now I hear you pop on your petticoat, and I know that in a minute you will be fully gowned, and there will be not a thing to show that you are not a solid saw-dust cylinder to a half-inch of your sandals, like all your cheaper sort of doll. Oh, I am calm, I tell you." He lolled back against the lintel of the window, and patted down a yawn. "Calm, and very comfortably tired! I can tell you that by the time we have had supper and talked our fill, I will be ready enough to fall into bed."

"So you shall," she promised, and from the click and tap of her heels it could be guessed that she was kicking on a pair of new shoes that the fool had bought too small. "And you shall have your sleep out, too."

"Ay, we shall sleep, and sleep, and sleep," he yawned happily. "And what," said he, letting his arms fall to his sides and his head roll back and his eyelids close, "shall we do in the morning?"

A silence fell behind the curtained window.

" What shall we do in the morning ? " he repeated.

But the silence was not broken.

Panic took hold of him. He had a fear that if he burst into the room he would find nothing but the circle of her dress on the floor. He ran to the door and rattled the chain, and cried, " Harriet ! Harriet ! are you there ? "

There came a faint murmur from within.

" For the love of God, Harriet, why did you do that ? " he asked fiercely. " I thought something had gone amiss with you ! But tell me, pet," he said, ranging himself cosily against the doorpost, " what shall we do in the morning ? "

Her voice was grave, and sounded something like the wind, as she replied : " I do not know what will happen in the morning." It seemed as if the silence was about to fall again, but her laugh trilled out, and she said, with a full measure of her natural levity, " And with that I will not concern myself, neither ! Have you forgotten that I was ever careless ? "

" Ay, and I liked it, as I like every element in your character, if one could so call that combination of negative qualities which somehow produces a positive effect," he replied. " But hark ! here are our friends returning."

And sure enough they could be heard treading the gravel path towards the house like great cattle.

Harriet opened the window wide and held out her

little tray. " Will you not stand beside me and say farewell to our guests ? " she enquired.

" It is my proper place," he answered, and stepped across the threshold. " What a crisp new gown ! " he said, putting his arm about her waist.

" Ay, all's new, all's new," said Harriet.

Bobbing up out of the darkness came the ruddy faces of the two policemen, their wet moustaches gleaming like clean hay.

The younger policeman put down his glass first, " Thank you kindly for the drink, ma'am," he said, and moved from foot to foot, because of his shyness. " 'Twas a very clever idea of yours, ma'am, to turn on all the lights in your house and leave all the windows open and the curtains undrawn. You cannot think what a fine show it makes from the end of your garden."

" Ay, it shines out like a Christmas tree," said his senior, smacking down his glass. " 'Twas good to look at while we were drinking our beer ; and it was good beer, too." He drew himself up smartly to the salute. " This has ended in a very pleasant evening. And we would both, sir, like to wish you and the lady

A Very Happy Eternity.

THE END

REBECCA WEST

Cicily Isabel Fairfield was born in London. Her father had come from County Kerry, Ireland, and she acquired her early education in Edinburgh. She adopted her pen name Rebecca West from the strong-willed character of that name in Ibsen's social drama, *Rosmersholm*, in which she once acted in her late teens. She began to appear in print as a journalist and political writer in London as early as 1911, in *The Freewoman*, and was soon deeply involved in the causes of feminism and social reform. These interests were prominent in her journalism and later were echoed in her novels, her biographical writings, criticism, satire, travel and history, which have alternated and supplemented each other throughout her long career.

Her first book, *Henry James*, was published in 1916. Her eight novels include *The Return of the Soldier* (1918), *The Judge* (1922), *Harriet Hume: A London Fantasy* (1929)—all three published by Virago: *The Harsh Voice* (1935), *The Thinking Reed* (1936), *The Fountain Overflows* (1956) and *The Birds Fall Down* (1966). In 1977 a selection of her greatest work, *A Celebration*, was published which included a portion of her latest novel, as yet incomplete: *This Real Night*, a sequel to *The Fountain Overflows*.

Her only child, Anthony West (b. 1914), was the son of the novelist H. G. Wells. In 1930 she married Henry Maxwell Andrews, the banker, and began a lifelong companionship at their country house, Ibstone, in Buckinghamshire, with visits to London and many travels together, including the journey to Yugoslavia that inspired *Black Lamb and Grey Falcon*, her two-volume magnum opus. She was created a Dame Commander of the British Empire in 1959. After her husband's death in 1968 she returned to London where she now lives.